You Can Smile on Wednesdays

A novel

Zdravka Evtimova

Fomite
Burlington, VT

ISBN-13: 978-1-947917-38-5
Library of Congress Control Number: requested
Fomite
58 Peru Street
Burlington, VT 05401

In idem flumen bis non descendimus.
We do not go down in the same river twice.

This saying is adapted from a paraphrase in Latin by the philosopher Seneca
of one of the famous sayings of the Greek philosopher Herclitus. Herclitus
is perhaps most famous for his saying, "panta rhei", "Everything flows".

He is a hare running away from hawks, a lonely man.
He has no bread, and his food is fear,
his life started yesterday
and will finish tomorrow.

Slivia Nedkova, Bulgaria,
from her poem "The Man on the Opposite Side of the Street"

"Yesterday I was eating my lunch and some dame sat at my table. I suspected — on the spot — she was not all there, no face, moonscape all over the place! I said to myself, 'Scram. Start your boneshaker and make yourself scarce, buddy.' I was right. Buy me a cup of coffee, she winked at me. Ok, tomorrow morning I'll get up earlier to buy you coffee, crater on the Moon, I added to myself."

The man deploying his arguments before the patrons of The Cat alehouse was as thin as a spindle, his beard very similar to the iron-hard grass around the premises. His sparse hair looked clotted and tousled. His voice hovered above the plastic chairs in front of The Cat's bar, a modest drinking facility, the favorite haunt of disreputable characters much like the speaker: everyone in dirty overalls that after long wear and tear had lost some of the block capital letters, informing all interested entities that the men worked for Road Civil Engineering LTD.

Here, a glass of brandy cost seventy cents, but no one had the vaguest idea who had made this hogwash or what he had used, zucchini or sunflower shells, to brew it from. Did the hogwash maker squeeze snake venom in it or sprinkle cheap Eau de Cologne on the foul-smelling concoction to kill its stink? The guys didn't care. They sat happily on the plastic chairs covered with thickly jotted inscriptions that offered an intimate contact in a manner lacking any delicacy whatsoever. Hearts painted gory red and pierced with three to five arrows at a time glowed like open wounds on the plastic tables.

Here, the men didn't talk; they swilled their brandy, the general intention being not to pay at all for their alcohol. Their debts were larger than the length of the Struma River from its source down to the Aegean Sea. The tavern-keeper, a tall taciturn character dressed in an immaculately clean white jacket despite the scorching heat, could hardly feel at ease among the tables with their grapes of obscene words. He insisted on being called Anno and no matter that it might sound illogical, at times he wiped off some debts more impressive than the Struma River, smiled at someone among the alcoholic customers, all anxiously quiet on their chairs, and offered the lucky beggar a drink. The other patrons, while still sober, argued if it would be Bourbon or 100 Pipers, but who could count one hundred pipers after the second glass of hogwash?

After the second glass, Anno didn't give pipers to the bloke he had taken a fancy to, and foisted turnip brandy on the poor devil instead. But in all other respects he was an honorable man and generously poured dirt cheap alcohol into everybody's glasses. He treated a couple of more clear-headed clients to free appetizers. Some gentlemen dropped hints that now was a propitious time for the tavern-keeper to give them more of the beverage with a hundred musicians drowning in it, but in the evenings Anno was a bad-tempered crank. He couldn't stand men who neglected their toes and failed to cut their toenails. The patrons of The Cat had a deep aversion to the bartender's haughtiness.

Now, Anno was smiling at the guy with the thin fair hair.

"It would be my pleasure if I could learn your name, sir."

The guy who believed women were moonscapes all over the place lost his ability to speak, gaped at Anno and began scratching his neck.

"What… what do you want?" he muttered as he came to his senses, but Anno already held a glass of Pipers in his hand, a brown fire that exuded its fragrance all over the room.

"I would like to buy you a drink and the sound of your name would be a pleasure to listen to."

The man with the shaggy hair stared, stunned by this complex sentence, but grabbed rapidly at the glass and poured the Pipers into his mouth.

"His name's David," one of the men muttered under his breath. This guy had cut his toenails, and his socks, visible above his sandals, gleamed white and hopeful. "But yesterday they fired him. He doesn't work for the Road Civil Engineering LTD anymore."

"Oh, really?" Anno said as he put his hand on the shabby man's shoulder precisely on the spot where the last letter of *LTD* had been scratched off. "What would you like to drink, Mr. David?"

"The same like the previous one," the sparse-haired man snapped, and Anno poured the beverage that tasted of fire, roast pork and fried vegetables all in one, i.e. alcohol that left one thirstier. David's glass was full to the brim of flames when not far from the thin rails of the railway overgrown with nettles and thorny shrubs, a figure appeared. It was probably a woman: the figure wore a faded blue coat like the ones the charladies put on every time they scrubbed the toilets at the village school. A very long blue coat that must have been bleaching in the sun for ten years before it perched on this woman's shoulders. The thing hung down to her ankles, unfortunately hiding her legs completely. The coat was wide and the stranger jutted out of it like a sword. All eyes remained glued to the seventy cent hogwash glowing in their glasses. Nobody in these parts cared about faded coats.

"That one again," rumbled a particularly raw-voiced patron behind Anno's back and spat on the grass as the bartender dabbed his lips with an immaculate white handkerchief. The customers treated the newcomer with total disregard although a couple of men spat on the grass as well.

The woman carried a load of books, hugging it to her chest as if the fat tomes were a newborn baby. Glancing at her, Anno remarked, "Wonderful volumes. I can see the first one is *Notre Dame de Paris* in French. The lady communicates with them in a very spiritual way, and, in my humble opinion, this practice is detrimental to her social development."

The woman went on her way, scrawny, silent like a stream that had run dry.

§

"Hey, broom, what are you looking for?" shouted the raw-voiced patron behind Anno's back.

Her eyes sank into the tome in front of her nose as if she was thinking she would be buried there soon. At that moment, the thin-haired man, fired from his road civil engineering job, froze in his tracks, staring at the woman. His hand twitched in midair, clinging to the whiskey in which 100 pipers were playing to the best of their ability. He looked at the scrawny walking-stick of a chick, his mouth open as if he was about to swallow his own teeth. He gaped at her, forgetting to drink his special brown beverage.

"That one's got a screw loose," commented the man whose white socks had not lost all hope. "She's constantly reading *Notre-Dame.* She can't buy you a drink and she's as poor as a rat."

In these parts, the peasants brewed cheap brandy, using moss or even hay. It was honest truth David shouldn't spend his resources on a gal that couldn't buy him a glass of the hay concoction the locals dubbed *stone death.* The chap who had been fired from his road job — the patrons wondered what Anno had seen in this bowl of bones and gristle — shouted, "Hey! Hey!"

For a while, the woman stood nailed to the grass under the load of her books, squirming under the weight of *Notre Dame de Paris*, then dashed across the nettles.

"Please don't go, sir," Anno muttered under his breath as he carefully put his hands on the deleted letters of the shabby man's overalls. However, David was staring at Notre-Dame of Paris; he watched her, petrified, unable to breathe. The only man with truly white socks on hinted, "Make her buy you a drink first. Why are you crawling before her, blockhead?"

4

In these parts, "a drink" meant plum brandy. Everything else was turnip homemade swill. It soon became evident who had drunk 100 Pipers; the dude smelled sweet of Eau de Cologne for a week and told tales about Anno's room, his huge TV set, and his black silk sheets.

David stirred under Anno's hands that still gripped the letters on his blue overalls, and watched the railway track that cut Bulgaria into two pieces: the first one belonged to The Cat and the 100 Pipers; the second one was the Motel and its glittering genuine leather sofas that calmed down the truckers' kidneys beaten black and blue during long journeys.

"Dear Sir, you drank my best whiskey!" Anno remarked, sad that the bloke with the tousled hair had left him in the lurch in the company of an empty glass and a raunchy joke, teeming with spelling mistakes carved in the plastic table.

A train heavy with summer heat hurtled through the valley. Its carriages had seen so many July afternoons that their walls and ceilings clanged. Drowsy faces at the windows shot past the pub as the patrons of the drinking establishment, enthused by the quantities of brandy they'd imbibed, made obscene gestures at them. Anno turned his back, trying to express his aversion to the National Bulgarian Railway Trust. The carriages had brought him neither a friend nor a heart capable of understanding him.

At their small station, the ticket collector evicted only illegal passengers, characters that hadn't had a bath for a month. Even though the customer Anno had invited to his apartment drank a gallon of his best whiskey, the ingrate plundered his office and left Anno with the lizards and the dirty outpourings of creative energy scrawled on the tables. Often on hot August mornings, Anno pressed exquisite objects against his chest, daydreaming about civilized folks who wouldn't swear at him or constantly beg whiskey from him, or snore like oxen on his black silk.

The shabby stranger rushed to the woman and the train hid him from Anno's view. This character that didn't have a square inch of cleanliness on him was an amiable presence, a cub smelling of dust and crushed stones that did not belong here. Every beard born far away from this insignificant village gave Anno fresh hope.

§

"That's all the money we have."

Their father did not look at her sisters. A couple of crumpled ten lev bills trembled in his hand. His veins trembled too, with the sleeve of his coat and the sky above them all. The house that used to be theirs a day ago seemed to shake. They sold their backyard, sold the old cherry trees in it, and the ancient quince tree that Pirina climbed after she turned four. She grew up amidst its strong brown branches. Now, the family stood in front of the house, waiting; she, her two sisters, their mother in her tattered straw hat, looking as if she had pulled down the scorching sun over her eyes. They had sold the days when the sky was their brother and didn't hate them, and the house, though small and gray, belonged to the family. The money in their father's hand wouldn't be enough to pay or spit at the trucker that was supposed to take everything, lock, stock and barrel, to Grandma's hut. Pirina didn't see the truck although its tires jutted out in front of her as black as the dry grass of August.

"Let's go," their mother said.

It was hard to believe that the house, the cherry trees, the backyard and their days in the past cost two ten lev bills that were shaking in the cup of their father's hand.

"You have to find jobs," their mother had said for the tenth time this morning. The sun got into a huff on her tattered straw hat and threw the woman's thin shadow under the truck tires.

Pirina's sisters said nothing. They were girls of few words, cautious and hard-headed, nodding their heads if they agreed with you, or keeping mum if they didn't. First Sara, the shortest one, then Luba, the tall thin spindle, turned around, their backs thin as clouds. The clouds in the sky said nothing. The girls' mother, light of foot and agile like a lizard, didn't speak a word. She grew the best peppers and magnificent tomatoes in the village of

Staro. Her pumpkins swelled like the moon and looked more beautiful than the silver in the moonbeams as they grew and ripened under the kitchen window. The girls had to find jobs.

Their father, a walking stick in hand, swayed his bad leg from left to right, trying to drive away the flies as the earth wobbled under him. He'd busted his leg in the coalmine years ago, now blackened under the weight of the summer and the two crumpled bills. He waited in the heat. He loved his house, the quince tree, the backyard and his mother's grave in it.

Brown expanse of dry grass stretched as far as the eye could see. It used to be a football field; ruined and plundered, today it was a place famous for thistles and scraggy donkeys, the torn sails of this stony land that the wind tried to drive towards the sea as the sun roasted the beasts tethered to old wooden poles. The summer had wrung every drop of moisture from weeds and shrubs, the river, a brown band of scorched mud, exuded heat. White bellies of fish and gray backs of tadpoles imbedded in the sand glittered like glass shards.

The sisters worked part-time at the motel that the locals had nicknamed *The Widow*. Then the establishment proudly bore the name *Venice*; however all the time it was a ramshackle affair buried in the ground, just a row of rooms as small as prison cells jutted out near the road, their windows looking on the parking lot. Each of these cells cost 20 levs an hour, plenty of time for the truckers and the girls to implement the plan they'd hired the room for. Only younger and less experienced truckers used the motel rooms; all others were quite successful on the seat behind the wheel, or in the shrubs. No matter where the men notched up another success, they had to eat, so Pirina's sisters cooked in the kitchen.

It was scorching hot in there in winter and summer alike. The sun thrust its yellow head in the ovens and that was why her sisters put on blouses so thin their breasts were visible through the fabric. Boys from the neighboring villages clung to the windows like bunches of grapes, their noses glued to the windowpanes despite the stink of burnt onions and rancid fat.

From time to time, the eldest sister Sara hid with a trucker in the adjoining room, a decent place where Yakob, the motel proprietor, had allowed the sisters to keep their goods and chattels. The devious driving souls, not only from the village of Staro, but also from the nearby towns, spread wild rumors about Sara, and many boys didn't drink beer and ate no lunch for a week, saving up money to visit that adjoining room. One of the lads as tall as a wall, all freckles and nimble fingers, often thought of Sara. He could draw dogs and snakes so well his colleagues, construction workers, were scared the beasts would bite them. This kid drew pictures of Sara — now her face, now her fabulous blouse — on paper napkins, on cigarette packs, sometimes even on the bricks he put in the walls of the buildings, so the houses in these parts of Bulgaria watched the passersby with Sara's eyes.

Sara, more beautiful than the moon in the sky, like everyone in the family, was headstrong. Her back was mist and the wind nested in her breasts. Even men from the town of Dupni came to the motel and drank no beer, saving up for her adjoining room, their voices thick in their throats.

The other sister, Luba, worked in the kitchen too; she, however, didn't go out on dates, although her breasts were a hot August night. Why didn't she, Pirina wondered? All day long, Luba cut mountains of onions, peeled potatoes, baked peppers, roasted loads of meatballs and dressed salads for the truckers, her fingers sticky and dented like the chopping log on which their father slaughtered chickens. Why didn't Luba pick up a trucker and take him to the adjoining room? She borrowed books from the village library instead, collected printed sheets of obscure poetry any Tom, Dick and Harry had thrown away, purchased mildewed tomes, huge and cumbersome all, from second hand bookshops in Radomir. This was what their sister Luba chose to waste her hard-earned money on.

Pirina liked to kill insects with the tomes, transforming their front and back covers into graveyards for cockroaches and flies; Luba read the foul smelling hardbacks at night, the lamp, a thief's shadow, languished in their room, its meager light crawling on Luba's pages. Sara didn't mind. Sara loved Luba so much that in the kitchen, when their eyes were holes of hot tears dug by the onions, Sara lifted huge crates of pork chops for her sister, thinking that a girl who was a slave to literature was either seriously ill, or worse. Luba would remain a spinster, sure thing, and there would be no men or lovers in her life.

Now they all had to leave the house. They had to pay their water bill with the banknotes in their father's hand. Their mother said they hadn't paid the thing for a year. Grandma had bequeathed her three granddaughters her hut and the debt she'd run up before she met her maker. Although the coalmine had ruined their father's leg, the man tried to lay new tiles on the roof, in fact no tiles, marble slabs; these used to be a sidewalk in front of The Widow Motel, but a week ago, their father, hanging like a flag in the corner of the roof, carefully put them in place. He could do nothing about the walls of the house built of wattle and daub. Grandma used to say, "The house is clay and I'm clay too. So we're friends."

To be honest, both the tumbledown hut and Grandma's grave belonged to Yakob. The marble slabs were his property too. He had made Pirina's father wrench the things from the sidewalk and put new marble in front of the motel. It remained marble only during the first day after the repair work was over, after that the truckers packed the new flagstones with the dust their shoes and clothes were covered with — a gray layer imported from overseas — and peed on the sidewalk. A chemical reaction probably took place, and the slabs changed colors, pink first then violet, but it was easy to scrub them. Pirina, in charge of the sidewalk, swore at it, and even at the rare moments when she didn't, she hated the marble's guts. It was impossible to remove the overseas dust or delete the obscene graffiti the local boys sprayed on the flagstones at night, all dedicated to Yakob.

"You must find jobs," their mother said again.

Yakob, the tycoon who owned practically everything in these parts, had fired the three girls. Sara had failed to give him a share of the cash she made off the guys in *his* adjoining room, he said. Luba… how much is a girl worth if she stuck her nose in stupid novels one can only kill cockroaches with, he asked. You don't give a damn for a chick that doesn't take truckers anywhere. Doesn't she have a room with a window looking onto the red fields heavy with thorns and wasps? A demoiselle as daft as a brush is no good for his kitchen and sauces. She doesn't cut the onions, no Sir! She cuts her fingers more often than tractor-trailers stop at the motel parking lot and her blood drips into the pot of soup.

Writers wrote lies in the books, and a decent person should ask why so much paper went to the dogs. They should produce toilet paper instead. Let this good-for-nothing Luba look for another job. If a guy saw something under her blouse and asked her a question, she wouldn't even say, "Bugger off". She turned to the onions in the frying pan or stared at cockroaches, crawling on the floor instead. On the shelf over her head, she'd arranged no plates or bowls, no sir! She'd left four thick books.

"It's a pity you're so pretty," her mother said. "It's a great pity. If you were plain, or if men didn't fall for you, I'd understand. Letting life slip through your fingers, that's what you're doing now."

Both Mother and Father suspected Luba planned to become a nun because she kept *Notre Dame* on her bedside table.

"You're on the wrong track," her mother scolded. "There's nothing in heaven and nothing on earth, if you don't learn to roast the onions the way guys like them. Throw away all your books. Drop them like hot potatoes. Your dad is a crackpot…reading newspapers and all, starving all his life. But you still have time to mend your ways."

Their father read quietly, like a mouse, his eyes stubbornly absorbing the words from the newspaper, his face taut as if he had a toothache. He kept a battered *Bulgarian Grammar: a Complete Guide,* and a book of fairy-tales, *The Gold Fish,* on his bedside table. He, not their mother, told the three girls stories. When their dad didn't work the nightshift, he often told them about the coal king who gave his gold ring to a simple country girl and married her.

"Keep your yap shut," their mom said. "How does Sara earn her living? By using her lower floor! Where will we go after Yakob kicks us out of this house?"

They had already loaded the truck. Their old beds in which the three girls had listened to the woodworms creaking at night; the ancient cupboard and the transparent glasses with which their father treated his pals to brandy. He no longer did that. One by one, his friends had vanished beyond the mountain fog and he remained alone, no job at the coalmine, his crooked leg like a tail in his wake. At a certain point, he learned to weave baskets and worked with the Gypsy folks from the Roma neighborhood. At times, he drank brandy with them in the same glasses that now waited for him in the truck. He'd taken everything he had, bag and baggage, out of the wattle-and-daub hut, far from The Widow Motel, its parking lot and the kitchen where the wind blew nobody any good.

Something jumped and shone in the distance, and if something whirred, was red and exuded the distinctive aroma of dollars, one could expect a slap in the face. That object was Yakob's red Mercedes-Benz sports car, Yakob's red Jeep Grand Cherokee, or at least Yakob's red Mazda. No matter if it was his Mercedes, Grand Cherokee or Mazda, the driver was always the same. Sara had taken this man to the famous adjoining room and already knew the weight of his fists; however, the 270-pound machine of muscles, gristle and lousy mood didn't scare her into obedience, especially when the machine had downed some whiskey beforehand.

This was Kiro, Yakob's chauffeur and bodyguard, a guy notorious for his habit of sinking his teeth into the end of a rope to which a heavy cart was tied. He was rumored to tug the thing all the way from the village of Staro to the town of Dupni. Kiro had said to Sara, "C'mon."

In his mouth, this phrase could mean: "I want it this way," "Give me bread and meat," "I'm waiting for my bottle of brandy," etc. Sara knew if a guy was scum by the way he gripped the cash in his hand, but even she couldn't translate the bodyguard's "C'mon" into simple Bulgarian. It meant,

"Move in with me". It was after the villagers stumbled on three young men Sara was particularly fond of, all beaten into a pulp, that it became clear Kiro's fists had been involved in these events. He was keen on Sara and made no bones about expressing it.

So, as far as Sara was concerned, she could secure a roof above her head, not that Kiro had any substantial property to boast of. He lived with his mother, a gloomy, towering crag of blood and bone, her wrists as big as huge hoes. On weekdays, she wore the same enormous dress, cheap and faded, spots all over the place as she dug in the garden, loudly threatening her husband and son. The woman hated it when her house stank of Yakob's cars and sleazy pubs.

Kiro's father was a 300-pound log of brawn and a belly heavy with brandy. He, too, gave Sara the eye, and the young gypsy girls didn't leave him indifferent. The only woman he neglected was his own wife, a thundercloud that in the evenings poured bean soup into his bowl as she called bitter curses down on him.

Now Yakob sat in his posh car next to his giant driver. The smile on the tycoon's face seemed like an ill omen. Yakob took money from you anyplace he showed up. The ten lev bills in their father's fist trembled with his blood. Yakob would snatch the house and the backyard. If he didn't pocket anything, he wouldn't go away before he crushed you under the tires of his Mercedes-Benz. Their father busted his left leg in the coalmine, and if the huge red car ran over the man's right leg, how could he wade through the sedges and pick willow branches for his baskets? Yakob didn't care for the house, the quince trees and the cherry trees. Their mother, as silent as a stone so far, hissed, "Girls, you're still dawdling! If we'd cleared off, he'd have seized the dust under my sneakers."

However, she knew she was wrong through and through. Had Yakob drawn a bead on you, he found you no matter if you were at home or on the moon. Kiro would grab you by the neck and drag you to the red Mercedes. Yakob had bought up most of the lands in these parts. He already owned the meadows lining the highway, and rumors had it he intended to build another motel, *Black Tigress* or *White Tigress*. If the tycoon planned on importing chicks from Sofia for the truckers then how could Sara and the girls from Staro earn their daily bread? The librarian said that the city folks from Sofia looked for donkey thistles to brew thistle tea. If men drank it, she added, they remained men ten years after their hair turned gray, and women's hair didn't turn gray at all! So Sara and the other girls could go into business: pick all thistles and keep donkeys on short rations, water from the river, clean air and couch grass.

§

Dad speaks a lot, using outlandish words he's learned from the newspapers. These are all old tabloids and weeklies that a scatter-brained pal of his keeps on giving him. Dad and his pal did their military service on the Bulgarian-Turkish border, so Dad's friend collects moldy gazettes for him, mostly in the Town Hall. These dailies are five or six months old, but Dad reads them all the same. The words bite you if you arrange them in an evil row, he says, but they can also sing to you about the summer when you sleep.

The second Yakob's Grand Cherokee screeches to a halt in front of us, Dad hides the tattered bills he's got for our house, thrusting them into his pocket. At least, the money isn't on show that way. He grumbles something, a sharp coalminer's curse the locals use instead of *Good morning* in the village of Staro. The morning is no good in the first place. Yakob gets out of the car and grinds mom's shadow underfoot.

This man tramples on everything: the sun, Dad's broken leg, cockroaches; nothing seems to make a difference to him. He buys our neighbors' house for the girls from Sofia who will arrive in Staro to do intimate things in the motel that's not built yet. Like bags of charcoal, our folks move out. They will smolder and smoke in another village somewhere near here. What else can the poor devils do with a couple of crumpled ten lev bills glued to their blood at the bottom of the trouser pockets?

When I'm flat broke, I sing; not that I know the tune or the lyrics. I just hum — hum, hum — under my breath. Dragons live in my song and they bite you savagely, but this is a closely guarded secret. I've hummed so obstinately that in the beginning Mom thinks I am not all there. She tells me to shut up, but I hum and buzz on, like a squeaking hinge, jarring on the ear. She says to herself I've gone deaf and I can't hear her. If someone is hard of hearing, Mom gives her a spanking, so that the girl keeps her mulishness to herself and doesn't fuss. We are decent folks that don't spin yarns for anybody.

Now, after Dad has sold the house, we are no longer decent, and I can prattle on into the night, discussing my dragons. They protect me against the boys that stalk me when Sara doesn't want them. I could clout the intruder between the eyes with a stone — I've been carrying one in my pocket since I turned ten.

After Mom forbade me to hum, the dragons stopped protecting me, so I had to fend for myself and I learned to wield the stone. I knew a bloke that had tried to roll me into a ball the way he did to Sara, and I didn't like that. I came up to the guy, and took a last, careful step as I hurled the stone, aiming at his neck. I broke the guy's head. The wretch stayed in hospital on account of his insolence, but after the docs stitched him up he came to our place to consult with Mom on a sensitive issue. Everybody consulted Mom on important issues, leaving Dad alone to peruse the old newspapers or hobble through the sedges, sticking knee-deep in the mud that teemed with leeches and water fleas. At a certain point, the guy asked Mom, "Slava, I didn't mean no harm. Honestly… I have a marriage intention…. with … with respect to Pirina. I'll take her to the Town Hall. The Mayor will marry us for free, if you don't mind."

"Pirina is not yet a girl of a marriageable age," Mom snapped. "I don't mean you're a bad guy, or that you're poor."

The truth was the guy was as poverty-stricken as the parched cracked mud along the riverbed. I had no boyfriend, and willy-nilly, I trudged through the nettles to Grandma's hut. Dad had told me the place abounded with tree frogs.

"I wish you could sing," Mom said. "You could have made a pop star. These morons wallow in money and store the cash in bags I've heard. But you squeal like a pig. If a man listens to you, he'll either start stuttering or cut off his own ears. Or worse, Pirina, you'll have dreams of marrying Yakob for a week!"

What was I to do when Yakob's red Grand Cherokee crawled to Dad? Should I summon the dragons? When I was a little girl and Mom was intent on boxing my ears, I climbed the quince tree and stayed at the top for hours. At the end of July during the scorching hot Dog-Days, the sky as so huge and heavy it petrified your brain, and you wished you were dead. You cried and Mom gave you a spanking to bring you back to your senses. I learned to be smarter. I hid in the room with its window to the north where Sara slept, and Luba, her eyes glued to the pages of her next *Notre Dame*, read like a saint. I stared at the matrimonial photograph of Grandma Pirina and Grandpa Todor and I was happy they'd named me after Granny. She used to admire gold.

A gold bracelet put out of sight in an old shoebox was our treasure. A trucker from Algeria had given it to Sara as he burned like a bale of straw out of his passion for her. The bracelet was so exquisite I got a throbbing headache every time I stared at it. So, I climbed the quince tree and stayed with the cobwebs as strong as fishing nets. Flies, bees, wasps, even gadflies writhed, caught in the sticky threads. A spider watched them. I'd never seen a more horrible beast, his back wider than the palm of my hand, his legs long and hairy, his body as huge as a plum. He was an elephant among the other spiders, and I sang to him — hum, hum —in my impossibly false voice that could make you see Yakob in your nightmares. The spider didn't recoil in horror from the dragons in my song, on the contrary, he surely was their relative and they got along just fine. The spider and I shouted at the top of our lungs, but no one gave a hoot. It was so hot that the snakes hid under stones, looking for a drop of moisture.

One day, Mom got a splitting headache, and why she asked, why did this stupid head of hers drag her into a mess? Perhaps she had a brain tumor; perhaps she was going to kick the bucket even before she married off her three daughters. Then a thought crossed her mind: she didn't have a tumor in her head; most probably something was bothering her and she knew: my mooing was the worst of her peeves. Mom was a resolute woman, and after spotting me in the tree, she concluded that I had a screw loose. Girls my age boasted of their baby bumps. What was I doing — sitting in a tree in the company of jackdaws! Sara, may God keep her safe in the brothel, was a sight all over the place, not a normal girl, not by a long shot. God knew if she was barren or not. Luba, and the daft ideas she carried in her empty head! She'd make no man lose his head, she wouldn't earn enough to feed a cat, and no baby would drool in her lap if she, the idiot, slept only with her *Notre Dame*. As far as I, Pirina, was concerned, Mom thought that a worm knew more about love than me.

Mom complained that yes, she did have three daughters, but no grand-child was in sight as she scanned the horizon. Dad had used this word, and she suspected that the horizon stared at the threshold and ended near the well in the corner of the backyard.

We sold the well, the threshold and the horizon. A fortnight ago, Mom made a vow to cut down that crooked quince tree, but I doubted she'd do it. She was crazy about quince jam; in winter she brewed the seeds, producing a cure to treat Dad's lung ailment. The man had a hacking cough and hawked up phlegm; this was the gift the coalmine had given him, so I was pretty sure Mom wouldn't harm the tree. She didn't. She killed my elephant-spider instead, and I didn't have anybody to sing to. Hope dies last, I said to myself. Perhaps my spider, the lion among other bugs, has fathered baby spiders and I'll tell *them* everything about my monsters. If I didn't have someone to sing to, I'd die, or I wouldn't be all there just the way Mom thought I wasn't.

That man that was as poor as mud visited me every evening. He spoke softly, the words blossoming like dandelions on his lips, but his was a dialect we disliked in these parts. Don't be afraid of me, he told me and I wasn't. I had no fear at all, and was truly sorry I'd broken his head with my stone.

I loved granite. I didn't have anybody to protect me, so I went and took the stone I'd broken the smart aleck's head with, removed the blood stains and put the thing into my pocket. Even the huge spider's offspring lost their nerve as I started to hum. The panic-stricken long-legged fellows ran for their life, abandoning me to sing in delight to the caterpillars that guzzled leaves of the quince tree until Mom exterminated them, spiders and cobwebs altogether, using B-58, a white powder that the druggist sold her.

The druggist was a good woman, so I went and swept her backyard for her. She had a son, a quiet, black-eyed boy, Kalcho, long thick eyelashes all over the place, and after I finished cleaning the backyard, his mom thrust the package of B-58 into my hands.

"This is for your mother," she said. "Give it to her."

If I had suspected that the poison would kill my spiders and caterpillars, I wouldn't have touched the druggist's broom, but that was another story.

I said to Kalcho, the pharmacist's son, "I'll give two levs, if you listen to me sing."

It was the same bill that Kalcho's mom had put into my bag together with B-58 powder. Ok, go ahead, Kalcho agreed, and I started crooning to my dragons, hum-hum-hum, droning for a century and a half. I didn't look at the guy, fearing the worst: his distorted face gaping at me, his jaws clenched. Mom stuffed cotton balls into her ears, yet her mouth compressed into a hard line when I burst into song.

"Take your two levs back," Kalcho said. "No need to give me money. I'll listen to you for free."

"You're nutty as a fruitcake, man," I told him. "But I like you. Listen to me now." But... if he wanted the same thing like the filthy bloke whose head I'd broken with my stone, then... "Hey, Kalcho," I went on, "Look at this stone. Can you see this spot here, the dark one? It's a bloodspot. You can't wash it or clean it under a running tap. If you're planning the intimate thing with me, another bloodspot will appear on the stone. It will be your blood."

"No, no way," Kalcho said. "Can I hold your hand, though? Is that ok with you?

My hand? Every day, I peeled heaps of onions, gutted fish and cut up chickens, deep-fried meat in rancid oil, so I feared my fingers smelled.

"This is the most beautiful hand I've seen," Kalcho said, and I didn't think he was nutty as a fruit cake. He held my hand, I hummed at the top of my throat and I was happier than on the days when I sang to the spider and the caterpillars in the quince tree.

Now, Yakob's Grand Cherokee ground to a halt. Dad's sweat must have drowned the bills that Yakob gave us for the house, the cherry trees, for the moon hidden in the biggest pumpkin, for Mom's magnificent tomatoes, for my spider and my caterpillars. Yakob got out of the car, but I thought of Kalcho. I was sure he was my spider's best friend.

§

The sun trampled us underfoot, my mom, my sisters and me. It must have tightened its yellow grip on Dad's bones for I saw him shudder. His arm twitched and he hid it behind his back; I'd seen Dad's hands shake like this after Mom said he was a hobbling wretch unable to feed his girls. Why, she asked him, why should Sara put up with scumbag truckers, why can't we pay for Luba to study at the university? She'd make a good teacher, if you ask me. And what is she doing now? Rotting with her thick *Notre Dame*! Who knows what nonsense this fat book puts in her head! Dad's fingers locked and unlocked behind his back as he tried not to listen, not to hit her.

"I'm sorry for Pirina," Mom said about me.

I didn't go in for truckers, the hounds on the road I dubbed them, nor did I rot, a *Notre Dame* tucked under my arm. I didn't even hate cockroaches. Peeling onions and potatoes, that was what I did. I washed dirty clothes too, and once in a blue moon, when nobody was listening, I very quietly sang to my dragons.

"Why are you bawling and squalling now for?" Mom would asked. "We are broke, bawling or no bawling."

She said those nasty things to me, and I didn't want to listen, so I cooked bean soup in my mind — great soup did I bring to a boil. I cut more carrots, added dried mint leaves and couldn't hear a word of what Mom droned on about me.

I hated to watch Yakob and Kiro, his henchman, drive up to the house, so I cooked bean soup in my mind. Kiro's long pinky nail scratched my shoulder, and I saw that the nail was not only long, it was dirty, a ton of mud wedged under it. If my stone was in my pocket this filthy finger wouldn't dare touch me again.

"You," Kiro's long nail said as it pricked my shoulder again. Dad's shoulders twitched, Mom's lips turned blue; they turned blue every time she called Dad "hobbling wretch." My sister Luba, her hands clinging to her *Notre Dame* like burrs to a coat, whispered, "Don't touch her."

Only Luba could say, "Don't touch her" in front of Yakob.

Yakob reached out and placed his hand on my shoulder. His fingers wriggled like worms as they slowly slipped downward. On that day, I wasn't wearing a bra. I hadn't been for years. My sister Sara, the prettiest girl I'd seen in my life, Sara with her sparkling eyes — the color of the clouds behind the windowsill in winter — Sara took a step to Yakob and pushed his hand away. How beautiful were Sara's fingers! Her teeth were beautiful too. I saw them sink into Yakob's wrist. Her beautiful teeth would have drawn a pool of blood if Kiro, the 6-foot 6-inch roof beam, had been in another place.

When we were little kids, I used to cry a lot. One day Sara wanted to make me shut up and bit my calf. Her teeth sank into my flesh through the trouser leg, and on that day, I wore thick pants of homespun wool. She drew a bucket of my blood, or so I thought. Mom hit her over the head with the sieve, and this made my heart bleed for Sara, so I stopped sobbing straightaway. I hated it if Mom gave my beautiful sister a good hiding on account of my whims and vagaries.

Kiro, Yakob's chauffeur and bodyguard, kicked Sara, and she collapsed on the ground — like a waterfall did my pretty sister flow down to the dust, her hair glossy, a whole lake of it, her skin clear and soft. Sprawled across the path, Sara looked beautiful. I didn't know how the men felt when they kissed Sara goodbye in that adjoining room with a window to the highway. Were they aware that my sister was the most magnificent lake in the world? Yes. They didn't drink beer for a month, dreaming of making their way to her in The Widow. One day, Sara gave me a thin bundle — it was the men's money she'd saved up for a week — and said, "Buy a pair of sandals and put them on. You'll catch fire in your brogues in this heat."

Now Sara lay on the ground, her white skin a glowing puddle at Yakob's feet. I didn't think of his thick fingers as they groped me, I cut Yakob into pieces for the soup I was cooking in my mind. I slashed him and hacked him. He had knocked down the most beautiful girl I knew.

I was roasting Kiro the chauffeur in the oven of my mind, his beard, unshaved for weeks, bursting into poisonous flames. Kiro stood, a speechless lamppost, a white umbrella in hand, guarding Yakob against the summer and the donkey thistles. I mashed him up like a bag of potatoes. He'd been explaining left and right what Sara did to him in the adjoining room, and how much he'd forked out for her services. The slob lied to young and old, saying that he had money to burn. One day, he sneaked into the kitchen of The Widow Motel and showed me a bundle of hundred lev bills as thick as the 7th grade geography textbook.

I kept this textbook underneath my international passport and read about different countries in the world I wanted to see. I wouldn't have money to go there, but the dragons in my songs flew over their capitals every day. Sometimes in the evenings when I wasn't dog-tired, I visited these countries in my mind, starting from Albania and then, in alphabetical order, I journeyed to Australia, Austria, Belgium, and so on till I reached Zimbabwe. I loved this geography textbook as much as I loved Luba and Sara. Kiros's bundle was fatter than all the pages, starting from descriptions of Austria

"How about this *Notre Dame* here?" barked Kiro as he pointed at Luba. "Didn't *Notre Dame* say Pirina wasn't ill at all?"

Yakob paid no heed to anybody as if we were sand under his sneakers. Wait a minute. We were no sand. You could tread on sand, but you could not tread on us. Mom wouldn't let people trample all over her, even Dad wouldn't, although he'd hidden his shaking hands behind his back, making efforts not to hit Yakob.

Yakob produced a bundle of cash twice as thick as my 7th grade geography textbook.

"Take it," he said, but it wasn't clear who he said this to: the crows perched like black gourds on the fence, or to Mom. "This is an addition to the price of your house if Pirina comes to cook for me and clean my place."

"To clean Yakob's place" meant that after a month Yakob would throw you out like a rag. No girl that had cooked his meals said a word about what Yakob did to her. Was it the same thing the truckers did to Sara? Mom hinted strongly that the fat cat had given them money to consult a woman's doctor in Sofia.

We knew Yakob had hired a man, a blue-eyed Marko from Pernik, to work for him. In Greece, childless couples were keen on adopting blue-eyed babies. A blue-eyed kid cost five grand more than a black-eyed one, so the girls who cooked and cleaned for Yakob all had blue eyes. This Marko guy, blue-eyed like a grass snake, his gaze steady, five grand more expensive than a black one, visited Sara in her cell at The Widow Motel. The grass snake didn't do anything to Sara in the adjoining room, just sat at her side as she ate the bean soup I'd cook for them, and after she finished, Marko said, "Sara, no woman has such dark beautiful eyes like yours," and that was the most honest truth I'd heard a man say.

Mom saw the bundle of money, as thick as all the countries in my geography textbook, and I thought she'd say, "Ok, Pirina, go cook and clean for him. The Greek families don't want dark-eyed babies. You'll bear a black-eyed one, and we'll raise it here."

How come the kid remains with us, I thought to myself. The donkey thistles in the field were all over the place, but they were not wheat you could harvest and eat. Shall we milk the mules to get milk for the baby?

This reminded me of the express train.

The trains passed over the bridge across the Struma River, a strong construction — all iron beams and bolts — with a narrow passageway on its left side for the railway workers to inspect the rails. When I was a little girl and still didn't have dragons, I lay on the passageway and waited for the train. Dad's hair turned gray within a day, no, within an afternoon. He thought that I'd got run over by the express train. The cars smelled magnificent of shores the Struma River went to. I slept with my geography 7th grade textbook glued to my chest with electrical tape. I slept with Coalminer, my teddy bear, which used to be Sara's, then Luba's and finally became mine. In the mornings, I used to sit under the bridge and, in my mind, I took the train. On Mondays, I journeyed to Greece, on Tuesdays to Africa; on Thursdays, I didn't travel anywhere because I had to gut the fish in the kitchen.

"Why do you read these fat books?" I asked Luba once. "Don't you have fairytales in your head, or at least a story about a big field and donkey thistles, a purse full of cash for mom or perhaps earrings for me? What about a tale aiming a kick at some smart Aleck that hangs around The Widow, one that gawks at our sister Sara?"

"It's only crazy men that have books in their heads," Luba said.

No guy, young or old, talked to Luba. Nobody cared for her maybe because she didn't have books in her head and bought old ones written by writers who obviously were not all there. The rest of us — Dad, Mom, Sara and I — had enough stories to tell. Luba retreated to her favorite *Notre Dame* that surely loved her a lot, and stayed there. In the evenings, she walked to the town of Radomir to buy now bread, now a box of cough medicine. No man alive spoke to her. I wondered why. Luba had tons of December snow in her soft white skin. Are all these men blind, can't they see how pretty she is? A guy had tried to kiss her at Radomir railway station, a drunkard all over the place he was. She didn't send him packing, didn't even shout at him, although he'd made a mess of his clothes and beard. This ginger-haired drunk came to our place even before we knew we had to sell the house. He saw my sister's books, gaped at her *Notre Dame of Paris*, muttered under his breath, "You belong to some crazy sect, eh?" and made himself scarce. I never saw him again.

The same ginger-haired coward visited The Widow Motel, stole a glance at my sister Sara and couldn't breathe for a while. They poured a pail of water over his head. He sold his coat, watch and shoes, hoping to spend an hour with my sister in the adjoining room, her cell. At a certain point, Sara realized he was the sot from the Radomir railway station, the one who'd kissed our Luba. Beautiful Sara gave him back his money and kicked him out so rapidly as if fleas were crawling on his cheeks. Speaking of fleas, I loved Ugly Eye, my tomcat, although at times he, too, was full of fleas. Ugly Eye was as courageous as a storm cloud, and when Kiro killed him, his thin cat's blood seeped into the gravel. I had refused to accompany Kiro to his shack, and this was the clod's revenge. I adopted a new Ugly Eye, and now he was the king of all tabbies in the neighborhood.

"Hey, look," Kiro said through his teeth as if he was speaking through the Grand Cherokee exhaust pipe to the white umbrella over Yakob's head. Yakob produced another bundle of hundred lev bills. I hated to watch money; I imagined what men did to Sara before they gave it to her. Mom, however, enjoyed staring at bundles, and loved pocketing bundles even more.

"I repeat," Kiro thundered. "Yakob gives you this. It's an addition to the price for the cherry trees. He wants Pirina to cook his meals. He wants her now. You must be crazy, if you don't let her go."

The girls from our neighborhood had given birth to babies enough to accommodate a whole village of childless couples in Greece. This Marko guy fathered them, and they all had blue eyes, Sara said. He told her that whenever he saw a blue-eyed tot, as thin as a grass snake, near Thessaloniki,

Greece, he thought the toddler was his son or daughter. Yakob paid him generously. Near the town of Thessaloniki dozens of blue-eyed babies were born; Marko was no longer a victim of circumstances, on the contrary, he told Sara he'd struck oil and was going to buy a big house. So, if Sara agreed to marry him, then "Come, come quickly, Sara. Let me kiss you, dearest." He hoped their daughter would have brown eyes and autumn sunsets would give bronze to her face. It was always a rainy afternoon in Sara's eyes, Marko had said, and he loved rain so much.

"Pirina won't go to Yakob's house," my sister Sara snapped.

"Shut your trap," Kiro gnashed his teeth. "Pirina will cook for him."

"You'll get the cash. I'll give you a strong donkey. Take it or leave it," Yakob said. "Kiro will bring the beast to your place. And you can stay in the house. Pirina, come on."

Mom clutched the two bundles, staring and staring at the bills. Dad seemed to have lost both his hands, or perhaps something had gone wrong, and that was why his fingers shook behind his back as he tried hard not to whack Mom with the bills. I couldn't believe they were swapping me for a donkey. Ok, I said to myself. At least they won't cut down the cherry trees. My spiders had built their nests up there. I loved cherries, and in July, I slept among the branches. Even if I gave birth to a blue-eyed mite, so what? I prayed to the clouds, "Help me. Help me! I'll bite the dust if they cut down a cherry tree, and if they take away my baby, even it's a blue-eyed one, then I'll bite the dust a dozen times."

"Go," Dad said.

"Go," Mom said. How happy her fingers looked as they held the money in a firm grip: two thick 7th grade geography textbooks. They both could describe the shores that smelled of new railroad lines. "See you," Mom added, avoiding my eyes.

Sara kissed me. Her lips were so warm that I knew, the summer, the cherry trees, the river and the railway bridge were all there, in her lips. Sara loved me so. She always let me put on her fine clothes. Luba hugged me hard. She was drowned in her ugly denim coat like the ones the cleaners wore at school. It hid her legs, but it couldn't hide her face, so I thought that the drunkard from the Radomir railway station was nuts. Why didn't he kiss Luba until the night thinned and dawn broke over the rails? She was so pretty, this silly Luba. Why should she try to bury her beauty under the weight of thick books?

"Don't give them your dragons," Dad said as he rumpled my hair.

I liked it when Dad rumpled my hair. His hands were rough, coal dust had filled the lines on his palms and if a donkey thistle seed landed there, a donkey thistle would strike roots and grow as high as the hill on his palm.

Yakob was already in his red Grand Cherokee; Kiro jutted out, an active volcano, his eyes pouring lava over the cash. *Honk-honk* sang the Grand Cherokee jeep, the car horn, the serviceable loyal dog, woofed as Kiro dashed off to the steering wheel.

"Get into the car," he shouted, goading me with the umbrella towards the grand red vehicle.

The house we had sold nodded sympathetically, the field waved its dry grasses at me; the other houses Yakob had recently bought winked, their gray walls trying to smile. Even the brightest color would have turned gray if the owner hadn't painted his hut for twenty years. In Yakob's car, the winter had set in. On the radio, a pop star shouted at the top of her bottomless lungs, a big screen TV spewed flames while two hunks blasted away at each other. Then, out of the blue, a cute chick showed up on the screen. She can't compare to Sara's pinky toenail, I thought.

$

"I'm David," the man said. "Who are you?"

She looked at him. Her eyes were the color of his dark-blue coverall before he'd put it on for the first time. A whirlpool in the Struma River were her eyes, so he stared as if he'd just got a fishbone stuck in his throat.

"They say you're as poor as a rusty rail. You tried to seduce a plumber. You fell flat on your face, they say. I come from a village by the Black Sea, but I'll beat it for Spain. I'll start the motorcycle one of these days and I'll say 'bye-bye' to this lousy place. What's your name?"

"Luba," the woman said as she pressed the heap of books against her ugly coat that had lost most of its color.

"You can try to seduce me if you want," he hinted. "I've given you the eye. I like you. Are these *Notre Dames*?" the man asked as he pointed to the books. "Sell them as scrap paper and you'll earn some cash. We can buy two glasses of brandy: one for me and the other for you."

The woman quickened her step, struggling with the coat that was hiding her ankles. She dropped one of her books, and it hit the nettles with a thud.

"Listen, I can do it for free with you. Save up your money, girl," the man said. "Look here! This old book costs one lev!" he added as he caught up with her, trampling on the nettles. Then he snatched up the book. "Wuth… Wuther.. ing.. Wuther-ing Heights," he muttered under his breath. "O, give me a break! You don't wuther the heights, you either leave them or defend them, girl. Come on. Don't you want something? Are you a silly woman, or what? Take off this coat. Let me see what you have to offer under it."

She took the book from him, clasped the paper pile in her hands and darted across grass and thorns, stumbling on the skirts of her coat. Her ankles gleamed, all silver in the green quagmire of the nettles. For a second, the long coat showed her knee, so white that the man with the tousled hair didn't know why he bolted for her. If a decent fellow meets a silly woman, he should explain the situation to her. David was a *gentleman*, damn it. He simply couldn't let her run like this among the donkey thistles.

"Look here, I'll buy you a glass of brandy, OK? No? You don't want brandy? Have you started losing your marbles?"

"Go away," said the woman. Well, what kind of a woman was she? A puny thing! And her denim coat looked older than the shaky passenger cars of that train.

"They gave me the boot for swearing at my manager. My mother met her maker, so I'll beat it for Spain," the Tousled Hair began, his shallow eyes intent on the girl's face. "The village is empty as an empty cupboard. What am I supposed to do here? My dad's gone, too… used to be as strong as flint… got drunk like an honest man, and in the morning woke up dead and cold."

It was hot. The sky, a bucket of gray clouds, pounced on the yellow ball of the sun. The railway line sweated, endless and indifferent in the heat.

"This coat's boiling you alive," David remarked as he pulled one of her tomes towards himself. The girl cowered.

"Don't touch my books!" she whispered.

"Listen, woman," the Tousled Hair said. "You don't know how many things I've read, volumes and novels both. You can't count up to that number. They don't have as many glasses in The Cat Pub. You can't impress me with books, woman. Write that down and read it three times a day. Hey, wait. Wait! You started it, woman!"

The girl walked on, not even glancing back, so he followed her.

"Listen to me. Hey! I earned eight hundred levs per month before the idiots fired me. Look here. I'm not like any Tom, Dick and Harry! I can plaster walls, strip off wallpapers, lay bricks, glue solid parquet flooring, fix a running toilet, eh? I want you to know this. They'll fork out two grand for my skills one of these days."

She stopped, her face hidden behind the pile of books.

"You're killing me! What will you do to this brick?" David asked as he touched the thickest book with a forefinger. "You read this bullshit? No… give your mom this one. She can burn it in the kitchen stove. Ok, let me carry the textbooks for you. Watch carefully, you may learn something. Look at my chest, muscles all over the place. You're thin like a shoelace. Ok, let's get things going." He took all the books, put half of them under his left arm, the rest under the right one, and added, "A buddy from the Cat Restaurant told me something. You offered him a bottle of brandy to get him into bed. Is this true?"

She didn't say anything, her denim coat, as old as the nettle seeds, wrapped tightly around her.

"It's ok for a woman to offer and pay," David blurted out. "Let's sit down. Let's get some rest under this plum tree, ok? Those plums are staring at us like puppies." She didn't seem to mind the sun as she trudged through thorns and bushes. At times her coat fluttered like a raven's wings. If it didn't show him her ankles and her milky-white knees, David would decisively give her the slip. "Stop, I tell you, or I'll be an experience you'd rather forget! Stop, or I'll throw your books in the river. Oh, the river's run dry. Ok, then, I'll set fire to them. Here's my cigarette lighter. See?"

The woman stopped in her tracks. Then she came up to him and, uttering no sound, extracted the *Notre Dames* from the trap of his arms.

"Mulish, aren't you," Tousled Hair concluded. "I haven't seen a woman as silly as you, honestly. I know plenty of dames… I've had more girlfriends than there are paving stones in front of The Cat Restaurant. Do I make myself clear?"

The girl plodded on through dust and dry grass. The path ended, but she plowed directly through blackthorns and wasp nests. David watched, sticking his neck out in the scorching sun.

"You're pretty," he muttered under his breath. After a while, he flopped down on the ground and tried to hide his legs under the scanty shadow of the small tree. Beads of sweat started to roll down his cheeks, neck and nose. He undid his shoelaces, took off his sneakers and sprawled out on the grass. Ants rapidly advanced on him and he cursed the dry yellow field.

The denim coat, as old as the train cars, returned to him. David sat up. The woman didn't say a word as she left her discolored textbooks to the mercy of the ants and sat down by his side. He could see the rotten sleeves of her coat and the dusty heap of her French *Notre Dames*.

She didn't look at him, and just sat rigidly by his side in the heat.

"Come in under the shade," David suggested, but the tree was too young, just a handful of leaves. Its shade was too narrow for the two of them, so he crept out in the sun. The woman refused to budge and the shade remained between them like a moat. Tousled Hair decisively reached across the moat then buried his nose into her face. This measure, in his opinion, was both the first and the last step towards a kiss. The girl recoiled from his touch.

"Hey, why did you come back if you don't want me?" he asked, disappointed. She retreated behind her paper *Notre Dame* Saints. "Ok, ok, look at me. My hands are behind my back. See? I won't do bad things to you. Don't be afraid."

She sat up, silent, trembling, bristling at him. At a certain point, David noticed that the skinny runt had grabbed a stone. In these parts, the soil was all rubble and mud. The sharp pieces of yellow rock yielded no crops to speak of; you could harvest only undersized spuds, but no one bothered to grow them here. Either the Roma guys or the Colorado beetles ate the spuds even before summer set in, so the potato fields had no potatoes. The potato bugs tried to eat stones, failed and died en masse. Heaps of Colorado beetles as big as popcorns lined the highway and the little Roma kids quarreled over them. In the evenings, the boys threw dead potato bugs into the fire, and their wings burned like Bengal lights. Tousled Hair thought that perhaps the State of Colorado was a fireworks show featuring dead flaring beetles.

The woman sat by his side, stock-still, a dead bug, waiting for a gypsy lad to hurl her into the fire so that she'd explode and become a star in the state of Colorado.

"Come on," David said. He lay on the grass, the sun beating down on his bare feet, his belly comfortable in the shade of the plum tree. She did nothing. He was on the verge of telling her about his native village, all deserted streets and abandoned houses. He'd better explain everything to her. After old villagers cashed in their chips, they started the motorbikes and decamped to the world beyond the Black Peak. The village was ok, clean air and stuff, but David would skedaddle as soon he made enough money. He'd go to Spain. His mother, may she rest in peace, breathed her last a year ago. His cousins, a heavy drinker the elder, a gambler the younger, were bad eggs, so… The girl collected her books and struggled to her feet.

Tousled Hair drew himself up to his full height.

"What?" he said.

"Be here tonight, 9 pm. The express train for Athens is due at 9.30," the girl whispered, avoiding his eyes.

David wanted to tell her that the railway station swarmed with drunks. All they wanted was a pretty girl like her and then… but she started the motorbike so quickly he could not warn her to be careful. He had a century to kill before the express train for Athens arrived, so it would be wonderful if he could get drunk at The Cat. Well, this seemed impossible. David had one lev, and if a guy wanted to drink like an honest citizen, he had to have at least three levs. That rotten express train for Athens was a snail. The heat would roast David, for sure. The thought of snails and high temperatures drove him to despair. Then something happened. The owner of The Cat showed up in front of the railway station. He was a generous one, wasn't he? The dude had let David guzzle down brandy that played 100 bagpipes. The bartender had drowned 100 pipers in his whiskey, and this was a good thing to do. But what would he want with David? Make him pay for his drinks, perhaps? It was obvious that the devil had come to collect his due as a stupid song said. David didn't have a penny to bless himself with.

§

The darkness in the backyard was as thick as the dust on the empty bowls and pans in the cupboard. The morning had lost its way in the village of Staro, and you didn't know how long the summer would stay on. The rain was a coward. Vasil, the father of Sara, Luba and Pirina, had forgotten to take the unloaded gun with which he guarded Yakob's sewing workshop. The man sat on the ground behind a pile of tattered newspapers, his eyes gazing at the columns of printed text. He looked abandoned; it felt like the articles were covered with frost and the letters perished one by one in his hands. In front of him, his daughters had put a glass of water on a piece of oilcloth, its roses so faded as if the autumn sat next to the man. He'd forgotten to sip at the glass. His eyes waited for something that didn't come.

"Vasil, peel the roasted peppers," his wife Slava said. To her, any newspaper was good enough to start a fire with and her wood-burning iron stove had tried many things; old clothes, scraps of paper and her three girls' old shoes. Those all were worn-out boots that remembered the children's heels, the school in Staro, cold autumns and winters. Some pairs remembered even Miss Petrova who recited the poem *My Little House in Bulgaria*, her eyes gleaming dangerously as if she was out of her mind at the end of the school year.

The stove remembered the kids' clothes too. With much dignity, old T-shirts had slowly turned into rags. Sara wore the dress, the pullover or the pants until she outgrew them all, then Luba put them on, and finally Pirina's turn came. But how could a stove learn anything about Sara's tears when she lost one lev and couldn't buy sweet cakes for her sisters? Sara still remembered the way the three of them stood in front of the convenience store, staring at the cinnamon buns, their mouths open. She felt she'd hate that lost lev until she breathed her last.

The stove knew a big secret: the letters that Slava had received from a miner from the town of Bobov Dol. "*I'll wait for u Behind the post office*" or "*I'll wait for U in the corn Field*". The poor devil was no good at using capital letters; any time he felt he'd written for a long time without using one, he penned a word in which the first letter was as tall as a chimney. Slava, who ordered her husband to peel the roasted peppers, Slava, who grew the most magnificent tomatoes in Staro — she made their roots strong with water in which she dissolved chicken droppings — this woman hid sometimes behind the post office or went to the cornfield. Then, after the miner, she rushed back home to her girls who played with their rag dolls in the shade of the quince tree. She was as strong as a peal of thunder.

Slava looked at kids. They were pretty. She, their mom, was a pretty girl too; why should this miner from Bobov Dol fork out fat ten levs for the ancient rattling bus to Staro if she wasn't? Why should he sneak up behind the post office, a place overgrown with nettles where gypsy lads kissed their sweethearts?

After Slava kissed the miner goodbye, she ran to the bean soup pot, swooped down on the brown sauce then cut the stale bread. She nodded at her husband who sat behind his pile of tattered newspapers, his wife running away from his eyes like a thief. Vasil must have seen her slink into the cornfield; her limping Vasil had surely noticed when the miner got off the boneshaker bus. Slava had even packed her things — were there things worth mentioning that a woman like her could boast of in the first place? Her three daughters were playing with the rag dolls she had made for them from her old skirt. Slava had thrown her only new dress into the suitcase, the one she put on when she went to the cornfield. She had taken the old coffeepot as well. She wanted to cram the only enamel cast-iron saucepan in her suitcase too, but couldn't find it in her heart to do it. How would Vasil cook nettle soup for the girls after she moved in with the miner from Bobov Dol?

Her eyes often settled on his busted leg, short and crooked as their dog Gasho's tail. The glass in front of him on the faded tablecloth was on her mind: he poured water into it. Vasil felt like drinking brandy in the afternoons, she knew. He drank water instead, saving up for their rainy years. He'd given up spending money on newspapers or clothes, he didn't waste money on anything at all. The only thing Vasil bought was sunflower oil, bread and pants for the girls. And he — wasn't the man a numbskull! — squandered the family's levs, hard-earned, drenched in sweat and blood, on books of fairytales as if the dumb yarns the pages spun were roasted peppers or chicken soup to fill the kid's bellies with. Vasil is a rainy day, she thought, so quietly did he sit by the faded tablecloth, a wind-blown leaf of the quince tree her husband was. Her Vasil, who was always saving pennies and dimes, took a ten lev bill out of his pocket and said, "Buy yourself some nice sandals, Slava. You can't go to that miner in that scuffed pair."

Then she put her new dress back in the lowest drawer of the chest and didn't go to the cornfield. For a couple of weeks, Slava would remain in front of the cracked mirror in the bedroom, staring at her reflection. What a pity she was so pretty. She had married at seventeen, and like a pig, she'd given birth to three kids. They were pretty, weren't they? She'd look at her girls playing under the quince tree with the doll she had sewn for them... Yes, they were pretty. Every time she thought of Vasil and his glass on the faded tablecloth, of the man limping in the backyard, she heaved a sigh and said to herself, "It might've been worse. Let me be pretty for him, for Vasil."

Vasil had finished peeling the peppers. In Radomir district, women called these small wild spears "gleaned murder." Hot as snakes all they were, and Slava's backyard smelled of murder and snakes all summer. The sky smelled of long winter, her eyes and thoughts stank of dill pickles that her husband was making, and she... she didn't know if she should be happy or ashamed that her strongest daughter Pirina was staying in Yakob's holiday villa. Slava's heart, as sharp as the peppers she picked, sank when she happened to catch a glimpse of Luba, her daughter that had gone astray.

It was cold and gray outside, and Luba had again drowned in her faded blue coat. Her daughter put it on when the afternoons were glowing embers in August; she was wearing it now under the black rain of pepper skins and, while Luba was roasting a heap of gleaned murder, she was reading a book loaded with lies as big as a horse cart. Otherwise her girl wouldn't have lost her head. She used to be a perfectly normal child, played hopscotch with the other kids, and now she went and burned the vegetables. Luba was off her rocker, like father like daughter. Too bad Slava cared about this man. Vasil had ruined her thinnest and silliest daughter, damn it! Slava was just thinking that Pirina had sunk to the bottom of Yakob's mire — at the villa that the locals called the Stronghold — when her eyes were drawn to the trees in their backyard. So far, so good, they'd kept the house, Slava picked quinces and immediately transformed them into jars of jam.

What could Yakob be doing to Pirina now? Why had he allowed them to live in the house? Pirina used to be a beautiful kid. What a pity! Wait a minute, Slava didn't let the sneaky word "pity" get the better of her. She fought and climbed higher than it. Time will come when I will have grandchildren, she thought. We're in our house now. Even their youngest dog inspired by Gasho barked as powerfully as a church bell, and that was a good sign. Too bad that Luba was reading this fat ledger of a book and burned the peppers. Well, the hooligans had stopped scrawling dirty sentences on their fence, like Luba had a screw loose and paid to have sex with men. If Slava were in her daughter's shoes, she'd pay a thug her last cent to have these chickens beaten black, flat and blue. No, she'd cut off their thumbs or find such poisonous words for them that they'd shoot themselves dead, every one of them.

She hated the filthy lies they chalked or sprayed on the fence. A month ago, Slava caught a drunk red-handed. He was scribbling, "Luba pays", but it was not Luba who paid; they did. Slava set Gasho the mutt on the idiot, then rushed axe in hand to chop off the moron's head. Who else would protect this girl, as timid as cotton, a fool who saw no further than the end of *Notre Dame's* nose? If Vasil hadn't plodded through thorns and nettles, chucking his tattered newspapers to stop her, Slavka might have knocked the living daylights out of that drunken schmuck. If the bats in his belfry were that active, let him spray-paint obscene graffiti on someone else's fence. One way or another, Slava managed to strike him with the axe, and his shirt got soaked with blood. Exactly like a decent woman soaked beans overnight in water before she cooked bean soup, the jerk's shirt soaked in his cheeky blood.

"The crazy shrew here cut my throat!" the guy roared as Vasil hobbled down to him, speaking reassuringly, "Wait, she's not done yet."

Slava didn't have fears about her firstborn, Sara. Her eldest daughter read neither musty newspapers nor anything else about this *Notre Dame* or another. She was constantly getting bad grades in Bulgarian at school, the teacher often visited Slava, repeating the same story, "Please pay close attention to this child. She can't read fluently and can't spell long words."

The more poor grades Sara got, the prettier she became. Slava wondered how it was possible that so much beauty had gone into a small, narrow girl's face.

"One day you'll come to me as you go to church to pray," her daughter had blabbed. "You'll see, Mom." Slava slapped her across the face and that was all there was to it.

"If you get another bad grade, I'll lock you in the cellar with the mice," her mom threatened after boxing Sara's ear. "The church steeple will come crashing down if you attend a service."

"Bring her to the study hall at school in the afternoon," the teacher Miss Petrova asked Slava. "In the afternoon, I teach students to learn to read better."

After Sara started attending the additional lessons at the study hall, all 8th-12th grade male high school students joined the afternoon classes.

The lads, however, didn't seem attracted to grammar; they stared at Sara and instead of studying classical Bulgarian poetry and fiction, they were fighting it out over who would carry Sara's bag for her to her house, a shabby building with a shabbier board fence in front of it. Every day, 9th graders, 11th graders and other students got into fisticuffs and came back home mauled, their T-shirts bloodstained. Their mothers visited Slava and bitterly complained to her, "Tame this wild daughter of yours, woman. They'll close down our school for good, and our sons will have to plod through mud and rocks to Radomir."

Miss Petrova, the Bulgarian teacher, felt forced into giving Sara passing grades with the sole purpose of discouraging her from attending the additional classes, thus putting an end to the bloodshed. Passing grades or no passing grades, Slava was not at all worried about her firstborn.

Her skinniest daughter, Luba, got all straight A's in the semester, so it didn't come as a surprise when Miss Petrova visited Slava. The harebrained educator asked Slava to raise money and let Luba enter the Bulgarian language speaking competition in Sofia. O, come off it. Returning from school, all the kids avoided Luba, and she slogged along by herself as if she had the measles in 1st through 9th grade. Luba sat at the first desk in the middle row, her eyes trained on Miss Petrova as if every word the Bulgarian literature teacher uttered was a gold piece.

Scraggy Luba was always writing down something in her notebook. In the evenings, instead of directly coming home from school, she left the gravel road and walked across the field where the villagers tethered their donkeys. There the girl read the next thick book the Bulgarian literature teacher had given her. One day, seething, Slava went and quarreled with the pedagogue.

"Petrova, you're driving my Luba crazy," Slava fumed. "You're off your nut if you think I'll put up with you. Don't give her books. I'll make you cut your own ears and eat them if you do. Mind my words."

At a certain point, Luba started to show up in Staro, lugging a heap of *Notre Dames* in a heavy bag, and the neighbors dropped hints she paid men. How could she pay these morons? She didn't have two pennies to rub together. The teacher stopped giving her books, but Luba must have already gone off her head because she moved into the village library and stayed there hours on end. It was a narrow room full of dusty reading matter, so one was in big danger of dying from asthma. In the library, Luba sat on the only good chair, all the others broken one by one with time, and the librarian felt free to burn them in her stove. On the one hand, the woman's coal bin remained untouched, and on the other, she was rid of annoying readers.

Years ago, Slava's husband, too, went and killed time as he perused volumes coved in a white cobweb. Now his daughter Luba did the same thing while the librarian dug her potatoes, weeded her garden or picked strawberries. Luba read and read, a girl as useless as the wind that shook the branches of the thorny bushes in the forest. The librarian declared that in the library there were books that adhered to Old Bulgarian grammar rules, adding that those rules applied at the time when Slava's grandma was a toddler. So far so good, however, after Luba read all the books, including the ones loaded with ancient grammar and lies, breathing in their dust, she took to poring over the tomes initially stuffed in plastic sacks and stored in the school cellar. This was the final straw. Slava rushed to Petrova's place, firmly clutching a pole she had pulled out of the ground in her tomato garden.

The teacher, a confused soul, had hoofed it all the way from Radomir to Staro. Slava reasoned that if Petrova was a decent demoiselle, she wouldn't bury herself in their backwater village, no sir. She'd have found a husband. What did she do, I ask you? The wacko goggled at her books day and night!

"Can you see this pole in my hand, Petrova? It's for you!" Slava shouted. "I'll flog you. Your mulishness unhinged my girl!"

Slava hit the teacher once with the pole, not very hard, for the woman had taught Sara to read. That was the honest truth. Not that reading was a useful thing, mind you. Petrova had taught Pirina to read, too, and Slava knew a woman was worth her name only if she could worm her way out of the whoppers the big fat liars published in the newspapers. The single blow of Slava's pole seemed to have done the job, for on the following day, the teacher packed up her things and vanished, for better or for worse. Where had she gone off to — to Radomir, to teach rich guys' kids, to Sofia where big money was, or perhaps she'd bought a train ticket and journeyed to Spain to pick olives there like a decent lady? It was a total mystery.

After Petrova made herself scarce and Yakob bought her place, lock stock and barrel, Slava felt constantly out of sorts. She shouldn't have run the poor demoiselle off from the village; should have scared the pants off her, yes that would be ok, or simply should've sworn at her to straighten things out. Slava had grabbed a pole. What a shame. Thank God, Petrova dragged herself back to Staro… well, it didn't turn out the way Slava had hoped.

Luba was down and out, deaf and blind all the time Petrova was away from school. The girl ran a fever. Her forehead was as hot as the boiling water in the teapot. Pirina, too, seemed to be in low spirits, and even Sara who earned one bad grade after another shed a tear when the teacher was gone. On the day Petrova disappeared, Vasil, Slava's limping husband, didn't drink a drop of water as his eyes dug and delved the faded letters in the newspapers. He opened a bottle of brandy, the one they kept as a cure for flu and tuberculosis, and slowly drank it. Gulping hard as if he was swallowing stones, Vasil moaned. Slava was struck dumb as her husband heaped the tattered newspapers in the backyard, threw dry grass on them and set fire to the yellow pile. He stood still, the smoke getting into his eyes. Her man was losing his mind. He didn't step away from the fire, he pushed his way through flying soot instead. Her man sank into the thickest flames, his eyes growing damp. That must be the smoke, Slava muttered to herself. That must be the smoke.

§

"Look here, my girl. You'll embark on an adventure, I warn you." David had made efforts to shave, although his razor was as blunt as a hoe, and he'd cut himself twice. He'd even washed his shirt, but didn't have an iron, so the thing was clean but wrinkled all over the place after he put it on. He had washed his head in the river as well. "Hey, sugar, you're an hour and a half late," David accused the girl. He hadn't asked her for her name, but he had recognized her faded denim coat. "Tell me honestly why you are late."

She didn't say anything, and David, fearing the girl might think he was gay, clasped her in his arms. Something went wrong under his fingers. The girl was shivering, her blue apron was shaking and her skin shrank like a caterpillar you poked with a twig. "This chick is out of her mind," David said to himself. Running the risk the gal might think he *was* a pansy, he withdrew his hand from her shoulder. His threat that she'd have an adventure must have frightened her, so he said reassuringly, "Don't be afraid, this won't be any kind of adventure." The trick worked. She did give a start, but didn't appear to panic. On the other hand, her body did run away from his fingers to the thorns and the brink of the Struma River.

Now the Struma was a puddle of mud, the duckweeds a bone-dry green crust in the evil heat.

"I could've bought you a pork chop at the pub," David said. "But I don't have a penny to my name. I can't spend more than fifty cents a day, you know… I've already drunk away my money in The Cat. No fear, I still have one lev and a dime in my pocket. These will keep body and soul together until Monday. Look here, do you want me to pluck sorrel leaves for you?"

She nodded. Her gesture reassured him; the girl had reacted well, therefore she wasn't one of those bitches that would give a decent guy the boot because he had only one lev and a dime until Monday. Courage came back to his heart. He ran to the field and trawled every inch of it for sorrel. The grass was as hard as pig iron. He didn't know what to do.

"I'll have to start the motorbike and steal tomatoes from the nearby gardens," he explained to her. "There's not a single sorrel leaf, damn it."

The girl didn't say anything as she thrust her hand under her apron and produced a mini loaf of bread; not one of those smelly cheap things you could buy at The Cat. It was an honest small white loaf.

"You have bread," he said, surprised. "It's still warm and smells good… smells of fried sausages and bean soup". David tore the loaf into two pieces. Its crust smelled of her hand and of bean soup, and he was suddenly so hungry that his head throbbed. He gobbled down his half; hers smelled even better. "Listen, kiddo, will you eat this bread? If you don't want to eat it…"

Then David remembered he hadn't had a bite to eat since morning. At The Cat, the White Silk, the bartender, gave him a glass of 100 Pipers. This time, the White Silk's hair was up in a ponytail — David had noticed the ponytail made the guy particularly generous — and the Silk added a bowl of soup to the whiskey. David drank the soup and washed the dishes in White Silk's kitchen, set the table in White Silk's room, and White Silk gave David a white shirt that was too large for him.

David had hoped he could swap it for two loaves of bread at the bakery in Staro, but it turned out he had hoped in vain. So, he ate the girl's half of the mini loaf as well.

"Hey, listen, what did you say your name was?" he asked her. "I tend to forget my sweethearts' names. Don't you worry. I'll write down yours and I'll commit it to memory for good."

The girl didn't tell him her name. She produced another mini loaf as tiny as a kid's sand bucket. David stopped asking questions, his teeth sank into the crust instead. He hadn't tasted anything so delicious since he took his salary a month ago before they fired him. He bolted down the baguette-like thing even before the moon showed its gloomy expression on the sky. How long would it take for a moon to show its face at the end of August, I'd like to know? Ten seconds and it shone as brightly as a tin box amidst the clouds. The moon was the owner of the sky, the month of August also belonged to it, and so the heavenly body gleamed undisturbed above David's head.

"Do you have any bread left?" David asked, then pounced at the third mini loaf she fished out of her gray bag.

"Your bread is a miracle!" he said. "I wanted to buy you something delicious to eat, but I've wasted my fifty cents on booze, you know. Tomorrow I'll catch some fish for you." David knew pretty well he could hardly catch any fish at all. The Struma had nothing to do with the savage river that in November rampaged through the valley, wrenching the trees from the soil, their roots grabbing at the dark air. Now the Struma was all dry stones and green slime. "Look, I can catch some frogs for you," he offered, trying to put her mind at ease. "I can see no fish, but don't you worry, I'll get going, and I'll sweep the floor at White Silk's pub. Then I'll be able to buy you something, I promise."

He reached out for her, put his hands around her neck and again something went wrong under his fingers. The faded blue apron shook and the thin girl stopped breathing.

"Hey, are you nuts?" he asked her. "I mean, are you in your right mind? Well, if you're not all there, don't waste my time."

She scrambled to her feet, taking away the sweet bag with the mini-loafs that smelled of pure gold. Her face was as soft as the last day of August, and David calmed down after he glanced at it. Women that had the end of August on their faces were not nuts.

"Hey, stop, stop, I didn't mean you were nuts!" he assured her. "Come here. I won't hurt you. If you have some bread, I'll eat it."

She didn't have any bread, and David wasn't hungry anymore. He simply felt like looking at her, as he ventured into the unknown, "Why don't you come and sit by my side?" He didn't expect she'd do what she was asked. As if the autumn hurled her off the highest branch of a big tree, so rapidly did she sit down at his feet. David touched her hand, and a disquieting thought popped into his mind, "*Her hand's freezing. She's sick today. It's a bad thing for a woman to be cold at the end of August.*" He touched her fingers, and the sweet smell of bread hit him again.

"I wish you had something to eat," he muttered under his breath as he stopped himself from rummaging in her bag where she kept her mini loaves and her secrets. He kissed her. Her face trembled under his lips, and this almost made him laugh. In the pale light of the evening, her old apron looked like the path of the moon to him.

A year ago, David drove to the Black Sea coast to buy sand, nails and hammers, and it was then he saw the moon's path; her apron was the same thing, silver and blue; that explained why the girl smelled of the moon. He kissed her again, but she wriggled out of his grip, just like the water did when he tried to stop a swimming pool leak. It dripped, trickled and was gone, no swimming for the owner and no money for David.

The girl dashed off, her apron opening a moon's path for David. He ran after her. She was totally nuts, crazy all over the place. It was the first time David had seen such a girl, her hands as soft as breadcrumbs.

"Stop. Hey, stop," he called out helplessly. "I won't eat your mini loaves anymore," but she had already jumped over the Struma River and stood by the dry duckweed behind the boulders, hotter than hotplates in the heat. *I didn't ask her her name*, a freezing thought carved his mind. *I'm nuts all over the place.*

At *The Cat*, he had to ask White Silk Shirt what the chick's name was and maybe why she'd run away from him. *She's in awe of my determination, the blockhead I am*, David said to himself reproachfully. *My impatience broke her neck. You have to have a soft voice for chicks and that means you have to drink two glasses of stone brandy. Then you're as gentle as a heap of feathers. I drank half a glass and scared her out of her wits.*

He saw her sprinting to the poplar trees. Ravens had built hundreds of nests among the branches and sat in them, cawing and squawking, so David thought the poplars were croaking too. Behind the raven poplars, the girl froze in her tracks as the moon-path waited for her.

"Don't ever chase a skirt, little buddy," Plamo, his best friend instructed him. They didn't fire Plamo, so the dude could say anything he pleased. "Skirts are mean. They wait for you to chase them and can't stop bragging about it. All they say about you is that you're a stupid pair of shoes."

A highway maintenance worker could scoff at skirts as long as his tongue caught fire in his mouth, he could hook a call girl in the first place, but if one had one lev and a dime in his pocket to keep body and soul together until Monday… David came to hate both this lev and this dime. He forgot all Plamo had taught him about skirts, he saw her and her bag in which there was no bread anymore.

David rushed across the river, through frogs and bare stones under which tiny carps were waiting for the autumn. He was about to catch her up when she dashed off. This chick ran like a wolf, damn it. She seemed to know all hare and goat trails in the district as she scuttled up the hill through thickets of briars and hawthorn bushes. David caught his pants on every thorn that came his way, and the ravens, old black rags, sons of bitches all of them, cawed at him at the top of their lungs. When the girl noticed he'd got entangled in weeds or had tripped and tumbled to the ground, she stopped dead in her tracks and waited, her eyes studying him.

This missy was positively loony but wasn't David loony, if you think about it? Why should he run like a moron in her wake if he weren't? At long last, a cottage came into view under the old gossip, the moon.

David couldn't say if it was a cottage or a hencoop. The walls were the color of September night, brown like lizards, a dwelling place for screech-owls at the back of beyond, yet the girl entered the room. She sank like a stone into the shack, and it would be a pity if David didn't find out why she'd pushed her way through nettles and briars to get there. *Perhaps she'd hired a gang of thugs to slit my throat*, he thought. *The bitch will sell my kidneys and my heart, and she'll get drunk on the money at* The Cat.

One way or another, he followed her. He'd plodded across the dry, hot field and would not give up. No way, he wasn't that whacko. On entering the hovel, he felt as if a bullet had hit his brain. If the thugs had chopped off a portion of his nose, they wouldn't have left him that astounded. If ten screech-owls had built nests on his head to hatch their eggs there, David wouldn't think this was as weird as this room. What he found inside was out to lunch.

A candle burned in the hencoop, but he saw no hens there. The place was full to the brim with books. Twenty-eight million books lay on the floor, arranged neatly like crates, some as huge as roofing slates or bricks, others thin and yellow, still others no bigger than boxes of chocolates. The windows were all blocked up with fat volumes, and a gap-like porthole half-jammed with notebooks let the moon slither into the dust. The faded moon's path on the girl's skin was mute and miserable. Her apron lay on the floor, and the girl waited, naked under the naked candle flame that illuminated only her knees. The candle could, as easy as pie, set fire to these papers thickly heaped up one on top the other.

David and the hencoop would soon be roasting in the blaze. Too bad for the girl. What a pity the candle couldn't illuminate all of her. Her knees, gleaming in the dark, told David nothing.

"We'll sell the used books, then we can go to the Black Sea," he suggested as he took a step to her. "Are all of them yours?"

She remained motionless as David took the candle and slowly, gently lifted it up towards the fattest tomes at the top of the book-hill. He waited for the light to climb to the biggest volume, a green hardcover. The girl kissed him. Her cold lips, even though it was still August, missed his mouth, brushing his cheek exactly where his blunt razor blade had cut his cheek. Suddenly, he smelled trouble, a fire that would destroy the grass, the trees and everything around him.

"I can't," he said as he bent forward to the only thing that was not a book, her faded apron, and threw it over her shoulders.

She didn't say anything; surely after she put on the apron she'd lost her tongue, or perhaps was struck dumb because the candlelight was too feeble. The girl ran outside to the bats that were catching something to eat in the dusk. David remained with the candle that would gobble up all greasy books, lying prostrate, like cabbages, in front of him. He could live on this mass of old paper for five even six days — enough food and a glass of Pipers every evening — if only he could sell these brown tomes.

§

White Shirt, who insisted David address him as Anno, put his faith in the shaggy-haired man, entrusting him with a second-hand minivan acquired in Germany in the obscure past. The vehicle was perhaps thirty years old, and if David tapped its roof, a hailstorm of rust dropped onto his head. Furthermore, the thing was guzzling gas as if its present owner had bought it in some backwater desert village and not in Frankfurt. The boneshaker behaved as if it hadn't had a drop of gas for a century. David was supposed to drive the van to Sofia and buy minced meat, frozen chickens and an assortment of cheap vegetables for the pub.

Some of White Silk Shirt's loyal customers envied David, others wolf-whistled at him every time he strolled along the street under the furious sun, an *At the Cat* cap tipped over his eyes, a fashion item Anno had paid a designer in Sofia a handful of greenbacks for. The same designer sewed Anno's white silk shirts, using high quality French fabrics. Anno had his slips made of a French patterned-silk blend, too. Every two days, the bartender treated a loyal customer to a glass of Pipers, and the lucky dog hung these expensive items of underwear on the clothesline to dry in the wind in front of the drinking establishment. The patrons, pleasantly warm with the stone brandy in their stomachs, admired the silk slips, clicking their tongues.

David slept in a narrow room that even at the end of August stank of mold; however, the bartender paid a housepainter to renovate the chamber and put a white prime coat on the walls. Often at night, before David went to sleep, he imagined they'd wrapped him up in a white medicine storage box. Anno addressed him as "sir," rarely as "illustrious sir," and soon all drunkards used this appellation. The pub landlord hired a barber that trundled through the valley in his ancient Volkswagen jalopy, a virtuoso selected to shave David and trim his hair. Anno even gave his assistant a couple of his immaculately white suits that were too big for the rope-thin guy. In an enormous snow-white jacket and pants, David looked like the pregnant female doctor who was in charge of healthcare issues in the village of Staro, dreaming day and night of kicking healthcare's ass and beating it for Germany where science and technology flourished.

David went twice to the place where the girl in the blue coat had let him eat all her bread. He asked two drunks what her name was, but they kept mum like the cobblestone path in the graveyard. He treated each guy to a glass of turnip brandy to mollify him, but the drunks thundered indignantly, "Chasing the blue coat, eh? Is that why Anno pays the barber to shampoo your dirty locks?" The boozers shut up for good, and that was all there was to it. It seemed these guys had spat out their tongues into the Struma River.

Then it wasn't necessary to ask anybody anything. David saw her.

She was in the schoolyard. Before David arrived in Staro, they said the school used to be entirely yellow. Now it was brown with gray patches under the windows, the plaster had fallen off the walls, and he could see the crumbling brickwork. The mayor didn't have money to repair the building, they said. A crowd of youngsters had gathered around the girl — gypsy kids as small as plums, pencils in hands, and she, in her blue apron that had the path of the moon in it, sat in the shade of a chestnut tree. What is she doing to them, he asked himself, but did not say anything out loud, feeling so happy he forgot where his voice was. He let the frozen chickens sweat in the 50 year-old minivan, ignored his terror that the catfish fillets would turn into muddy paste in the heat as he rushed to the school's naked brickwork.

"Hey!" David shouted.

The Roma kids, little ostriches all, bristled, a brat clutching a knife, a smaller one brandishing an awl as a street urchin as tall as a chair hurled a rusty nail at him. David couldn't tell if they were boys or girls. Everybody's heads looked the same as if a moronic barber had trimmed their hair with a wood cutting saw. At places the scalps were shaved to the bone and shone threateningly, at the back, untidy tresses hung down scrawny necks.

"I won't beat you, guys," he assured them, but the sprogs didn't understand a word and the tallest kid tried to stab him with his awl.

"Zachary, please stop," the girl said, the moon gleaming in her voice.

Suddenly the gypsy awl drooped in midair an inch away from David's head.

"Hey," David said startled. "I went ten times to the river. I saw no sign of you."

"Sir! Illustrious Sir!" the kids shrieked, jumping on him, groping him, tugging on his white short-sleeve shirt and his white shorts of finest French fabric that Anno had given him.

"What are you doing to these kids?" he asked.

She didn't answer, she got up and crossed the cinder-covered part of the schoolyard. The cinders were the pupil's gymnasium in winter and in summer. The other part of the schoolyard, thickly overgrown with thorn-apples and thistles, used to be the school's experimental area. The brats stopped barking "Sir! Sir!" and followed her, a shabby peacock's tail, scraped to the skull at places or bunches of bristling waist-length hair trimmed with a Husqvarna brush cutter.

"Hey, where will you take these kids?" David trailed behind the peacock's tail, completely forgetting about the chickens that were melting in the van. The catfish fillets flashed like lightning in his mind: Anno would bake them, then he'd invite David to a delicious dinner and a couple of Pipers in the magnificent glass the bartender had bought him.

"What are you up to, eh? Stop. Hey! Stop!"

"She teaches us to read and write. We don't want to be blockheads like you," said the big boy as he brandished the awl, the small hairs under his nose dark like poison. "I'll break your neck if you touch her. Do I make myself clear?"

"What's in your pockets? Let me see what you've stolen." David overtook the kids, or rather caught up with the big boy's back. He couldn't make it to the moon's path of her blue apron. No one cared a hoot that David should be in the restaurant and his catfish fillets, 30 levs per pound, had turned into mud in the minivan. "What have you hidden in your black plastic bags?"

"Our moms gave us food. Give this to Luba, your teacher, they said. She teaches us to write. We don't want to remain stupid and un'ducated like you," a kid explained, probably a girl, for the nipper wore a skirt, long and brown like the heat, so tight that David said to himself, *this must have been one of her dad's trouser legs.*

"Your moms and dads filch stuff and things from honest guys' gardens," David muttered under his breath. "Woman! Hey, wait. Wait! Why did you start the motorbike? What are you up to? There are only trash bins behind the school. What will you do there?"

But the girl did have something important to do there for she neither turned back nor said a word. The boy with the awl thundered, "Go back or I'll cut your thing, if you have one!"

"Mom says men that wear white clothes like you don't have such things," the girl in the trouser-leg skirt hinted.

"Tonight, I'll wait for you at the place where I ate all your bread. Do you hear me, woman?" David shouted.

The deep shadows of the chestnut trees heard him.

The kids and the plastic bags full of stolen tomatoes for their teacher vanished behind the school building. David dumped all empty Coca-Cola bottles from The Cat in the trash bins here. He tailed the bunch of brats and the minute he saw the rubbish heap in front of him, the air was thorns and needles in his mouth. The gypsies and their teacher had built a house, all transparent walls and roof, with empty Coca-Cola bottles. The place stank of plastic and sour soft drinks, but the kids' house was so dazzling and magnificent that David froze in his tracks, spellbound by its translucent Fanta and Sprite door.

§

Then bulldozers started to put up a fence around the mountain. The machines dug a moat that surrounded the hills exactly the way the serfs did in the Middle or Black Ages; Pirina didn't remember how the teacher called this time at school. Pirina had flunked most of her history tests, leaving Miss Petrova as hopeless as a beaten track. All she knew was that the noblemen burrowed into the mud and rubble, excavated ditches full of slime, crocodiles and adders in order to protect their wives' panties from other blue bloods while the barons carried out a crusade or two, or mauled one another in a war near their warm castles.

Now the bulldozers bit into an endless meadow, so big Yakob couldn't drive around it in his Grand Cherokee jeep for three days. The ditches filled with grass-snakes and grasshoppers. Not a drop of water was in sight. One couldn't smell the river for the Struma was dry duckweeds and dead tadpoles in August. The bulldozers fenced in oaks, mushrooms and hares.

Pirina had the right to crisscross the forest and wander all over the place if only old Martusha trailed along behind her, muttering a volcano of curses under her breath. The old woman droned on about what she should expect from scumbag Pirina; no sooner had the floozy smelled Yakob's Grand Cherokee vehicle than she lifted her petticoat.

Pirina roamed the hill and, to put it plainly and more directly, she ran all the way, but Martusha, although old as the riverbed, trotted in her wake. Yakob had ordered the old boots to be all eyes. Pirina should meet no one. How could she meet anyone here, at the back of beyond? Doc Stoim was admitted to hospital on the very day when he got drunk for the first time in his life to honor a woman. Doc Stoim, a decent healer, had treated young and old for years; he brought some through sickness and saw others off to eternal treatment in heaven, he personally went to his patient's grave, and, bottle of brandy in hand, shed a tear as he stared at the modest tombstone.

"You're no healer, doc. Not in the least!" Martusha fumed. "Why should you sob your heart out for these worms?" She said those words before meals and killed two birds with one stone: on the one hand, she wasn't tight-lipped like a hammer, on the other, she at least verbally, approached the topic that hadn't stopped stinging her heart: he, Doctor Stoim. She always had the man on her mind and his name on the tip of her tongue. "Guys choose their docs to make death easier for them. Sob and snuffle, Doc, now that Pirina, the sleazy bitch, went and knocked you dead. You're off your head, man. You are! What a waste. It's the first time I'd felt like having a guy since my hubby Gercho bought the farm. I buried him with my own hands. The guy I wanted was you! You seem over-the-hill, Doc, it's true, but the older you get — even if you'd collapsed and then crept along the pavement — the more I'd have loved you. Now I don't give a hoot about you, Stoim, old fart. I want you to write that down on your kitchen wall and read it twice a day, Doc."

...Pirina burst into song. Today she imagined she was singing in Greek so she savagely thundered on, "Hey, Greeks, they've trapped me among four mountains, a moat and a wall. A frigging moat like the ones fat kings dug in the Middle Ages to protect their wives' socks. Mom weeds the cornfield without me. Dad drinks water. He's saving his brandy for the future, his eyes glued to the newspapers, every evening without me.

Doc Stiom is dying without me. My sister Sara sleeps with different guys every night. She can tell you man's love is greedy and evil. My poor sister Luba… If only Luba chucked out all her nutty books! I hope against hope she's learned to fry onions, or she'll bite the dust, a moth pressed between two pages. I wish they didn't give Dad those old newspapers. I can see him by the heap of paper, his eyes flowing out, losing their way among the printed letters."

…After lunch, Yakob took Pirina to the scarlet room. Everything was red in it, the inlaid floor, the walls and windows; there was no ceiling there, a red mirror from Switzerland reflected Yakob's back as the man worked hard to lose weight through copulation. Pirina hated her 10th grade geography textbook because Yakob bought her clothes from all countries mentioned on its pages: shorts from Jamaica, a blouse from Sweden and boots from Germany that were so strong they could crush a train under their heels. Pirina had the world, its gowns, shoes, refrigerators and sandwiches in the mountain fenced in by a moat as deep as a volcano. The food-laden table exuded warmth and delicious smells of recipes from Greece, Shanghai and the North Pole.

She could no longer let loose her spiders. They couldn't chase the rain and tell her in the evening what they'd seen. Locked up with the old crone, Pirina hated the world that knuckled under Yakob, serving him chocolate, shoes and sexual enhancement creams.

"I want to go home," Pirina told Yakob one day.

He didn't say a word or stop the activities he was involved in; the man kept active by making love after love to her, the only physical exercise that, in his view, burned calories. When Yakob was fresh enough, he and Pirina went to red room with the Swiss mirror. In case the lord was dog-tired, he installed her on the leather couch where Pirina's obligation was to breathe slowly by his head in the green room. There even the mirror was green, and the reflection of his ass appeared green too. If business was slack, Yakob locked her up in the brown room. There was no bed there. Its floor was a carpet, so thick that one couldn't see Pirina after she'd sunk into it.

Yakob swore and hurled abuse at Pirina in his black room. No bed, no chairs, no lamp, the place was black silk walls and black silk sheets. He hissed obscenities at her stomach, breasts, womb, and Pirina wondered how it was possible for a human being to put bread in his mouth and swallow it after he'd pronounced those filthy words.

"I want to go home," Pirina said after a week. Yakob went off the deep end every time someone interrupted his efforts in his colorful rooms; at least that was what the girls before Pirina shared with old Martusha. Pirina didn't care if Yakob was livid with rage or danced with joy.

"Do you have a boyfriend in the village?" Yakob asked.

"No," Pirina said. "Let me go."

They were in the red room with the Swiss mirror.

"If I let you go, I'll kick your parents out of the village, I'll burn down your house and I'll kick Sara out of the Venice Motel. Do you want all this to happen?"

Pirina shut up, feeling the red walls inside her bones.

"Yes," she said. "I have a boyfriend in the village. I want to see him."

Yakob kept mum as he threw his love into her like a load of clay. A guy's love is so heavy it breaks your ribs. Martusha is sent for and soon an ambulance comes.

That night, Yakob forbade Pirina to eat dinner.

"I gather you've got a boyfriend in the village," he said.

"Yes," Pirina said. She thought of her sisters, her mom and dad.

Her mother grew the most awesome tomatoes in Staro, her father had a heap of old newspapers and her two sisters were pretty.

Pirina didn't eat anything that evening. In front of her, old Martusha and Yakob chewed their Chinese style roast duck, jamming pieces of China into their guts, drinking wine. Yakob had a swig every now and then, the crystal bottle from the Netherlands igniting flames on his lip as Martusha gargled and swirled Dutch mineral water in her mouth. After Doc Stoim was banished from the neighborhood, her blood pressure wound its way through hot afternoons like an adder ready to strike the old woman between her eyebrows. I'll die like a mouse, Martusha thought. The next slut will plant her scrawny ass in my chair, after Yakob has had his fill of nutty Pirina.

Pirina didn't have a bite of the Chinese style roast duck and didn't drink a drop of mineral water from the Netherlands. The whole night, her stomach was a duck bristling with hunger as it hovered over the Himalayans.

"I want you to let me go," Pirina said in the morning on an empty stomach as the duck in her belly flew away to Asia starved to death.

Yakob raised his index finger half an inch as he ordered Martusha, "Don't give her anything to eat at lunch."

That day, Pirina didn't have lunch. When Yakob dropped in intending to lose weight through love and copulation on the grass, Pirina fell asleep under him. The sun above her forehead simmered: a big bowl of creamy soup, the earth under her ass was a slice of brown bread and the moat that surrounded four mountains was a sesame roll in her dream.

Pirina passed out. After she came to, Yakob took to feeding her the way he pampered his Irish setter, a mutt notorious for his mean biting habit. The beast was itching to bite strangers around the clock. Martusha was behind it all: she sprayed the victims with special Scottish deodorant, and the vile smell of carrion infuriated the mutt.

Yakob doted on Yanko, the Irish setter. Yanko had been a comforting part of his owner's life five years now. On the other hand, at least a dozen girls had writhed in the scarlet, green, brown and black rooms of his mansion. Evan Martusha, who provided her boss with a blow-by-blow account, putting down names, ages, weight, height, etc. in a special leather-bound notebook, got confused as to the precise number. Yakob fed raw Finnish salmon and German raw pork to the setter, offering him chunks of meat he himself cut with his Swiss army knife.

Yakob arranged pieces of Finnish salmon on his thighs and waited for Pirina to eat the pieces, licking his thighs clean the way Yanko, the Irish setter did. Pirina lay prostrate, immobile; perhaps at that moment the last spider in her thoughts gave up the ghost, or perhaps she hated to eat pieces of salmon as thin as a subway tickets, licking hirsute thighs. She opened her mouth and sang. The song had no words and no tune, but her old loyal dragons squeezed their way through her clenched teeth and soon caught up with the Chinese duck that was flying over the Arctic Ocean.

"I have a boyfriend in the village," she shouted.

Pirina had no boyfriend to speak of, had nothing at all, but she wanted to jump over the moat and its adders, with which the dukes protected their wives' stockings from other dukes during the Middle, Black and Lilac Ages. Pirina did not intend to spend another age in Yakob's luxury mansion.

§

Her hands went numb the minute she saw him: a guy in a shabby boiler-suit so thickly packed with dust that his skin and the fabric must have cemented together. Kalcho! She immediately knew it was him.

Kalcho was Koyna's son, and Koyna was the druggist who used to have a tiny chemist's shop in the town of Kustendil. Robbers ransacked it twice and the woman moved to the village of Staro. She gave the old wives aspirin and helped them fight against death. The hardy souls battled, struggled and lived on, making death sick. The drunkards comprised a considerable part of the drugstore's clientele. They paid the old pharmacist in empty beer bottles, dug or weeded her small strawberry beds in return for remedies to help heart failure.

The drunks could barely breathe, the problems in their chests as heavy as the hills. They were die-hard fellows committed to getting totally sloshed; most of them loved to slurp heart-cure syrup, hoping to survive the long day. Five men, completely frazzled by the sun and the fabulous heart cure, sat in front of Yakob's mansion, their heads bending low. Yakob personally sprayed them with the special Scottish deodorant.

The youngest among these scruffy guys was Kalcho, the druggist's son. Why should the poor bugger volunteer to get sprayed with antiperspirant that reeked of manure? Even before Yakob had selected Pirina as his best weight-loss tool, Kalcho would sit in the chemist's shop late in the evening. When the month of July was all over the place with its red-hot crates of ripe tomatoes, Pirina would drop by his place and would sing to him. He was the only human being who could listen to her without grabbing for his liver or spleen, panic-stricken. She wailed quietly, on Mondays in Greek, on Thursdays in Italian or in Hindi. Her yowls and howls sounded poisonous; however, Pirina imagined that she sang in the language of the country for which the train in her thoughts was bound. Once Kalcho held her hand in the shadow of his mother's drugstore; he'd kissed her pinky finger, a silly thing to do that left Pirina speechless. She felt as if a stranger had shot her dead and stared at Kalcho as though the stranger had shot Kalcho dead, too.

"Are you ill or something?" she asked the guy. "You should kiss your girl on the mouth."

But Kalcho didn't dare to do this. He just stood there, looking at her, looking at her so long that she finally kissed him the way one should because evidently the guy was not all there, and didn't know what to do.

"Pirina!" Kalcho shouted from the row of the drunkards.

Pirina didn't say anything. She knew what had happened to a plasterer that had called out to her, "Love you, sugar!" as he waved from the top of the wall he was plastering.

"Love you," she'd shouted to him from the other side of the moat. "What's your name?"

"Gosho," the plasterer had thundered back from beyond the mountain, and that was it. Yakob fired Gosho the plasterer. This was a mean thing to do. In these parts, you could sweep the floors at the Venice Motel or fry chicken livers in the kitchen to make a living. A pretty woman had a different story to tell: she could sneak into one of the motel rooms with a trucker, or if the guy was knowing and smart, they did it in the cab of his truck. Gosho the plasterer had probably gone to plaster houses in Spain, a country that most adult males from the village of Staro favored when it came to eking out a living under a foreign sun. No one heard of that plastering chap again.

"Pirina, I am Kalcho!" the druggist's son hollered, his blue coveralls glued to the ground. "I'm Kalcho! You sang to me. Don't you remember…"

"She sang to you, eh?" Yakob asked, immaculate in his black business suit.

The drunkards didn't dare budge.

Two of them said, "Yes, she sang to him, Sir," and Kiro, Yakob's bodyguard and chauffeur, gave each man a kick to restore silence. The other two thundered, "No, she didn't sing to him, Sir," but Kiro kicked them as well, so all four wobbled indecisively back and forth, their eyes on their heels.

"So you're Pirina's boyfriend?" inquired Yakob's business suit with two hundred acres of forests, the moat, the lizards and snakes in it.

"Yes, I am," Kalcho said.

He must've been totally off his trolley, the poor devil. Maybe the aspirin he gave out was to blame, or the folks he dispensed it to: old women and drunks, the only local citizens willing to go into any therapy at all, unlike the gypsies who didn't care about medication or pills. The month of July cured everybody of the flu, lice and stomach ulcers. If the heat failed to do the job, two gravediggers successfully treated all diseases, terminal or common ones alike. The gypsy folks, however, flatly refused to breathe their last. Even without aspirin, they remained alive and kicking. They coughed, it was true, snot dripping from young and old noses, but when finally the last virus broke the camel's back, they had a way out. A sick toddler's mom would steal a chicken from a neighbor's backyard. She'd swipe a rooster even from the druggist's hencoop, then would say to Kalcho's mother, the druggist, "Give me a cough medicine, woman. Quick! Or my little Prodan will die like a dog!"

Often, the panicky gypsy mothers didn't bring anything at all, but Kalcho gave them the medicine all the same. The gypsy girls, pretty and decent most of them, offered him the way an honest lady should, "Kalcho, come with me behind the board fence. I'll pay you there."

Most of the wise Roma gents, old hands at dealing with crises of any shape and depth, suggested to the gray-haired druggist, "Koyna, I'll pay you behind the board fence. Fairly good-looking, that's what you still are, woman. Honestly. I wouldn't throw you out of my house."

Kalcho's father had died in the worst coalmine accident Staro had known, a strong man buried under two hundred yards of mudslide, sand and rocks, and to make things worse — the man's molar was of pure gold. All gypsy lads from the village dug and plowed into the mountain-face intent on wrenching the gold tooth from the dead man's mouth. A Roma young man and a Bulgarian miner got stuck in the shaft and their wives dropped food in buckets within their reach to no avail. At long last, after the firemen extracted the squashed body of Kalcho's father, it became evident that the gold tooth had vanished from the dead jaw. It remained a mystery as to who had knocked the precious thing out. Ultimately, the locals saw a gold molar, hanging on a chain around Anno's neck, and Anno was the only honest connoisseur of French silks in these parts. He explained he'd bought the precious tooth from a client for five glasses of his brown whiskey, 100 Pipers.

A week later, the same tooth tied to a gold chain sparkled on David's chest, and David was the cook, sweeper, senior manager and caterer at The Cat, i.e. the small guy who put on Anno's expensive designer suits, and in them looked like Doc Ivanova, six months into her pregnancy. A kind-hearted soul the Doc was despite the fact that she'd planned to beat it for Germany. Martusha, Yakob's informer that nosed into drawers and dirty laundry, one day sneered at Pirina, "Your sister, scrawny Luba… eh, has she gone bats? Couldn't she find herself a normal guy? No, Sir. They tell me she's hooked up with that *David*, Anno's little filly. You know him, the flea!"

Martusha's grunts, boos and hisses gave rise to the story that Anno purchased a personally designed blue suit for his sweeper from a high-end luxury tailor in Sofia. It wasn't only a rumor. In the evening, the pub owner ordered all the customers out of the premises and scrubbed the floor.

Although the man broke his pinky fingernail, he lit five candles, fell to his knees in front of David and gave him both the suit and the gold molar that used to belong to Kalcho's father.

…No matter what, every time a gypsy kid was about to give up the ghost, the brat's father raced to Kalcho's mom, the poor druggist, and said, panting, "Koyna, come with me to the barn. I'll pay you there, woman."

Koyna didn't go the barn. She kept silent, and her gray frizzled hair looked grayer. She gave the kid herbal remedies free of charge, and if it turned out the gravediggers had sweated for nothing as they dug a tiny grave, both the father and the mother came to the drug store and silently kissed Koyna's coarse hand. This time Death must've said to himself again, "*I've got no business here.*"

"God bless you, Koyna," the kid's father said. "Tell us what you need. I'll steal it for you. You'll have the thing in half an hour, woman."

The drunkards adopted a pragmatic approach. When an honest man sensed that the heart cure he'd taken, generously diluted with brandy, didn't work, he and his best drinking buddy went to Koyna. The two men hurried to the druggist, the sick one on his last legs, the healthy one holding up his pal. The healthy guy said, "Koyna, give Anton some strong medicine, quick, or he'll kick the bucket like the mutt that died yesterday eaten by his worms. I'll pay you in the barn."

Koyna found the medicine on the highest shelf in her store. Once more, a wretch got off cheap, the gravediggers didn't bury anybody and the grave they'd dug remained empty, new as a shiny penny. Even if it was Tuesday, it felt like Easter Sunday in the village of Staro. A yawning hole, three times as long as broad, kept its big mouth open in the hill. Gradually, the slope became the graveyard of the village. Every time a villager cashed in his chips, the family planted a cherry tree on his grave, and now instead of graves, good cherry trees blossomed, producing good fruit, and so the gypsies were all able-bodied and muscular. Young and old slept in the cherry shadows in summer, while in winter the swarthy ladies snapped dry branches to use them as firewood. So, if a drinking patient didn't stretch out dead and cold in a hole inside the cherry grove, a week or two later he would come to kiss Koyna's hand and weed the peppers in her garden.

A rumor got around that just once Koyna accompanied a drunkard to the barn. After this event, every night he made additional payments, and his persistence paid off in the long run: the drinking bloke moved in with her. The locals knew for sure he'd thrown his things in the room where pants, shirts and socks, all belonging to Koyna's deceased husband, were stored in a big chest of drawers after the man was buried under a mountain of rubble in the shaft. Koyna's husband was a hard working coalminer, may he rest in peace. Now his gold tooth they'd knocked out of his mouth was a glittering talisman on a gold chain David wore around his neck, and David was the dishwasher, waiter, manager, plasterer and supplier to The Cat restaurant. Little David loved to strut his stuff, dressed up in Anno's old suits, which made him look as bulky as pregnant Doc Ivanova.

The drunkard in question hung around Koyna's house for a while, in the evenings he even played chess with Kalcho. The gypsy lads believed it was at that time that the druggist's son lost his marbles. Last year, they said, once in a blue moon, Kalcho would accompany a gypsy girl to the barn. There, she expressed her sense of deep gratitude to him, but after his mom visited the barn too, he caught an obscure disease, took to retching and puking and was unable to stop for a month. Neighbors said Pirina's mooing and howling cured him of his ailment. A lady swore she'd heard Pirina declare, "Kalcho, I'll give you a fiver if you listen to me sing."

Kalcho took the fiver, and on Monday he puked less, on Tuesday he stopped puking altogether and even trudged up the hill to watch Pirina chop onions at the Venice Motel.

Kalcho had given the drunkards medicines for chest infections, bronchitis and pneumonias, had dispensed ointments treating scabies and itch. The boys didn't pay him, didn't weed his tomatoes or strawberries because, Kalcho said, man must not be racked with pain, by no means! Man was the crown of creation and was born to the world to listen to Pirina's songs. Wait a minute. What crown are you babbling about, man? So far, no one had seen a crown in the village of Staro. Ok, ok, how come a guy becomes Pirina's boyfriend only because he's listened to her snort like a pig? Her cawing and squawking, even if it put an end to his retching, doesn't qualify her as his girlfriend. No way! Was it possible for a guy to catch a particular illness only because his mom had cured a poor boozer in the room where his dead father's clothes had been gathering dust for years? You couldn't be a girl's boyfriend just because you had stopped puking, could you?

Within a fortnight, the tippler Kalcho's mom had accompanied to the barn stole her new clothes, lifted her TV set and her electric cooker, filched Kalcho's money-box and took to the woods. In these parts "to take to the woods" meant that the small-time crook beat it for Sofia, the capital of Bulgaria. There, even Elijah, the prophet who brought fire down from the sky, wouldn't find him for the simple reason that the pubs in the capital were more numerous than the city's inhabitants. The well-to do, fashionable ladies in Sofia, willing to administer on the spot treatment to bad guys were more plentiful than the pubs. To make a long story short, the drunkard had pinched the medicines, pills, capsules, herbal remedies, ointments and vitamins from Koyna's drugstore. Villagers from all walks of life called down curses not only on the creep, but also on his mom, dad, his grandma and grandpa. If now a poor bugger was about to fall off his perch, what medication could Koyna offer the wretch to bring him back to his wife? The only therapy she could think of was elderberry tea, and even toddlers knew elderberry wouldn't heal lice bites or gastric ulcers, although Koyna had tried to make a go of it.

On these days of distress, the Roma wives who had brought up their kids thanks to Koyna's skills, the drunkards who had kept their hearts safe and sound by dint of Koyna's cures and the old ladies, too, everyone as best as they could, produced fifty cents, a lev, a fiver, apples, a bowl of beans or lentils, and raised money to help Koyna's drugstore to its feet again. Only

Koyna and perhaps a doctor or two on the train that puffed its way to Athens, knew which medicines treated this or that disease. The gravediggers, the most ungodly riffraff in the village of Staro, gave Koya a twenty lev bill each; their wives also got themselves into a fix time and again, and Konya brought them through pregnancy and sickness as gently as a whisper.

"Pirina, I am your boyfriend, remember?" Kalcho called out, grieved that she didn't acknowledge him even as an acquaintance and miserable because of the expensive dress the girl wore. In it, she didn't look like Pirina. In this red velvet thing, she looked like a lady from London or America that the TV foisted on him night and day, but Pirina was more beautiful than America and London put together. "I am your boyfriend, Pirina!"

After a month, the drunkard who had robbed Koyna the druggist, returned to her –a-limping, a-hobbling and wobbling, stumping along on long thin legs. Like a horse dying of starvation, the worm sneaked into the drugstore that he had robbed with his own hands.

"Take it," the dog said as he produced a bundle of banknotes — such a thin bundle that it did not look like a bundle at all. In truth, the thing was a fifty lev bill folded four times, from right to left then from top to bottom. "That's all I have, Koyna. May I come back to you?"

Koyna didn't answer as she continued stirring some thick salve. Her gray hair, dyed brown, didn't budge.

"I have no one else to go to, Koyna. Let me come back to you. I'll give you back everything I stole from you. I gradually will."

How could he give her back the TV set, Kalcho's moneybox, her husband's old clothes, the electric cooker? These things cost much more than his measly fifty levs! They cost at least five hundred. This snake slithered across the room to her, caught the woman's hand as she blended the salve with thick oily liquid; he started kissing her fingers one by one as if Koyna had given him pills for his sick child, and made death go home empty-handed.

"Do me a kindness, Kamen. Go away," Koyna said to him, but he didn't do her a kindness and stayed on. In the evening, the drunk remained in the street. The August night was warm. He stretched himself out in front of her drugstore and slept.

"Shall we kill him?" the Roma guys turned to Koyna. Her reddish-brown hair hid her face, and she didn't tell them anything, neither "Kill him," nor "Don't kill him."

If a *Gypsy* kid — in the vicinity of Radomir folks were proud of this adjective although no one knew what the hell "adjective" meant — so, if a Gypsy had the option not to do a certain thing, he positively wouldn't stir a finger, and Kamen the drunk went on snoring in front of the drugstore buried under the old women's curses and maledictions.

"We've had enough of this idiot's cheek," the population of Staro shook their heads in an outburst of indignation. "As brazen-faced as a manure heap, that's what the creep is. He'll fleece this saint once again, I bet you."

The saint said nothing, and three consecutive nights Kamen the crook slept in front of her drugstore, stray mongrel dogs whining by his side. On the fourth day, Koyna took him back to the narrow room, which was empty, no old clothes belonging to Koyna's husband, no blankets, just the drunk's fifty levs on the floor: she had left the money there before she let the man move in. On the following morning, Kalcho had a prolonged bout of vomiting, then another one, and no medicine in the drugstore did him any good.

Then tall and quiet Koyna, the biggest heart of gold in Staro, accompanied by the drunk — the scoundrel, trudging three yards behind her like a lamb the ewe had weaned — went to Pirina's mother.

"Slava, may I ask your daughter Pirina to come over to my place and stay for an hour or two?"

Slava, who was grinding tomatoes for sauce, could not believe what she'd just heard.

"Perhaps it's Sara you're looking for, Koyna. Everybody looks for Sara… She's the prettiest of the three, you know."

"Please ask Pirina to drop by my place. Kalcho started vomiting again," the druggist said. "He'd like to see her."

"Why should he want to see Pirina?" Slava asked amazed. "Pirina is not Sara. She can't help him."

… In the evening, Pirina entered the room where Kalcho lay in his bed, yellow as a quince. Koyna touched her hand and said, "Sing to him, girl, please sing to him."

Pirina burst out singing. Within ten minutes the dogs in the yard began to bark, the rooster, getting into a panic, crowed a third time although the moon had already shown up in the sky as glossy as a pair of expensive shoes. The roar in Kalchos's room sounded so deafening that the donkeys awoke and happily brayed along.

Koyna hid in the drugstore, and the drunkard she had put up for the night fled for dear life to The Cat. The other guys refused to drink with him. He sipped on his beer bottle, alone at the shabbiest plastic table on the premises, and at a certain point one of the patrons pissed on his feet.

On the following day, Kalcho stopped vomiting altogether. In the evening, he went to Slava's place, hoping to see Pirina again, but Pirina wasn't available. Yakob had taken her to his dazzling mansion.

Now Kalin, known far and wide as Kalcho Who Throws Up, thrust himself out amidst the other drunks, looking Pirina in the face, insisting that he was her boyfriend.

For a long while, Yakob stood silent and distant, then he produced a bundle — a genuine bundle of banknotes as fat as a 10th grade geography textbook, as thick as the telephone directory Anno used in The Cat — and addressed the drunks, his voice a heap of stones, "This money will be yours if you give this wretch here a good hiding. Do I make myself clear?"

The four guys who didn't dare budge, their eyes fastened simultaneously on their heels and Kiro the chauffeur's boots that stood in readiness to beat them black and blue, suddenly came back to life. The bundle lay under their noses, a beautiful fifty dollar bill wad, a heap of dough they couldn't earn for two years even if they toiled and moiled 24/7 on the highway. On the other hand, who'd hire them to work on the highway, them of all people, juiceheads all of them? The boss hired them for a day or two and their bellies didn't explode with hunger, but each drunk grumbled it was about time to push off. Beat it for Spain. Let's shove off tomorrow.

"He means nothing to me," Pirina thundered.

She saw the men, dizzy with heat and the fake alcohol, form a tight circle around Kalcho. He looked as thin as a five-cent candle in the village church that opened its doors only at Christmas. This church remained closed even when a dead woman's son arranged his mother's funeral because if the priest unlocked the front door and wasn't careful, both Gypsies and Bulgarians would steal everything that could be stolen there.

"Do you still puke five times a day?" Yakob asked, scowling at Kalcho. The boy, the five-cent candle, didn't say anything; it was one of the drunks who was quick to explain, "He's stopped puking."

"It seems to me you don't care about the money," Yakob said.

The four men kept silent. The incredible bundle remained as big as the telephone directory under the scorching sun… two years of drudgery on the highway to the Greek border. The guys were on the verge of doing something, kicking Kalcho in the teeth perhaps. They were itching to get started, their trouser legs shaking.

"Hey!" Pirina shouted. "He meant nothing to me. But now he does. He's my boyfriend."

None of the four unshaven boozers reached for the bundle. Were they thinking of their wives' ulcers that this kid — Kalcho Who Throws Up — had made bearable? Did they remember the horrible flu last winter, and Koyna who drove it away from the village? Perhaps they saw the patches of land under the stunted cherry trees where they'd lie under sand and stones if Kalcho hadn't given them a bottle of heart cure?

"Kalcho," Pirtina whispered. Then she said something in Greek, or maybe in Hawaiian or Islandic. Even she didn't know which language she said it in, "I love you."

She clasped her hands together in a hard knot. This way, she could not scratch herself. Her body itched, her legs, toes, neck, everything hurt as if someone was cutting her into pieces with a razorblade. The itch ignited the space between her fingers, her belly was a festering wound, and her faded blue coat seemed to burn. She couldn't find peace in the heat. It made her scabies much worse. The gypsy kids by her side scratched their arms, legs, stomach, and stayed on, all ears, all eyes.

Luba taught them how to write the Bulgarian alphabet — a good bit of work, that alphabet, thorns and traps all over the place, but the kids stayed on. Who would hire you to work for the Hygiene Municipal Company, even in the town of Radomir, if you didn't know how to write a couple of letters or couldn't spell your own name? Scabies belonged to the natural order of things. The nippers thought it was perfectly normal for their bellies and backs to itch. Their mothers told them, "Your belly is ok. Ants are crawling on it, child," but how was it possible for those ants to bite you all the time? Didn't they fall asleep, these little buggers, didn't they get tired?

Luba got scabies all right. She clasped her hands tightly, unwilling to scratch her neck in front of the kids, trying hard not to think of the itch as she showed the letter H to Valia, a little girl who loved the alphabet above everything else in the world. Valia had cut out a number of black printed letters from a discarded whiskey packaging box, and carried the pieces of cardboard, pressing them to her meager chest. The letters on the 100 Pipers whiskey packaging box were, of course, Latin, but the child didn't know that. In the evenings, the family baked potatoes in the open and her mother burned a letter or two in the fire that roared in the unfenced backyard. The little girl sobbed bitterly. She believed she'd lost the letter for good and would never again find another like it. Her mother was a decent woman. She slapped her daughter across the face to calm her down, but Valia did not calm down. She cried quietly for her burnt alphabet, and on the following morning asked Luba to write a new, more beautiful letter for her.

Although Valia was the youngest in the group, she could already spell out some short words. At noon, she hid in the shadow of the chestnut trees in the schoolyard, produced an ancient newspaper she'd taken from a trashcan and tried hard to read the headlines. The kid didn't know if the printed text was in Greek, Polish or Bulgarian, she read on, making sense only of the tiniest words and thinking up all the rest. So she read a fairytale, always the same one, about a little girl who burnt her most precious letter of the alphabet and about a young woman called Luba, the kindest one that lived in the world. At the end, she took the kid to a big palace, its walls milk chocolate, and the rooms full of chicken soup. This Valia girl suffered most terribly from scabies — or was it mange they called the itch? Scabies bit into Valia's heart, clutched at her throat, the kid's stomach and back itched, but her mother said, "Don't worry, little one, you won't die. If your back doesn't itch, you sure will die soon."

Luba could not stay at home with her mom and dad, and Sara, the cleanest member of the family, the most beautiful one who smelled good even while she slept. Luba should not go home, she'd give everyone the disease, and their skins would explode with scabies. Her mother would have to boil and sterilize sheets, blankets and quilts. In the evenings, Luba took shelter in her deceased grandma's hut — the old dear met her maker as illiterate and unlettered as a grass snake. Luba filled her wattle-and-daub shack with a waist-deep layer of books: tomes with inconceivably difficult Old Bulgarian orthography, books with no pictures and novels with modern orthography from the village library that had closed down. The volumes would have been used as firewood had Luba not collected them.

In the dusk, Luba went to the deserted mud house and thought of that girl, little Valia. She shouldn't teach the kid to spell because if you read books your mind becomes unhinged; because she, Luba, was able to talk to books and could not talk to people. Only the street urchins she taught the alphabet thought how beautiful the letters looked.

Valia, the little gypsy girl who made up a fairytale about a house with chocolate walls and rooms full of soup, prayed to God day and night that Luba would become her mom. Valia thought that God was the roof of their house and that was the reason why He protected them all. She used the knife with which her mother slaughtered the stolen chickens and carved LABA into the roof beam, Laba because the child still didn't know that there was a letter U in the Bulgarian alphabet.

Luba cut onions, gutted fish, fried peppers and eggplants, peeled a dozen crates of potatoes all through the afternoon. In the gathering dusk, she felt scabies eat into her hands and feet. At noon, she could feel scabies creep into the soup she was bringing to a boil, and her itch sank into the beefsteaks she grilled for the truckers. Her scabies made the sky claw at the moon.

At night, Luba went to the hut of her deceased Grandma Luba who was surely planting peony flowers, dill weeds and cabbages in the sky now. Her granddaughter slept with three thousand books. The air, rife with scabies, smelled of paper and love. There, in the narrow room, thinking of her favorite poems, Luba could scratch her legs, feet, hands and back as much as she pleased. Of course, clawing at her neck only made the itch worse.

The skin between her toes looked bad and hurt, numerous small blisters spewing hot pain. Luba was spreading crushed dandelion leaves on her feet when the door creaked open. Sometimes her friends, the kids, dropped by to see her at her grandma's place; from the Venice Motel, Luba took bread and leftover scraps of meat for them, explaining she'd give the food to stray dogs. She was happy when the gypsy children came over, but now she'd rather take care of her sore skin. The moon was big and strong, there was enough of its light and she could read for a while. Luba had bought a book with a strange-sounding title, *A Clock without Hands*. Her life was a clock without hands and scabies on its face.

"Come in, it's open," Luba said. She had no money now. Yakob paid her wages on the 20th of the month, so she would scratch her sore back for twenty more days. She had made up her mind to buy scabies medication from Koyna and cure both herself and the kids of the itch, but would this change anything?

Back home, they'd start scratching their legs and backs again. In these parts, scabies was as common as the dust on the streets. The wind took it everywhere: you'd just shoveled it out from your threshold, and a minute later a huge cloud of sand landed on your kitchen table.

The dark shape silhouetted against the rectangle of light at the door was none of her pupils. The shadow of a big, heavy man pushed the night out of the room.

The moon gleamed hard, but Luba could not puzzle out who the man was before she heard him speak.

"Take your clothes off," the unexpected guest said. "We'll do it here." It was Kiro the giant who guarded Yakob against the sun, the wasps, the potholes and the thugs. Kiro catered to his boss's every whim, procured special alcoholic beverages for Yakob and drove him around town, to Athens, Paris or Sofia. "Don't make it hard on yourself, kid, or I'll have to rape you. Just now I'm worn out, see. Why rot here lonely like a spider… They say you're nutty as a fruitcake. It's ok with me. Nutty or not is none of my business," the big guy concluded as he lit a cigarette. "You're crazy, but I don't give a damn. Come on."

She didn't budge, her eyes fixed on the clock without hands as if the brawny guy had not spoken to her, as if his words were meant to stir the dust that had gathered on three thousand books.

"Come on. Take off this coat… shabby as a shit hill…the thought of touching it makes me sick," he gave her the once over. "I can bring guys to you. They won't be stinking rich like the sugar daddies Sara has. They'll give you two levs per full service. Don't moon over your stupid books and papers. Earn cold hard cash instead."

"No," Luba lisped or perhaps she said it out loud, but the beefy guy couldn't hear her.

"Don't make it hard on yourself," he said, not a grain of malice in his tone. "I'm showing mercy to you. You're in luck. Or you want to rot away, an old spinster moldy like these ancient beams above your head?"

"No," Luba said.

"You think I'd trudged up the hill to take your shitty no as an answer? No way!" Kiro caught her feet and pulled. She was thin; if he squeezed harder, half her bones would be crushed into splinters in his hands.

"I am ill," Luba whispered.

He lifted her in the air, shook her, pressed hard his right hand against her forehead then snapped, "Bullshit. You don't have a fever."

Kiro threw her on the heap of books whose authors' names started with B. And he tore her blue coat, putting almost no effort into it, but the old buttons flew like small shot, scattering between the faded covers.

"You'll catch scabies," Luba's words sank into the dust and were lost.

"What's scabies?" he grunted.

"The seven-year itch," she said.

One doesn't die of the itch, seven years or no seven years, Kiro thought. He made up his mind. His large, heavy body pressed her against poor Blake who rolled into a ball like a ring-shaped bun under Luba's scabby skin. Books from the other heaps wobbled and shook; these were tomes whose authors' names began with the letter H: Heine, Hegel and Hölderlin hit his back then crashed into her scabies. Luba began to cry, but Kiro had seen more tears than a large lake held. Sobbing could never interfere with his love.

Luba cried under the moonlight, under *Paradise Lost*. She cried for Pippi Longstocking, she sobbed quietly, the way she did everything, her eyes hopeless in the dusk, all ten thousand lines of Milton's verse stuck into her back. She cried for the swarthy kids because they didn't know anything about *Paradise Lost*.

"I'm your first, eh? Nobody before me has… O, come on. I'll be damned," Kiro exclaimed. "Can't believe it…. I'll be damned."

After a while, he kicked the books aside — their authors' names all beginning with S — and lay down on them.

"Do you have anything to eat? Give me a chunk of bread."

Luba was still crying, this time for the crumpled Schiller and Salinger, her sobs stifled, gasping and dry. She knew she had only a bag of sour pears she'd picked on the way to her grandma's place. She wouldn't give him the pears, not for the world.

'My buddies won't believe a word of it if I tell them," Kiro muttered under his breath. "Ok, why should I tell them? Every little squirt would jeer at me. And rightly so. He's flat broke, the wretch, they'll say. Stooping so low... rolling in the hay with the crazy *Notre Dame...*"

He reached out his hand and touched her face.

"Are you whimpering, woman! You're wet as a wash-basin, damn it."

He flung her to Blake again.

Kiro was very hungry, yet his powerful body had enough strength to lift the hut, her books, her and her torn coat high in the air.

Even before he got up, he started scratching his arms, legs and neck. His big head hid the night and the moon as he stood by the door. The thick-muscled man snatched a book, tore a page and wiped his neck with it, then made a grab for another tome. His chest was wringing wet and he needed more pages to dry it and keep the itch under control.

"No!" Luba shouted.

She picked herself up, naked like the moon. Her arms, below the elbow, were dark brown, baked by the sun like paving stones. Her face was a baked stone too, but the moon gave a glow to her body, and her skin was the gleaming path in the night. Kiro stopped breathing as he rubbed his legs with a sheaf of torn pages. His body was the color of Yakob's new car, silver metallic. Luba's body, at the same time a moon and a palely glittering Mercedes in front of him, struck him dumb.

He forgot he was in a hurry to eat, he stopped thinking about the books he'd made up his mind to sell as waste paper and get drunk on the money later. He could see only her and came back, gasping for air, enormous.

This time he didn't throw her on Blake. This time, he didn't throw her at all; he carefully put her, her tears and wet chin on a heap of thick square books. He licked her salty face. He licked the tears off her cheeks, and yes, he surely was off his rocker, he was the biggest idiot in the world, but he'd never tasted anything more delicious than the salty water on this thin whimpering face.

"I'm not all there," he said. "I'm out of my mind. I won't send guys your way. I won't allow any man to touch you even if he forks out five thousand levs … No one'd believe me, damn you. I've never stumbled on a fool like you," he muttered as he pressed her against his ribs. It was very hot. Was it the moon or the stars above the crab apple tree that gave off so much heat? He didn't want to let her go; he thrust his unshaven face into her tears, the most delicious thing he'd tasted since the time he could open his mouth.

§

That was the stupidest and the most fearful thing one could possibly do. David waited in ambush for Kiro, planning to knock the living daylights out of him.

David, the driver, supplier, house cleaner, Anno's right-hand man; a thin guy who ran The Cat and got lost in the folds of his silk shirt, sweet David, the envy of the neighborhood. The drunks bluntly asked him if the wine he drank with Anno by candlelight was strong enough for a willing lady, and if it was true the bartender recited love poems in between kisses.

Thin sweet David waylaid Kiro while the colossus was snoozing in Yakob's third biggest Jeep Cherokee, before he made up his mind to drink or not to drink. Kiro had parked the Jeep in his own garage that used to be full of hay for Mara, their cow; Kiro's father fed the animal while Kiro's mother cursed the old potbelly and told him she wished that he rot in fire and brimstone. The old codger had contracted a number of shameful diseases on account of the copious amount of moonshine he had swilled as well as the countless hussies he had chased.

Kiro was at his ease as his mom's curses spread across the night sky. His father spat an obscene word or two in response to his wife, meanwhile, from sheer force of habit, swearing at Mara the cow. The timid beast would die on the spot if its mammalian brain could understand the message the old crab passed on it. So, soothed by his mom's curses and his father's unshakable resilience, Kiro drove the Jeep into the garage and as was a custom with him, spat three times in the red-hot street, hoping to have a restful sleep this night.

No sweet dreams, alas, a silhouette showed up in the dusk instead, a thin face, and a caricature dressed in an enormous white business suit that hung on the bugger like old posters. The plasterer, supplier, Anno's highest-paid buddy, David the waiter! That was the guy who confronted Kiro in the night.

"I'll kill you!" David hissed, but it remained unclear who he was hissing at — was it the cow that had relaxed at last influenced by the curses muttered by Kiro's mom, or at the dogs, big and small, rolled into a hot ball on the manure heap.

"Hey David, is it true Anno kneels down in front of you every evening?" Kiro let out an explosive guffaw at the moon, scaring the pack of mutts.

"It's true," David barked or perhaps he didn't bark. Perhaps the French silks on his shoulders rustled. "I'll kill you."

Kiro didn't think it was possible for anybody to kill him.

"Is it true that Anno hired a painter from Sofia and paid the wacko to paint you in oils the way you snore by the empty beer crates in The Cat?"

"It's true!" the supplier, dishwasher, and The Cat's cook shrieked, a man that a talented postmodern painter from the capital of the country portrayed half-naked as he slept in the shadow of a chestnut tree.

David almost jumped out of his boundless silks, despite the fact that his suit could comfortably accommodate Yakob's Grand Cherokee Jeep. The cook lunged forward, grabbed Kiro by the collar and let his teeth sink into the huge man's neck. The bodyguard bled profusely. David hoped he had slit the ogre's throat as he pummeled his chest, forgetting the masterpiece love poems and the ballads full of wisdom that Anno whispered to him under the flickering candle flame. Kiro had the feeling that caterpillars were crawling on his back. His eyes began to itch, and when the measly little fellow bit into his face, the giant went off the deep end.

Kiro slightly moved his arms, massive as a hill and a quagmire rolled into one. Accustomed to being kicked and watching blood, the big man almost bled to death every once in a while, and if he saw another guy bleeding, he tended to fall into a sulk. Now Kiro lifted up his hands, then his fist landed on the supplier's forehead. A pity that Anno had ordered dark blue silk shirts from Sweden for his driver and cook, the underlying motive for his choice being the shirts were the color of David's eyes; to be honest, Swedish silk was a heap of dirt compared to the runty supplier's deep blue gaze. The silk suit was no good any more. Abruptly, David slackened his grip, didn't even have the strength to groan or sob as he opened his mouth already full of Kiro's blood.

Kiro hit him one more time, not hard at all. The bodyguard couldn't find any reason why he should whack the poor driver. On occasions, when David didn't show up in The Cat for an hour or so, Anno sank to the depths of despair, closed the pub, locked the door and dialed from his cell phone, his face flushed, drenched in perspiration. More often than not the owner of The Cat rushed to the highway to check if the puny man and his hundred-year old van came into view on the road.

"Hey, Dave, what's wrong with you?" Kiro asked. "Why did you bite me? Are you out of your mind, pal?"

The thin guy attempted to kick his legs in the air, to scratch and shriek as he made efforts to spit in Kiro's face, but the bodyguard's fist made him give up slobbering.

"What's wrong, Dave?" Kiro repeated, amazed.

Whenever the giant encountered a medical problem, his paw groped for the forehead of the louse he'd just beaten, trying to ascertain if the louse was running a temperature. It was evident little Davie wasn't, the kid was simply off his trolley for some obscure reason.

"I'll kill you!" David squeaked and left Kiro wondering as to how this could happen. If the bodyguard slightly pressed his knee against Anno's cook's chest, a handful of broken ribs and a pool of blood would be the only traces Davie would leave behind.

So Kiro boxed the little man's ears to sharpen his logical thinking. "Hey, Dave, it's me, Kiro, can't you see me? Tell me what you want."

But the cook, driver and supplier said nothing, his nose bleeding, his eyes overflowing with tears, his face swimming in a cocktail of sweat, dribbles of dirt and spittle. His mouth produced a series of stifled gasps that squeezed its way under Kiro's knee and probably meant, "I'll teach you a lesson, you clown."

Yakob's bodyguard loosened his grip on Anno's pint-sized employee who continued to spit blood and tears until he blurted out, "I'll kill you."

"Why, man? Why do you want to kill me?" Now Kiro was beginning to get in a snit. He hated it when he talked in a friendly manner to a fellow and the fellow wanted to kill you without offering any explanation. The bodyguard had learned an important thing from Yakob: if someone didn't talk or talked too much, give him a good thrashing, and he will understand you.

"Luba!" Anno's driver shouted, blood spurting from his mouth. "I'll kill you. For her sake!"

"Luba!" Kiro whistled shocked, unbelieving. "Luba? Ok. Can you hear me, moron? Hey, moron. If only you looked at her …this thin neck of yours… I'll squeeze your neck, ok? I'll squeeze it between my thumb and forefinger. You won't have any neck to speak of."

"I'll k…ki…kill yo…u" David gasped one more time as he bit into Kiro's trouser leg. "Keep your h… h…hands off L.. L… Luba!"

At that moment, the bodyguard's knee hit his chest, and the supplier's words were a peculiar squeaking sound in his throat.

§

He trudged through the nettles, his blood oozing slowly from his wounds, leaving a thin trail behind him, like a red grass snake. He slogged through thorns and dry brambles, past ditches and stakes to which peasants tied their donkeys. He was hungry, and his back hurt. The stabbing pain in his ribs chewed its way into his mind. He could see prickly shrubs, young plum trees, blackthorns, their roots open traps under his feet, their spikes hammers digging into his eyes, yet he pushed on. Behind the shrubs, the wattle and daub house came into view. It was hard to totter across the thicket, then cross the railway line and keep out of the express train's way, the cars almost running over him. The waifs and strays, catching the smell of death, went for him as the red trail of his blood crawled on the grass.

The homeless dogs of the village, seven or eight altogether, some big as calves, the others small as sparrows, trotted behind him.

A tiny poodle brought up the rear. It was the same little beast Anno had thrown out, seriously worried that it was impossible to handle the fleas on its coat. The obstinate creature had refused to stand up on hind legs in front of its master, so it soon relinquished its comfortable bed, a silver tray covered with a wool quilt, and landed at the back of the pack of mutts. All the dogs licked David's bloody trail as they followed him towards the wattle and daub house. Perhaps the mongrels waited for David to drop dead, silk trousers or no silk trousers, in which he looked like Doc Ivanova, already six months pregnant.

The mongrels hoped against hope that after the guy breathed his last, they'd eat him up at a big holiday party at the end of the summer. Summer was a season when pooches survived. In winter, some froze and croaked. There was no one to eat in the street, so they perched like rooks by the railway line, lying in ambush, waiting for the express train to Greece to meet its maker. The dogs honestly hoped they could chew on the carriages until they picked all passengers' bones clean.

In winter, the weather was so lousy that the big dogs killed and ate the smaller ones. Under these circumstances, Anno's poodle didn't stand a chance. The little darling should either come back home and stand on his hind legs for his master, or go and bark its way into the next world.

On reaching the hut, David burst into a fit of coughing. The air smelled of death and books, but no blood oozed from his mouth anymore. He saw the door gaping open. One of its hinges must have fallen off. A neat pile of books jutted out from the corner, front covers new and shiny; some leather-bound volumes and two huge fertilizer sacks stuffed with paperbacks sprawled on the earthen floor. David edged into the hut followed by his blood, dripping from some wound, and the pack of dogs as thick as his shadow. Even before he sank into the low-ceilinged room, he said, "Don't be scared. It's me," but one way or another, the books weren't scared. There was nobody in the room, just a ball of faded blue cloth, Luba's old coat. It had shown him a tiny white patch of her knee and the path of the moon. He noticed two bruised apples and a half loaf of bread; but the dogs instantly got a whiff of it, and the heaviest among them, chased by the pack's hungry eyes, gobbled it up.

"Hey, where are you?" David shouted as he slumped onto the smallest pile of books, his blood seeping down their covers. He sat up, leaning against *Bellum Gallicum*, and slowly ate the pears, their sweet juice mixing with his tears. It started to get dark, the dogs lost interest in him and one by one tails and haunches retreated from the sacks of paperbacks, some mutts seizing this opportunity to take a piss on a leather-bound tome. David watched the long string of beasts working its way up the hilltop behind the railway line.

At a certain point, the hill barked, the plum trees and the worms, the rails and the dust barked too. David's Android cell phone, the best on the market, sang the Italian love song Anno had uploaded for his manager. The cellphone insisted it loved David so much as he gnawed on the sour bruised pears. The driver-manager's back hurt and he stretched himself out on the floor. To be honest, there was no floor to speak of because the raw earth was carpeted with three or four layers of books: *History of Bulgaria, The History of Byzantium* and numerous other histories of five different Byzantiums.

David looked at the volumes, his blood a crumbling empire on the floor. An hour or perhaps a year later, the sound of footsteps broke the sour silence. Many footsteps, young and arrogant, drummed on the grass. It felt as if the express train to Greece had climbed to the wattle-and-daub hut, and the passengers, all drunk, had gotten off and were kicking the front door. A covey of gypsy kids muscled its way through the books and stopped in front of David, a disordered row of rags and eyes trained on him as he chewed the bruised pears.

"What are you doing here, faggot?" the biggest boy rasped and spat on his leg.

The other lads took to spitting helter-skelter on David. The driver-manager could rip them to shreds, but his ribs hurt. Suddenly, he felt sorry for the dogs that waited for food, a bone or two, their tongues lolling out of their mouths, the railway line a dying flame in the air. He lay prostrate on a *History of Bulgaria*, his white jacket of unique Swedish silk steeped in blood up to his bellybutton. A child with a runny nose came up to him, a girl, although her head was shaved and the front of her skull glistened like the dome of Saint Sofia's Basilica; in places, wisps of twisted hair hung loosely, reaching well below the kid's dirty chin. The little one had stuffed her puny ass into a skirt made from a trouser leg from her father's pants. She reached out her hand and touched David's forehead.

"Are you sick, uncle D?" she asked as she gently pressed her forefinger against the bloody spot on his jacket, half an inch below David's heart.

"I am hurt," the driver said. "I am dying."

But the Roma kids belonged to a tribe that wouldn't retreat before everybody had checked the pockets of a person on the verge of dying before their eyes. The biggest boy, some black fluff like sand on his face, brazenly pushed David as his dark hand dug deep into the pocket of the blood-stained jacket. There were fifty cents there. The gypsy boy took the coins and checked the other pockets, the other kids watching, ready to lunge forward. David couldn't move, couldn't stir an eyelid -— just lay quietly in his own blood like a skinned cat. The big lad found David's mobile phone in one of the pockets and indecisively hid it under his shirt.

"Give it to me," David said at last.

The young gypsy reluctantly produced the thing, kicked David's leg and walked to the door as proud as the king of peacocks who had nothing to do with these books.

The other kids followed him. Only the little girl in the trouser-leg skirt stooped over David and whispered, "I am Valia. Do you want me to bring you some water to drink, Uncle D?"

"Yes, please," David said.

Valia, her hair shaved in places, clipped short in others, brought from somewhere a Sprite bottle without a cap and some water at the bottom, in which a fly had drowned. The girl tried hard to remove the fly, but David couldn't wait. He grabbed the bottle from her hands and took a long swig.

The biggest kid, the one with the black face fluff, snarled as he punched David's shoulder, "Don't you dare pilfer any book of hers! Don't you dare spit on Luba's books! Look at me! I am Zachary. Don't forget my name. I know you. You sleep in The Cat. I'll set your black sheets on fire. Do I make myself clear?"

David did not understand a word of it, his ribs hurt so much, his legs felt as though someone had crushed them into dust. The gypsy kid thrust his hand into David's trouser pocket, found a pen, grabbed it and, saying no more, gave a sign to the rabble of swarthy children.

"You, dung-heap! I won't let you sprawl out on her books. You'll muck them up," Zachary, the ringleader, said as he and the other kids started dragging David out of the room. The driver swiped at the bunch of dark faces and it was good he didn't clobber anybody; if he had done so, the days of the victim would have been numbered. David's hand clutched at the air. The air was a substance that didn't hurt. The pack of kids hauled him into the yard. The only kid that wasn't pulling at his shirt was the little girl in the trouser-leg skirt. She looked at David, silent, as the night fell in her black eyes. The children dumped him near the pack of dogs that had hushed, tired of growling at the express train and its rails. David could use his mobile phone and call Anno; then within ten minutes, the van would show up to collect him. Perhaps Anno would personally carry him to the van… David remained with the dogs that seemed very interested in the blood on his white Swedish jacket.

"You go away," the big stripling said to the other kids. "I want to talk to him."

The children made efforts to obey as they shuffled down the hill, a torrent of shorn heads and twenty second-hand shirts and pants collected from garbage cans in the towns of Kyustendil, Dupni and Pernik. Watching these kids, you could gather what the fashion trends were half a century ago provided that your intellect was brilliant enough to guess at the true color of the clothes before they faded on their skinny backs. The black fluff boy waited until all kids had beat it, then squatted next to David and said, "Look here. Tell me, if Anno sleeps with you one night, will you be like him all your life?"

David kept silent for a long time. His neck hurt too and he didn't know why he felt sorry for this dark kid that crouched over his head, his black eyes hating David's guts.

"Hey, faggot, did you hear me?" the boy whispered.

"Why do you ask about Anno?" David asked amazed. It was still early, the daylight had not yet faded, but it was growing dark on the kid's face.

In the distance the hill barked, top, slopes, paths and all, even Anno's poodle, born far from these parts, joined the refrain of piercing howls. It was about time the passenger train to Dupni pulled into the railway station. Most of the highway maintenance workers got off here and drank at The Cat hours on end. After midnight, David collected them one by one. If the guys were very drunk, he drove them in his old van to their dormitory in Dupni in a block of flats where nobody had washed the windows for decades, the doors were broken and the guys slept on camp-beds in a big cold room.

"I hate Anno," the boy said, with no malice in his voice. "I'll set fire to his pub. Perhaps I won't set fire to your van," David had an itch to light a cigarette, in fact he was dying for a cigarette, but his chest hurt, and his brains had turned to mush from too much strain. "I want to marry her when I grow up," the kid muttered.

"Marry who?" David asked.

"Her," the boy answered. "She couldn't teach me to read. I'm stupid as a brush, the alphabet is too difficult for me, damn it. But I'll learn all about the letters for her."

The kid scrambled to his feet and spat on the ground like the workers who got off the passenger train to Dupni. Before the little fool made himself scarce, he hissed to David, "Hey, milksop, make sure you don't muck up the floor here. I'll skin you alive if you piss on her books!" His shadow, dexterous as a woodpecker, slipped into the thicket. David watched as it swam among trees and dogs, then slalomed down the hill towards the village huts, most of them occupied by well-heeled mechanics. There were, of course, villas, too, complete with pedigree dogs and sturdy garages. These belonged to bigwigs from the capital, which was the polite way of saying that the buildings were loaded like beasts of burden with state-of-the-art alarm systems. One way or the other, the electronic devices were small potatoes for the gypsy lads. So far, no genius had invented a system able to discourage the pilfering of the Roma lads that Luba taught the Bulgarian alphabet.

In his life, David had not taught anybody anything.

He heard Luba coming to the door a long time after the stray dogs had abandoned him. Anno's poodle was the only loyal beast that stayed on, a shaggy thing curled up against David's neck, his sweet puppy breath still smelling of Torino, Italy, the poor darling's native town from which it had been delivered to Anno.

David saw her.

She had put on a new coat, dazzlingly blue, like a blue cotton candy ball. She'd taken some book from somewhere and carried it like a shovel in front of her chest. The tactlessness of it irritated him. He hoped she wouldn't press the idiotic volume against her ribs.

"Hey," David shouted.

She recoiled, scared, then saw him and hurried on, quickening her pace, almost running perhaps because he reeked of onions and mutts. Splinters and spikes had sunk into his back, but David didn't think of them now. Luba turned around as her light steps, like a handful of coins, were lost near the railway lines in the tangle of weeds and stones. There thistles and thorns grew as huge as trees in spite of the fierce heat. The girl disappeared more rapidly than the flock of crows above David, furtively like the bunch of kids who had spat on him. He thought his veins were running dry.

"Hey, hey!"

Her blue coat twitched, and slowly, as if she was dragging the mountain in her wake, Luba took a couple of steps to his blood-drenched jacket of white Swedish silk. She left the book on the weeds, her coat showing him a small patch of her knee. The white purity of her skin made him feel giddy and left a bitter taste in his mouth.

"Luba…" he mouthed.

She leant forward and the legs the new coat momentarily revealed frightened him, the bitter taste in his mouth so strong it blinded his eyes. She, quiet like dirt, unbuttoned his jacket, wiped his neck then left him to his blackness, taking her knees away somewhere else, to the house perhaps. This felt worse. He shouted "Hey" so hard and long as if all the starving dogs were growling out of his mouth. He was sorry for her knees and her skin that had scared him. He felt miserable she'd left him with the dried blood that had starched his jacket, the most expensive article of clothing he'd ever had on his back.

"Hey, hey," David went on whispering so quietly you'd think his voice was dust.

Maybe the pages of her book could hear him, its brown front cover a sunset in the weeds. She had chucked her novel to the ground near his head, and now she had nothing, and he was sorry for her. The wind was shrieking, "Hey, hey," and there she was, coming back, a bucket and a blue rag in hand, part and parcel of her old blue coat. Luba was washing him, wasn't she? Her hands felt as soft as the poodle's hair Anno liked so much; nimble fingers and a wet rag were looking for a cure for his aching ribs as they brushed his face all soiled with blood. David groaned. She might think of undressing and washing him! She would unbuckle the thick Moroccan leather belt Anno had given him as a birthday present. He panicked, yet a part of the blood that ran in his veins hoped that she'd wash him as he lay naked on the grass. It was good her new coat didn't show him her knees anymore. Her hands were visible, though, thin ordinary fingers that gutted fish, scrubbed floors and thickened sauces. The sight of her hands soothed him. She stopped cleaning his chest, she didn't even try to wash him, and this threw him into despair.

"Can you walk?" she asked. These words, pacifying and soft, helped him more than her hands did.

"Yes."

When she leaned forward, her coat attempted to show him details of her body, but his eyes ran away. Luba put her face close to his, and he enjoyed it, wasn't scared a bit because she was a skinny woman, as scrawny as Anno's poodle that couldn't do him any harm. Luba helped him get up. It was good she didn't say a word as she threw his arm around her neck, then slowly led him down the hill to the cottages of the highway maintenance workers.

"I don't want to go there."

"Where?" Luba asked her blue eyes puzzled. This encouraged him. He didn't like eyes that knew everything.

"I want the *History of Bulgaria*," he said.

The smile on her thin face put him at ease. Luba knew you slept well, if the *History of Bulgaria* was your pillow. They tottered off to the wattle and daub hut, to the histories of Byzantium, Europe and Bulgaria piled on the dirt floor. It felt wonderful and peaceful to walk by her side, so wonderful that he turned to watch her. Her face looked calm, the sun seemed to have tanned her blue eyes; the frogs and the duckweed, the sky and the stones appeared brown at the end of summer.

Luba did not look brown to him.

She took him back to the books, to the dust and the smell of printed pages that made David's head swim. She let him lie down on the dozen Byzantiums.

"Are you hungry?" she asked.

David nodded. Suddenly he had ravenous appetite as he remembered the two bruised pears he'd gobbled up in the hut with her books. Now she gave him a piece of bread; it cost forty cents in the bakery, he knew, exactly as much as a glass of moonshine in The Cat. Come to think of it, a glass of fake plum brandy was much more useful than a loaf of bread. He ate slowly, gratefully, not letting go of her hand.

"I have scabies," she said. "You'll get it from me. It's contagious."

But he was not scared of scabies, so he chewed on, not letting go of her infected fingers. It was hard to believe the thing Kiro did to her had really happened. She was the girl he cared about, the only girl. Her new coat was ugly, longer than the old one, and its bright color angered him a lot. Now, he wanted to see her knees, and the damn coat got in the way.

"Shall I go to The Cat and tell the guys you are here?"

"I'll sleep in your hut," he said.

"No," she said as she lifted the book like a hoe in front of him. "I'll sleep here."

"Read to me," he asked her, hoping he could see her knees.

Luba read for a couple of minutes or even more about a crazy teenager and David, to be honest, didn't give a hoot for him.

He sat up and kissed the hem of her new blue coat. At first, she was taken aback, then she told him one more time about her scabies. She had to wait until the 20th when they'd pay her wages. Then she'd buy a remedy from Koyna the druggist, and then she had to wait seven more days for the itch to entirely disappear. Scabies was a nasty disease.

"Hey, look here," David said as he went through the pockets of his silk bell-bottomed pants, his impatience draining his strength. He sat there breathing hard, fuming with anger. She had given up on him. She had not washed him with the water from the blue pail. "This is what I wanted to give you," he said as he produced a thing that gleamed like a fishing lure as it caught the last rays of the day.

Luba looked at his hand and saw it, a yellow glittering thing that looked like a tooth.

"It's gold," David explained to her. "Get going. Run to buy the scabies remedy. This is the gold tooth of the miner who kicked the bucket in the coal pit. Anno gave it to me. I'll take the treatment with you. Whatever you do, I'll do it too."

She gave him back the piece of gold.

"I'll wait a few more days," she said. "I can stand the itch until the 20th."

David stirred uneasily on the floor as he complained his bones hurt. At that moment, her coat showed him her white knee, and he, full of gratitude, again kissed the blue hem, although her naked skin still scared him.

She sat down by his side. There were no books between them now, and the fact she was eating her chunk of bread very slowly reassured him.

"You may come with me to Spain if you want," David blurted out. "One can make heaps of money in Spain." He edged closer to her, kissed the shoulder of the blue coat, undid the top button, then the second, and the minute her skin looked like the moon — he had enjoyed its silver glow at the Black Sea coast in a little cove as he drove a dump truck full of beans — he was sure he could look at her until the moon turned into night. "Marry me."

Then he wondered why he had mumbled these words and why he had unbuttoned her new coat. It was good she had not said "yes" right away. He was lucky she had retreated behind a mound of histories of Byzantium and had not touched him. It was good she had buttoned up her coat shortly after he had unbuttoned it.

One more time, the blue coat hid her moon from him, and he was so sad he could hardly breathe. It was the saddest day in his life. She smiled and it felt as if someone washed the blood off his chest. I'll die, David thought. I positively will if I'm afraid to kiss this girl. She was still smiling, still smiling, perhaps at her books, perhaps at Byzantium, he couldn't say. He was sure he wanted to stay here, with the smell of printed letters and her books, with the barking hill, the blue coat and the two buttons he had unfastened. He wanted to remain in this room as long as he lived.

"Help me carry the books to the village," she said, and it astonished him. Why should she carry these books anywhere? Couldn't she set fire to the fat tomes herself? She could summon the gypsy lads, and they could brew plum brandy or roast chili peppers in the flames. "We'll take them to Zachary's barn."

David tried hard to remember who this Zachary was. Who was it that would pay David a pretty penny if he were to slog his way through the thistles a sack of thick volumes on his back, trudging down the hill to Zachary's barn? Who was crazy to lug moldy pages to Zachary's barn if this mountain of paper could honestly and decently burn down pretty well here? Zachary, the boy with the peach fuzz cheeks.

She shouldered a bulging sack full of Heine, Hegel, Harry Potter, Hölderlin and other guys David had not heard anybody talk about. She carried them all as she strode across the room, then pushed forward, hammering away at rocks and grass until her coat turned into a flock of rooks.

God, David said to himself. Anno often whispered "Oh, my God" as he stared at a sword fixed to the wall by means of two silver nails, so David guessed God was a sword that could chop your head off if you spoke too much.

Sometimes in the evening Anno unhooked the sword from its silver nails, put it on his chest and said, "Touch it." A fat lot of good that would do! Touching God! On and off, David groused yet he fondled the blade that even in the heat was as cold as death. However, Anno's skin was warm and set his mind at rest.

"Oh, my God," David said as he sat up. His ribs must have turned into a bag of cooked spaghetti. What the hell. He rose to his feet and shouldered another sack. There was this Victor Hugo guy on top, then some other scribbling colleagues of his. David had earned an honest "C" on Victor Hugo, he might have earned even a "B" if he had known how Gavroche had met his maker. This Gavroche kid was David's favorite among all characters from all books, both thick and thin, in the school library, and for this reason David's classmates had dubbed him Gavroche.

David couldn't say a word on Gavroche's death even if his life depended on it, and that was why he sank to "C". No matter what, ever since high school he'd held that plucky chap, V. Hugo, in considerable respect. Now David had to carry him on his back for a couple of miles, yet he wasn't mad at the writing dudes although his ribs were spaghetti and hurt a lot. He clutched the sack with V. Hugo and the other scribblers in it, and slowly schlepped it through the thorns, nettles and stones. At places, where the stray dogs had not licked at his dried blood, the bloody droplets shone on the ground, turning the weeds into wounds that wouldn't clot. Luba walked in front of him, Bulgaria and Byzantium on her back. He could see a wisp of her auburn hair, and this comforted him. He hadn't pressed her to go further on the issue of "Will you marry me?"

Now David quietly tried to adjust Victor Hugo onto his broken ribs. It was warm, the wind smelled of mud and tadpoles and the night air comforted him. He remembered everything Luba's new blue coat had shown him and felt as happy as a tadpole in a pool in the Struma that still hadn't run dry. David clumped after the girl, down the hill, further down the hill, and only once did he call "Hey!" so softly he could barely hear his own voice.

She stopped in her tracks, left the load of books on the ground and turned to face him. David hoped she'd wait for him a bit longer because *Les Miserables* weighed him down like a ton of bricks, Luba lifted up the sack and padded on through the dry grass, a walking new blue coat that hid her calves, her hands and back. It was ok with David because the girl's knees scared him. Luba dragged the books into a yard, its broken-down picket fence glowering at the empty sky. An empty barn, a rickety affair about to collapse any minute now, jutted out in the corner.

Not a straw bale was in sight under the low roof, no dry herbs or hay. A heap of rags and shabby mattresses, that was all. There, the villagers threw away their relatives' clothes after the old folks cashed in their chips and closed the world behind their backs. You could see mustachioed men, thin squinting women and seven or eight snotty brats arranged in order of descending height in faded black-and-white photographs. In the barn, on the dead men's pants and shirts, Luba left Bulgaria and Byzantium, then she drew nearer, her hands accidentally bumping into David's as she took the sack with V. Hugo conspicuous on top of the other tomes.

"Thank you."

Sharp rib cage pain bit into David, his throat hurt, yet he followed her up the slope to the wattle-and-daub hut where the dogs had laughed at him. The hill barked again and the express train to Greece began climbing the steep mountain to squash David. They walked side by side in silence, Luba and he, at times stepping on his dried blood in the grass. The dusk was thin and sweet, so he plucked up courage and took her hand in his.

She tried to pull it free.

"I'll have scabies until the 20th," she said, but David didn't let her fingers slip away. They walked on through the weeds, thistles and plum trees hitting their faces, no one saying a word. Not far from the river, shrubs and prickles were entwined in a thorny fence, so he let go of her hand. Suddenly Luba darted across the thicket. A minute passed and he was alone with the hill. The faint sound of her steps offended him.

It was not that she had scabies until the 20th, no. She didn't want him to hold her hand. That was it. No way! David started to run, soon caught up with her and, almost feeling no pain, blurted out "Oh, my God." He believed he said it to God who often dropped in to see how Anno's sword was doing in The Cat.

"Why don't you want the gold tooth?" he asked as he took the girl's hand in his.

Teeth, once pulled out, bring bad luck she said, or did she? He didn't remember.

They took two more sacks from the wattle-and-daub hut, a thousand books by obscure gents, Turks, Krauts, Americans, overweight tomes all, that could brew a barrel of brandy for sure, if you set fire to their fat covers and let the pages be, mind you. After Luba touched these shabby books, they were suddenly as strong as the sword on Anno's chest, and God himself peeking inside Luba's sacks. Then they walked in the dusk again, following the trace his dried blood had left, and he held her hand. Luba did not try to pull it away, probably she had despaired of explaining things to him, so David held her puny fingers, praying there would be many more books in the hut. This would mean he would go there with her ten more times. He liked the slight chill in her skin.

The stray dogs perched on the hill like hawks barked somberly and waited for the train to breathe its last on the rails. Then the beasts would hold a great feast, gobbling up all the passengers at the end of the summer.

"All right. Cut to the chase already," David said. "Why should we dump the poor volumes on the coats of guys who kicked the bucket ten years ago?"

Luba didn't say anything, so he scolded her, "Hey, are you off your rocker? Don't you like your grandma's hut?"

She didn't answer, and David was taken aback. Why should this girl keep quiet here? Did she suspect the villagers would set fire to her books in order to brew plum brandy, or more likely than not, make baked-pepper pickles as V. Hugo and the other big cheese scribes were burnt to a crisp? Luba said nothing as she pulled her hand free, and this angered him.

"Hey," David muttered under his breath. "You take your books from the hut because you're scared Kiro will come back to your grandma's place. Is that it?"

She kept silent for an age as the dogs waited for the summer to end. Then she nodded and his eyes seemed to bleed. No, it was his soul drowning in the pool of malice he bore towards Kiro. The idiot wanted his girl. The only girl he had dared to touch.

Her skin and her knees did not frighten him. He hated the thought of letting go her thin fingers, and he hated the tangled plum branches that didn't let them go to the wattle-and-daub hut.

"I'll kill Kiro," David whispered, then the plum trees put an end to his courage. He wanted to see her face, though. It was good he saw the moon gleam in her eyes, quietly, very softly.

"Don't be afraid," he said, then he kissed her.

It was the first time he had really kissed a girl in his life.

She recoiled from his touch, amazed, he recoiled, too, amazed even more, and it seemed the hill retreated to the railway line with the express train silent as a winter day.

"Tomorrow, I'll drop in to see how your books with the dead writers are doing in the barn," David said. "I hope you'll be there too."

She didn't say anything, the dogs waited for the summer to end and an age passed until Luba nodded her auburn head. Yes, she'd be there, with her books and the dead folks' shabby clothes neatly folded in the gypsy lad Zachary's ramshackle barn.

He felt like taking her to his room at The Cat where the walls were coated in silk and velvet. He wanted to show her God, taking a nap on Anno's sword that hung on its two silver nails; he wanted to give her the gold tooth, the one which belonged to the miner buried under mud and stones in the coal pit. David didn't believe teeth brought bad luck. Every man has 32 teeth, does that mean he was unhappy? And yes, Luba could buy a remedy for her scabies with the gold tooth. Why should the silly girl endure the itch until the 20th? She set out for the barn, property of Zachary, the gypsy raw-boned boy, the ringleader of the bunch of swarthy kids who tried hard to learn all the letters of the Bulgarian alphabet.

Luba told him this Zachary kid had two homes. He had chosen an abandoned house and squatted in it; the place's owner, a wrinkled old man dissolved in his glass of brandy a couple of years ago. "To dissolve in your cup of brandy" in these parts meant to die alone and unclaimed. The kid slept on the kitchen floor, having squeezed through a basement window. He had asked Luba to keep her books in the best room of the ownerless house until she got rid of her scabies. David was sure Luba wouldn't let rotten scabies infect her mom, her dad and her sister Sara. If Sara caught it, the thing would flare up in a flash, all-terrain vehicle drivers, chauffeurs and truckers would be scratching and clawing at their bellies. The itch would swoop down over Spain, Italy, Greece, the Near East, the Middle East and the Far East. It could reach Japan too, but Japan, as far as David knew, was an island, and he was not sure if trucks could swim across the ocean, carrying Sara's scabies in the driver's cab.

§

Luba could not stay in the old man's deserted house. The barn where the citizens of Staro threw out their dead relatives' mattresses was no man's land, and that was why Zachary had appropriated it for his own use. He had appropriated the hill, the fields and the Struma River, too. Now everything in Staro belonged to Zachary, but the land and the river were of no use. It was extremely difficult for him to soak up the Bulgarian alphabet. He had learned a thing or two, though. He knew how to write curse words, and he scribbled with spray-paint on the houses of the folks he hated. Two days ago, dirty phrases emerged on Kiro's garage, and Kiro was a big cheese in Staro, Yakob's lousy bodyguard. The same filthy expressions burst into bloom on Kiro's house and appeared, scribbled in indelible ink on Yakob's four Jeep Grand Cherokees. Things were serious, one had to shake the big stick and hit the criminals who wreaked havoc with the law-abiding citizens. No one suspected the perpetrator was Zachary, the scrawny kid, who knew only two letters, "L" for Luba and "Z" of the impossibly difficult Bulgarian alphabet.

Zachary could write the word "Luba" as well.

… David returned to The Cat, to the room with the black silk sheets, with God Almighty and the sword, hanging on its two silver nails. Anno had kicked the select clientele out of the pub. This evening his customers were unable to take their seats at the garden plastic tables thickly illustrated with obscene drawings; they couldn't enjoy the comfort of the rickety chairs either, so most of them lay prostrate by the Struma. The river had shriveled up into a gutter of sand and mud. The clientele swilled fake turnip brandy from lemonade bottles, muttering their indignation against Anno's black sheets. The owner of the drinking establishment had lit a dozen candles on the bar counter. A flashlight flickered on every table and chair, and a huge candle, which cost fifty levs in the local hardware store, gleamed like a glowworm on the threshold of David's room.

"Where have you been?" Anno asked, the minute David set foot in The Cat, his ribs soft as curds, his silk pants torn and starched with dry blood. "What's the matter with you?" The Cat's proprietor breathed. "Your nose is bleeding!" David paid no heed to him. "Everything is for you… the candles, the wine. Look. Let's feast. I got rid of the men from the restaurant… wanted to make the place cozy for you. Look. This bottle of wine is magnificent. It's for you. You are bleeding!"

David sat at the table, failing to notice the 50 lev candle as he pounced upon the magnificent wine, an exorbitantly expensive bottle from France.

"Why are you doing this?" he asked, the naked candle flames kneeling down at his feet.

The night fell quickly for the dead, the drunkards and the ordinary folk. The night wore on even in Yakob's mansion although every five yards a powerful lamp shone, illuminating the fenced-in hills, mountain ridges, weasels and deer.

A faint breeze drifted in Zachary's barn, in his two houses, and his fireflies enjoyed it, but the boy didn't feel like sleeping in the room with his four brothers and three sisters at the home distillery where his father brewed his plum poison. Zachary didn't feel like spending the night in his two houses either, although he believed that their dead owners' clothes did bring good luck.

He rushed to his barn. There, the villagers discarded the souls of their dead relatives, dead hens and stuff like rusted pans and sieves scrap metal dealers did not want.

Some guys used to throw out Coca-Cola bottles too, but the working people in these parts got smart and stopped burying plastic items in the barn. The younger ones lit fires to warm themselves or cooked the potatoes they'd stolen over burning Fanta and 7up bottles. No one was mentally retarded enough to dump burnable things, Zachary knew. He hoped that she, Luba — the only woman whose name he could write without spelling mistakes — had already taken her scabies to his building.

He secretly prayed to the roof beam in his father's hut. Without a shadow of doubt this roof beam was God, Zachary was sure of it.

"God, it hurts," his mom screamed when she gave birth to his brothers and sisters, staring at the roof beam above her head. So, Zachary prayed to this beam that Luba would have scabies for a long time, if possible all her life, but please, God, don't make her suffer. Let her itch be timid like dust. Ease her nasty itch, please. And, God, I'll carry you on my back to the mountain top. I promise. Let her scabies be caught between her skin and her blue coat, so she'll stay in my barn. Please.

Zachary could visit her in the evenings and ask her about the most difficult letters in the Bulgarian alphabet.

She talked softly, and he watched, the lonely Christmas night in her eyes waiting for him as blue as the whirlpool in the Struma River that teemed with minnows. Zachary caught them with his bare hands and baked them on a rusty iron sheet. Minnows swam in Luba's eyes too, meek, glittering ones; he could catch them with his bare hands, too, but he wouldn't bake these little fish. He'd take care of them, his heart a happy tadpole.

Last night, he found her in the barn. But who had lugged her books down there? He was furious with the guy who had touched Luba's volumes. Zachary could've carried them all on his back. If only he hadn't helped his pop brew plum brandy! It was true, brandy was the only thing Anno bought from his old man. The fat dirty words appeared on Anno's pub too. They were the only phrase apart from Luba's name Zachary could write without making spelling mistakes. The obscene expression materialized scrawled in a blue ballpoint pen on all Anno's shirts the pub owner had hung out to dry in The Cat's backyard. Well, who could suspect Zachary was the offender if the only Bulgarian letters he knew were L and Z?

So, last night he went to the barn and Luba was there, a prisoner serving time in a cluttered jail of books. Zachary had brought her cheese he had stolen from the Venice Motel; he had picked a bag of strawberries for her from a bigwig's garden, although the bigwig's fence was loaded like a camel with security camera systems. No security or insecurity camera systems could stop Zachary. He picked strawberries, cherries, raspberries and took everything to Luba, the convicted felon in the cell of paperbacks. It was dark and he could not see the blue whirlpools the Struma River had left in her eyes before it ran dry.

What was impossible to see in the dark made no difference to Zachary; he saw it all the same. Today in the afternoon Luba asked them to learn by heart some crazy poem "I am Bulgarian" by a crazy poetic guy Vazov who bent over backwards to talk one into believing that being Bulgarian was great. Well, if Luba said so, Zachary reckoned it was ok to be Bulgarian. He gave her the strawberries, the chunk of bread and the sausage he had filched from his mom, all the time thinking hard, so hard his head throbbed. Somebody else, not he, Zachary, had schlepped Luba's books to keep company with the dead men's clothes.

"Are you crazy, Luba, or what! Did you drag along those heavy volumes and stuff?" he chided. "I could have stolen a wheelbarrow for you. I know it's a bad idea to steal and thieve, but I'd have stolen it just for an hour, not a second more. Ok, ok, I won't steal a thing if you say it's a bad thing to do. I won't touch anything that's not mine. You can take my word for it. I'd have carried your smelly books on my back. The fattest tomes I'd have lugged, book after book, bag after bag. I'd have hauled them together with 'I am Bulgarian'"! But… Dad and me, we brewed brandy. I sipped brandy, then I sipped brandy and sipped brandy again. When I woke up in the morning, it was 10 pm on the following day. Those nitwits from the highway were just catching the night train to Dupni to travel back home. Then the brandy I'd brewed with Dad let me be. The moon broke my head. I ran to see what you were doing and lo and behold! It turns out you've taken your books to my barn all by yourself. Measly scabies makes your itch worse? I itch all over the place, honestly. Let me see your scabies. Do you have bubbles and bumps on your arms? I've got them on my legs, too. God — God stays on the roof beam at our place, you know — God, say I to the roof beam. You don't know Luba. The Struma River stops in her eyes for a while. Her scabies is awful. Her books are also awful, honestly.

This Vazov guy, too, must be hard hit by the itch. He caught scabies, I'm sure. Luba, you carried him on your back. You know what? I can write some, but you'd better not read the words I can spell correctly. They are dirty words, all of them. But I can write a clean thing, just one. One very good thing I can write. I'll show you."

Zachary, who had a fuzz of black hairs under his nose, took a sheet of paper and, sticking the tip of his tongue out, although he was well past the age of first grade, printed in shaky, very large capital letters "LUBA".

Luba said, "Good for you, Zachary. Soon you'll learn to write all the letters of the alphabet. You and Valia will read fairytales together. I have many books of fairytales here, in the brown sacks. I can read to you if you want."

That night, she read to him about the wild swans and a pretty girl, Elisa by name. It was the first time that Zachary had heard a fairytale and this was the most magnificent night in his life. He felt happy and so grateful he didn't know what to say. Should he thank the dead men's clothes or the brown sacks stuffed with books? All words of gratitude had fled from his mind; he only saw Luba, her pale skin that had the moon and the wind in it. He knew that Elisa in the fairytale was Luba. The swans looked like sparrows, but those were sparrows that lived abroad. The nettles stung you exactly as they did in Bulgaria.

That night, Zachary padded barefoot down to his barn; he didn't feel like sleeping or praying to God who lived in the roof beam. Under it, his mom had given birth to his siblings, whispering, "It hurts, God!", and God tried to help as much as he could.

Now, God was much stronger because Zachary had carved something on his roof beam with a knife he had filched from the fair in Dupni — he carved **LUBA** with the stolen knife and then everybody, God, his mom, his dad, his sisters and brothers, all became beautiful after Luba's name was spelled correctly in their room.

Now he ran to the barn, praying, let Luba be there! Let her be there, please. He had made up his mind to tell her. He'd tell her not to be afraid of scabies. Zachary would grow up real quick. He'd marry her and he'd learn all the letters of the alphabet from the beginning to the end. He'd buy scabies remedies for her, cherries and books he'd buy, too, the fattest tomes and volumes in Staro. If only Luba would agree to wait a minute and he'd grow up. Let her wait at least two years. But when should he speak to her? The minute he set his eyes on her? Or should he wait, let her read to him again about that Elisa girl from the sack of fairytales? He ran to the barn.

Luba was as meek as a breadcrumb while she was reading fairytales, her eyes a blue river for him. The minnows in the whirlpools scurried off to Zachary, mad as March hares all, jumping into his fingers of their own free will. Zachary loved the wild swans and Elisa fairytale. It was sweet as a melon and endless like the railways by the Struma.

He walked in the deserted field that belonged to him, every inch of it, every leaf of dry grass. He had a loaf of bread in his bag. Luba and he would eat it together. Quietly, like a woodpecker among the branches, he stole his way to the barn full of dead men's clothes and books.

§

Zachary peeked through a gap in the wattle fence, itching to shout at the top of his impatient lungs, "I'm here!" The words ran into his throat like a fish bone. He choked. The bag he carried slipped from his hand, the loaf of bread thudded to the ground.

On the volumes, on the dead guy's clothes, in the dust lay Luba. Kiro! The mugger as good as a grave, the goon who guarded Yakob and stopped the gypsies from stealing his tomatoes, Kiro… naked, his back glistening with sweat, as big as an airfield. Kiro climbed on top of Luba. The picture book about the swans wallowed by her side. A torn book fell in a pile on the floor, its pages a mess of dirt. Kiro the Tombstone, mudslide of muscles, flattened Luba against the hardcovers, squashed her under his greasy face. He made love to her. No. He made death to her.

Luba's face was wet like the wind in November. Her eyes had lost the blue river. Kiro didn't care about Luba's hands white as the icicles under the eaves at Christmas. She did not wail. She didn't tell God it hurt the way Zachary's mother did when she gave birth to his brothers. Luba bit her lip, Luba didn't scream and God couldn't hear her. Only Zachary could hear her tears seep into the snow of January. Her eyes kept silent.

Zachary would print the dirtiest words on Kiro's Jeep Wrangler, he could copy the most obscene curses the drunks had jotted down on the tables at The Cat. But what good would dirty words be? He'd set Kiro's Jeep on fire. No. What good would a burnt out car be? Kiro would beat Zachary's mother, his father, his brothers…. A guy Kiro had clobbered came back home without his gallbladder, without an eye or with a ruptured spleen. Sometimes the beaten guy's mom threw her son's clothes in this barn because the boy didn't come back at all.

Kiro crushed the girl who was pretty like a January night, like Elisa and the eleven swans. Kiro pushed his Luba, warm like the clothes of the living folks, like Zachary's most beautiful day when she read to him the only fairytale in his life. Big as a moat and the poisonous lizards in it, Kiro squashed the girl who had taught Zachary the most important four letters of the Bulgarian alphabet he knew.

Zachary looked and looked. He could not set fire to Kiro's lousy Jeep. Zachary looked on and could not kill Kiro, could not even hit him, Zachary was paralyzed with fear.

Zachary, a shivering heap by the chunk of bread that had slipped from his hands, looked at Kiro's ugly naked back, stared at the white January face of his teacher, the only person in his life who'd tried to teach him the beautiful alphabet. He looked, biting his knuckles, he looked and kept silent, black tears as heavy as the hill springing to his eyes, the hungry dogs black poison in the heat.

"Luba! I'm here!" the boy screeched. He jumped.

If Kiro catches you, you lose an eye. If Kiro beats you, you lose your spleen. If Kiro…

"I'm here!" Zachary lashed out at the beefy ugly back. "I'll rescue you! Luba!"

§

In the beginning, you can't climb a wall, but you quickly learn how to do it. Day in day out, you creep an inch higher, then another one, then one more.

Martusha lay, a pile of flab and greasy hair, nailed to her luxury bed, her blood pressure killing her.

"Give me my heart drops and two white pills."

I didn't give her anything. It was a pleasure watching a crone die. This particular ugly old woman had diligently counted and registered the number of times Yakob had shoved me into his green room. At times, he was too lazy to go on breathing. He didn't tear my shirt or panties off, he wouldn't have sex, he lolled back in his chair, silent, staring at me, whispering, "You are very pretty, Pirina, damn it!" This was a lie. He made me comb his hair and I did, taking my time, dallying with the idea of slitting his throat as he sucked in air, his eyes tired old slippers, fastened on me like a safety pin. I believed I could put him to sleep, although I didn't have a knife. Martusha hid all sharp objects, razors, nails, etc. I could snap a thick branch off and plunge its sharp end into his neck.

"Did you knock out Kalcho's teeth?" I asked Yakob.

"I thrashed him with a shovel," he said.

"Is he dead?" I asked, my voice a pile of rags.

No one spoke loudly in Yakob's green room. Death lived in it. I was thinking of that branch I had already chosen; I knew where the oak tree grew and I'd beaten a path to it.

"You're constantly prattling on about Kalcho the wretch. Why?" Yakob's words, a nest of vipers, waited at my feet, but I was not afraid of reptiles. I learned to capture snakes with a forked stick, just for the sport of it as I roamed through the woods in the mountain trapped within the wall. I became skilled at extracting snake venom, collecting the deadly fluid in a Mason jar. Why an oak branch stuck in your throat? Why not viper venom, Yakob?

"You didn't explain to me why you keep on chattering about Kalcho the blockhead." Anger gnawed at the big cheese's words and torched half of the green room.

"He treats sick folks, Yakob. I love Kalcho."

"What about me? Do you love me?" The vipers in his voice basked in the sun and their nest was at its worst.

"No, I don't," I said. I wasn't scared. I didn't care. Martusha would write down in her ledger "The idiot went and cawed she didn't love him. The numbskull!" or something in the same line. Tomorrow, they'd find a girl run over by a truck on the road to Staro. A pothole as deep as a swimming pool gaped near the village, and I knew a few strumpets had breathed their last in it. So? "Another filthy pair of panties the boss got bored with. Who is to arrange the funeral? Old Martusha with her stiff, achy knees."

"I'll tell you what makes me real mad," the old woman said, harping hard on the same string. "They'll force me to wash your body after the truck hits you. It's a nasty task to give a squashed belly a tub bath. Blood clots, stinking to high heaven. I'm not twenty years old, mind you. And I have blood pressure like everybody else!"

Now, Martusha's blood pressure was giving her hell.

"Two white pills… Pirina, give me two white pills."

I didn't give her two white pills.

"Slip your hand under that chest of drawers…lift the loose board…" she rasped. "I've got two thousand levs. Take the money. Give me two white pills."

I found a bunch of cash, big, magnificent bills as pure as a baby's tear, and waved them under her nose.

"Give me the pills."

Martusha's nose looked as yellow as the clay in the moat which surrounded the mountain.

"Did you calculate how many minutes Yakob rocked on top of me without a break, Martusha?" I asked.

Her eyes the color of pumpkin seed shells slowly grew cold.

"The pills…" she wheezed, her throat stalled, her lips wooden on her gray face.

"I bled… Blood on my legs…on my bottom. I bled like a slaughtered pig. You didn't send for Doc Stiom." It wasn't a trip down memory lane I took Martusha to. "You lied to Yakob that I was alive and kicking."

I took two white pills, tossed them onto the marble floor and crushed them into the dust under my boot.

"Please," she gasped.

"You collected ants for Yakob. They were as big as grasshoppers, brown dirty cannibals. You knew where Yakob turned these cannibals loose?" I chucked a handful of white pills onto the marble tiles. It was exciting to watch them split and burst under the soles of my shoes as I said, "Ten days I pissed blood. It felt like someone cut my crotch with a hand-saw."

"There's a shoebox in the wardrobe. I keep a gold ring in it…" Martusha was choking on the air, her throat, rattling dangerously, seemed to explode. "That ring… take it. Gercho gave it to me before… before we …got married. Take it. My daughter… she died," Martusha groaned in pain; however, here in the green room, pain, moaning and groaning had been my part of the deal. "My granddaughter… it's something I've never told anybody before… I took my granddaughter to Yakob. After a month, he let her go. He did. Nobody said a word about a car crash near that pothole, not in Staro… no girl run over by a truck. I don't know where she is now…" the old woman sobbed.

Folks sobbed a lot in these parts. If you didn't sob, you were either dead or you'd passed out after Yakob had fun with you. No other options were available, period.

"She couldn't make it in the red room," the old one mumbled. "She was weaker than you… lost twenty pounds…the poor girl…"

I took the ring from the shoebox — nothing spectacular, a thin gold wire and a tiny gemstone stuck onto it.

"She gnawed through her skin to get at her veins," Martusha gasped. "I saved her life… Yakob dumped her. I don't know where she is now." her words were the edge of a precipice, the branch I wanted to break from the oak tree and jab its sharp end into Yakob's throat.

"My granddaughter…She called down a curse on me," Martusha said as her parched lips started bleeding. "Even before Yakob kicked her out, I gave her all the money I had, every cent Yakob had paid me. My granddaughter… She took it. Doc Stoim couldn't make her bleeding stop," Martusha droned on. "I know you did it with sumac tea, Pirina. You bled a couple of days, no more. You are as strong as a crag."

I thrust my fingers into Martusha's mouth and dropped two pills inside it, her throat a panicked funnel.

"My mom is your age," I said. "My mom hurled stones at Yakob's Jeep Grand Cherokee. His goons dragged me out of our house. She threw stones at them too."

"Your mom hasn't seen blood gushing out of a woman's butt," Martusha muttered. "I see it again and again."

An ugly woman, big hands, thin arms, thin legs and huge belly, an egg that had learned to walk. That was what Martusha was.

"I'll tell Yakob on you," she hissed. "He'll know you tried to murder me."

I laughed my head off at her words.

"You are a witch," the crone blurted out. "He lost his head over you. He dotes on you, hussy. How did you do it? Where did you touch him? Is it because you moo your lousy songs? Or because you can outstay him in the red room? Your soul is a dung heap."

"You're right, my soul is a dung heap," I said. "You be careful, or I won't give you white pills. There will be no next time. Death will take you to your granddaughter."

Martusha's yellow eyes died, a couple of glowworms on which a housewife had tossed a bucket of hogwash.

"She's alive."

I had wanted to skin Martusha's brown face a thousand times. I'd been dreaming of dropping her scalp inside the jar with the brown ants she had collected for me… Now her cheeks were trembling, flabby as mud. Suddenly, her face looked like my father's. I saw him bent over his ancient newspaper. The woman's eyes gleamed, their yellow light scorching and desperate. I remembered my father's eyes the day when Petrova, the teacher in Bulgarian literature, left the village of Staro. A bit of skirt she was and I hated her. She turned my sister Luba into a beast of burden loaded with a cart full of books. Wait a minute. No, I didn't hate Petrova. This teacher opened my eyes. She told me no woman was Yakob's beast of burden. A woman must not put up with brown ants, Petrova told me, although only God knew where she was now. You didn't come into the world to watch an old woman pray to God, hoping against hope Yakob hadn't bumped off her granddaughter.

I could say to Martusha, "You know Yakob. You won't hear from your granddaughter again." I didn't say that. The old woman looked at me, her eyes shallow as my father's. He'd lost something long time ago as he trawled through old printed pages, blind to the road after Petrova gave up on Staro and left us, her students. She, the darned retard, knew "If You Forget Me" by heart and recited "The Road Not Taken" until kingdom come. She recited the poem from its damned beginning to its damned end, and you melted like butter in a frying pan. At times, you sobbed and felt like an addlebrained brat, tears and snot on your face.

"Your girl is alive," I said.

I saw Martusha brace up. Her face was parched clay no more. Old, cut by the gorges of wrinkles and lines, but it was a human face all the same.

"The boss kept you eight hours in the red room. You were a bundle of rags. I felt sorry for you…didn't give you water to drink," Martusha mumbled to herself. "The other girls were good an hour or two, no more. Your blood stopped gushing of its own accord. This surprised me. Honestly."

I still don't know why Yakob took me to the green room. Last Monday, he stared at me, his eyes digging into my face, obstinate, refusing to creep down to my breasts even though he hadn't drunk much.

"It hurts," he said as his hand perched on his ribs. "I'll throw up."

After a while, I started to sing. There was no voice to speak of in my throat, false and wrong sounds all over the place writhing like caterpillars you'd chucked into a saucepan of vinegar. Not worth a red cent, that was how much my voice cost. I roared for the dragons, my old pals. I knew they were listening while my blood was running dry in the red room, sturdy magnificent giants they were, my monsters, rancor every square inch of them, savage as the brown ants. I loved them and I sang, my anxiety melting, a lump of grease in the sun, my fear fleeing like a hare chased by a hound. When I roared I was a sea — I'd seen one on the TV — a place full of water, no end, and no shore in sight. I was that water. I sang and I thought of my sister Sara, the most beautiful girl I'd ever seen. Now I knew what they did to her in that stink hole, the Venice Motel. All men are made like Yakob — that was what *Gray's Anatomy* said; well, I didn't write that textbook, Gray did. Then a thought crossed my mind, Kalcho is not Yakob. Old Koyna, his mom, had saved the lives of every man, woman or kid in town. No, Kalcho was my friend.

"Sing!" Yakob ordered, and I did, my voice wriggling like a snake, its head smashed and dead. "I stop throwing up the minute you start to squawk. My belly doesn't hurt anymore."

One day, Yakob brought builders to the mansion, burly strapping fellows, their shaved pates glowing like my jar of snake venom the gorilla Kiro, a hill of paving blocks, made for me. His mammoth hand landed on my forehead and pressed hard. I suspected my skull was about to crack open.

"You don't have a temperature," he snapped. "Look at you. They're spilling yarns about you in Staro. Said you'd bitten the dust. Your mom goes to the graveyard, lights candles for you. The gypsy kids dug your grave. When a dame has a heart attack and croaks at Yakob's place, they don't bring the body to her mom. The family can't bury her properly. Kalcho's been puking for ten days in a row. Can't stop throwing up. The docks don't know what pills to stick into him. We're waiting for him to go belly up." Kiro, having thrashed more guys than the thousand stars twinkling in the sky, had learned from experience to tell if a bone was broken or not. He searched me, checked feet, stomach, tits, neck and scalp. "Wow! A ripped torso. You're cool. No smashed bones. I'll tell your mom. I'll tell her to stop making an ass of herself in the bone orchard. Your dad's much smarter than her. I only saw him once near your grave. He drank water like an eel and read his newspaper."

"How's Sara doing? How's Luba doing?" I asked, but he clammed up. Had the cat got his tongue?

I was good at opening mouths compressed into a hard line. I'd learned when and where to press, and conversations quickly took place. I tossed a bottle of vodka on the ground in front of the thug and the garbage dump of muscles blurted out, "Sara's ok," then he went on, gripping the bottle, "Sara's sitting pretty… wallowing in money. Luba… Luba… She lives near my place… I didn't burn her books. Didn't rip the cover off of a single sleazy tome. Honestly. I bought her clothes and stuff… She tried to run away from me. Twice. Why? Couldn't tell you why."

The builders wrecked the red room from the ceramic floor tiles to the gold chandelier, inside out, backwards and forwards. They painted the walls yellow, brought wardrobes the color of sunrise, dumped the red carpet in the street; however, Martusha collected it from the rubbish heap and stored it together with her white pills. The chamber shone as clean as a baby toddler nursery, sterile as a pharmacy, immaculate as a private hospital and cozy like a grave. In it, I sang to Yakob. He'd plant his head in my lap and I'd croon as hard as I could. I could daub some snake venom on the tiny cut he'd left on his smug face when he shaved in the morning. I could harm him in more than one way, so I wailed the tunes, hissed the songs and roared the carols. Martusha must've gone nuts on account of the nasty sounds I kept on neighing day after day. Her blood pressure was sure going to seed. Whenever I left the yellow toddler nursery, the clay on her face collapsed, the net of wrinkles, lines and furrows a quagmire of fear.

"It doesn't hurt anymore," Yakob sighed, relieved.

I knew what would come next, love vapid as a cup of tea for a terminally ill patient, but I was not that patient, my blood had stopped running dry, I crushed him into his own bed. My veins were brimming over with brown ants and I extracted malice from their narrow yellow throats. The soil outside the nursery squirmed hungry for rain. Yakob cringed at the sound of his own voice, a jellyfish, a slug I could stomp on. Blood stopped seeping down my legs a long time ago. They say damaged muscles which make up the buttocks recover very fast especially in female patients. Some girls recuperated from anal surgery more slowly than others. After the heaps of onions I had peeled and chopped in the kitchen of the Venice Motel, the word "slowly" didn't exist for me. I forgot the meaning of "fatigue and exhaustion. " Yakov choked on my breath, burst into pieces of happy skin, spilled like a quail egg I had cracked open for the builders to admire. They had excavated a second moat around Yakob's mountain, the morons.

You can't lock in frogs and robins, you can't button up the river in your trouser pocket. The mountain peak is God only to the man who is climbing the mountain. There is always sky above the peak. I was an ant that ate bones, skin and blood. Yakob was a wet shirt and I went and squeezed the last drops of energy out of him. I performed my mating dance on his belly, tattooed his chest, my teeth sinking in it, then my teeth scrawled obscene words on his thighs. I wouldn't speak of the ways I deleted these offensive phrases after he read them. This idea of mine was a sore that festered badly. Perhaps the dragons had a finger in that pie. Love was not one of Yakob's strengths, despite the cartload of muscles that was supposed to rope women into believing he was at his peak this season.

"Is the wall pink or black?" he asked me.

It's still yellow, I said, but it will turn black if I want it to. Are you keen on deep colors, on wearing a blindfold or perhaps on drops of honey on your stomach? Yakob wanted more of my colors and honey, so I dripped with sweat. It was unnecessary to think of snakes, I milked rattler venom as I looked at Yakob after I ditched him impotent, a lump of dead frogspawn in his bed, his mouth a well gone dry, his naked chest a captured enemy's flag.

I thought of my Bulgarian literature teacher, the only woman my father had fallen in love with. He must have been totally out of his mind, an aging man, getting hysterical like those knights in the Middle, Black or Purple Ages. Wrapped up in chain mail shirts and suits of armor, the poor bug-gers couldn't smell the cologne on the hem of Milady's ball gown, couldn't even sneak a glance at her face, an old and lined suitcase, drenched in cold cream and oils. I could imagine them sobbing their noble hearts out for

Her Majesty the Duchess, meanwhile producing a throng of infants for the maids who scrubbed and polished the Duke's chamber pot. I was glad Petrova taught me that there were other things in life more important than the Duke's chamber pot. While Yakob spent hours recuperating from the bruises my teeth had given him, I read his thick book on barons and duchesses. His order boiled down to the following: I had to drastically broaden my skills with respect to satisfying carnal passions by following the examples their Lordships had provided. This leather-bound volume had taught him everything he knew about the brown ants, Yakob told me.

I was eleven years old when Petrova, my Bulgarian literature teacher, hammered home a crazy message to me. A human being is nobody's slave. That was a lie, of course. If you are chicken-hearted, Pirina, I said to myself, if you cannot kill Yakob even though you've sharpened an oak branch to stick in his throat, then, my girl, spread him like broiler poultry manure on the floor, and leave him powerless and as mute as her Ladyship's dirty undies. He'd sure snore on the Italian marble tiles, the most expensive floor in southeast Bulgaria, he wouldn't make it to his bedroom with the four poster bed in which a month ago my blood spurted like an oil well, then ran dry and my buttocks were caked with blood clots. Kick Yakob's butt. I know you'd be afraid to. Ok then, let him snore, a brainless, boneless carcass, no nerves and a thick skull, no Grand Cherokee Jeep, no bundle of hundred lev bills as thick as my 10th grade geography textbook. No chamber pot. In the morning, he couldn't tell you if the wall was black, pink or yellow. In the morning, he wouldn't remember his first name. He'd be a package of beef.

"Sing to me please," he'd say.

Kalcho... Kalcho and his mom Koyna the apothecary in the drugstore... the gypsies, brave souls... on All Souls' Day the dark kids ate even the grains of sand that had stuck to the slices of pie women had left on the graves of their dead sons. All Souls' Day... In my mind, I saw Kalcho, a flickering candle, now going out, now burning again as he stared at my grave in which I had never lain.

…Kalcho cured Dad's whooping cough that had plowed his old chest for a year ever since my Bulgarian literature teacher left the village of Staro. My father shook and staggered as he tried to hide his hacking cough in the hollow of his hand. Koyna said you wouldn't find medicines good enough to fight this disease not only in her backwoods drugstore, but also in much richer parts of Europe.

Kalcho cured Dad's nasty cough all right. He received a postcard of Lion's Bridge in Sofia. On its back, a bunch of neat block capital letters said, "*I am keeping my fingers crossed for Luba, Pirina and Sara. Say hello to uncle Vasil for me. He is a wise man. My best, Petrova*"

Uncle Vasil is my father and he's not wise at all. What could you learn from a suitcase of yellowing newspapers you constantly pressed to your ribs? Dad didn't watch TV, didn't listen to the radio; he spent his nights perusing every word of the printed texts, studying paragraphs, poring over nonsensical articles just because my Bulgarian literature teacher had touched the ancient weekly. I knew she had underlined certain passages in the same red ink in which she had given me a bad grade on my *Iron Lamp* essay, the only Bulgarian novel I cared about.

This Lion's Bridge postcard put an abrupt end to Dad's whooping cough, and he departed for Sofia. He had stopped drinking water from his bottle, he ambled through the field, holding the postcard tight in his hands, staring at the Lion's Bridge intently as if the bronze lion statue was pure gold.

Kamen, the good-for-nothing wastrel who had robbed druggist Koyna blind — out of pity the woman had taken him in and let him share a pillow with her gray hair — this deadbeat told my mother he'd seen Dad knocking around Lion's Bridge. On the following day, Kamen saw Dad at the Housewives' Market. Dad didn't look good. On the contrary, he was at a loss which way to take. He roamed the streets like a beggar, a shabby bag in hand, a clod lost in the capital city. Koyna's wastrel shadowed my father, thinking Dad had completely lost his mind after all those freaking newspapers he'd read.

"Have you seen a… a… woman… with a suitcase?" Dad asked the construction workers who were digging a tunnel below Lion's Bridge. "A woman… tall, scrawny, not pretty… at all. She lugs her suitcase, an old and brown one."

One of the workers told him that every day he saw many women, not pretty at all, tall and scrawny, lugging brown suitcases.

"Her name is Petrova," Dad added desperately and bought the worker a glass of plum brandy. The man said he had trekked across the mountains both of Turkey and Bulgaria and landed in Sofia, stone-broke.

My father produced a meager bundle of two lev bills, folded in half. "*That was the money his daughter Sara gave him,*" the good-for-nothing wastrel said to Koyna the druggist. "We all know what Sara does at the Venice Motel, and we can imagine what she's done to earn this measly bundle. She fleeces her clients, if you ask me," the wastrel pointed out. "But even if a guy forked over his whole paycheck, every single cent was worth its weight in gold. After an hour in the Venice Motel with Sara, a man became immortal," Koyna's drunk explained. Then he added that he mowed the meadows and dug the gardens of every big cheese in the region. He saved up every penny, the boozer said. Sara was on his mind all the time, so he'd been hoarding nickels and dimes in order to bring a dream to a good end: to take Kalcho to her. The wastrel's heart bled for Kalcho. The boy would soon drown in his own bowl of tomato soup, he would. The poor kid puked all the time, and when he didn't, he mumbled, *Pirina, Pirina, Pirina...*

After my father saw the Lion's Bridge, he didn't cough anymore. He collected all yellowing newspapers and set them on fire in the middle of our backyard. Our neighbors said Dad seemed to shrink. He kicked his lame leg so hard that he looked shorter than his own wife, they said.

On that ground, I concluded that literary work dedicated to dukes and duchesses had nothing to do with me or Dad's old newspapers. After a closed session with me, Yakob lay hacked, dead beat like Dad's useless reading matter.

"Sing to me," he said.

I produced no sound.

It never occurred to Martusha that I could be that stubborn. Yakob hoped Doc Stoim would knock some sense into my thick head, but the doc looked me full in the face, smiling as if I was the wine in his glass. You're electricity, he told me. If I drink this wine, I'll have you in my bones and you'll light my way to the village hospital with my long-stay patients.

"Marry me," Yakob said.

I knew love was sharper than a razor-sharp tooth: the deeper it sank into you, the hungrier it became. I didn't let Yakob get any rest. My hands had learnt everything worth knowing, brown ants, sharpened oak branches, mud and moats, snakes and kisses as I thought of that absurd stonemason who fell in love with me. He was building a wall to imprison the mountain in Yakob's black ages. I didn't fear black blizzards or brown ants. Neither ages nor hours scared me.

"Marry me, Pirina," Yakob said.

I wasn't listening.

Kalcho was on my mind.

Kalcho was a totally different man.

§

That day the pub near the railway station was closed; however, the TV was on and an enthusiastic TV channel broadcast a EUROCUP football match. No fans watched the heated rivalry; nobody sat at the tables on which anonymous hands had scrawled insights of such depth that even the plastic tops had blushed with shame. The chairs had been neatly folded, their rust-eaten legs quiet, the plastic seats sporting images that looked like female faces or female posteriors — depending on your mood — all produced by local drinking talents. A genius having an affinity for the boundless ocean of poetry had trumped up a poem dedicated to Anno's white shirts and pants; however, the author's enthusiasm was primarily concentrated on the charms under the bartender's garments.

A short sentence was printed on the wall of the best room above the pub, the one in which David, the manager and house cleaner of The Cat, lived. Anno read the text and ran a temperature, his nose bled and a drunk who the fake stone brandy hadn't hit that hard fetched Doc Stiom. It was the doc that gave first aid to the pub owner. The emotional uproar this set off was considerable. The loyal customers rushed to the wall and read the obscene libel, stars swimming in their admiring eyes.

"Who wrote this filth on the bricks? Great job! Well done! How did the rogue climb up there? Bravo!" The drunks fully appreciated the culprit's skills. When David showed up, that puny wisp of a hero the foul writing was dedicated to, everyone stood up, applauding, cheering wildly, pointing at his back. Why should they do this? The little feller's huge white suit had been delivered from Marseilles, France; it used to be Anno's property a few days ago, dazzlingly clean, immaculately ironed. The jacket shone, putting to shame the sun that had sucked the clouds dry. Anno witnessed the admiration his employee got from the barflies, and his nose started to bleed again. Doc Stoim suspected the bartender was at his wit's end, so the doc drove him to the village hospital. Fortunately, Anno's medical A-Z tests said he was still alive and ok, although the man whispered he was on his last legs. The drinking establishment was temporarily closed, a fact that drove its faithful fake-brandy aficionados to despair. The drunks were so attached to The Cat that they scraped off, on their initiative, the filthy text, which had driven Anno to exhaustion and helplessness. When David showed up wrapped to the eyeballs in his white silk, as lonely as the only bottle in an empty cellar, the aficionados bowed down to him, then the neatest one among them dropped a hint, "If Anno cashes in his chips, you'll be the owner of the joint, eh? We hope you'll bring down the price of booze, David. Make it sixty cents a glass, won't you, baby?"

It transpired they'd reckoned without their host. David didn't throw open the doors of The Cat. On the contrary, the shrimp covered the tables with tarpaulin and pushed the chairs underneath the shed roof. Then he made a mistake. Instead of showing his drinking buddies the door, the little guy treated everyone to a free Piper from the best 100 Pipers bottle. The Cat's shabby and very grateful clientele lifted David to their shoulders, thundering, "Hip-hip hooray!" David, startlingly diminutive in his magnificent French jacket, ordered a bottle of stone turnip brandy for every single drinker and poured himself a glass of turnips. The drink tasted like the blood of a tapeworm and smelled like a snake's anus and mud, but it warmed the cockles of all hearts in the restaurant. The Struma River refused to go away, so it tried hard to run dry and stay in Bulgaria for good, the railways melted and the trains stopped dead in their tracks. David, assisted by three drinking talents, produced a fifteen-gallon — or was it thirty-gallon — glass tank full to the brim of turnip blessing, then schnapps boozing began, so powerful and formidable that the Struma could not remember such an impressive act of courage, although its waters had flowed in these parts many centuries before Christ.

The turnip mystery spilled out, filled glasses, bowls and cups, the smarter chaps grabbed the plastic vases in which, as a rule, refined Anno put wildflowers. Some poured the turnip without removing the nosegays meant to adorn the drinking establishment, and gobbled down blossoms, leaves and flower stalks alike. Others took a fancy to national dances, but being drunk as eels, confused the steps and fell full length on the ground, roaring songs and military marches. In these parts sprawling oneself out was a means of gaining additional free stomach space to fill with stone-turnip schnapps. It seemed possible that glass aquarium held fifty gallons, for that matter. You wouldn't be surprised. The Cat's customers grabbed at David and, elated at the prospect of more Pipers and turnip magic, threw him in the air a couple of times. What astonished the boozers was how sensibly the little man drank, how wise he was, may God give him good health and long, long life. Let's hope Anno will soon have a heart attack and croak. Let our small friend run this unique place for centuries to come.

After half an hour, the chaps started kissing David. You're the smartest guy under the sun. You are the most handsome dude in the world. Bravo. You are God. You are much more than God, you're one of us. You are the best. David poured turnip mystery after turnip mystery into his glass, refusing to mount a high horse, at least not openly, although it was the first time strangers had proclaimed him a hero.

No sooner had the boys started kissing his shoes and his socks — the Struma River, the stones and fish in it hadn't seen a man as loyal to alcoholic concepts as David, one clever guy said — than Anno parked his grey Mercedes-Benz in front of the pub. He got out, saw the empty enormous glass aquarium that jutted out in the center of the backyard like a cross over a grave, watched the customers swill turnip brandy straight from his flower vases and counted fifty-seven smashed wine glasses; however, these sad details were not the only reason that broke his heart. David, the purveyor of health foods, the waiter, the manager, The Cat's soul and the purest person in this part of Bulgaria, lay sleeping on the laps of three patrons. The first one, a dark smiling man, had just forced the little purveyor's lips apart and kept his mouth open by thrusting two big spoons into it. The second drinker held David's tongue between his thumb and index finger so that the little guy wouldn't choke on his own chops. The third sponger slowly and amply poured stone turnip concoction into David's throat.

"Out!" Anno thundered.

Get out — but where? They all were under the open sky. The three drunks, caught pumping turnip and stones into David, trying to imbue him with the original pub spirit by singing patriotic songs in his ears, got up rapidly. As a result, The Cat's manager and cleaner thudded to the ground like a sack of cabbages.

"David!" Anno whispered, smelling sweet of shaving cream, dressed to perfection, his suit immaculate despite the heat and the unbearable month of August.

The customers wormed their way in a single file out of the pub's backyard as David lay bathing in a pool of malodorous fake brandy, his gigantic silk jacket black, not snowy-white. Anno made up his mind. He shouldered his manager and slowly, taking his time, carried him upstairs to the best room on the second floor. No one noticed that on this happy day the obscene statements slandering David, no doubt a case of ugly defamation of character, had again flared up on the front wall of The Cat. This time, the libel against the honest waiter, manager etc. was printed in gray letters, each one as big as David who was snoring in his room.

Within an half an hour, Anno himself drove Doc Stoim to The Cat. David was sick. He constantly muttered 'Luba', or shouted at the top of his small lungs, "Come with me to Spain. Luba… I… I'll kill this dog," then went on, his stifled moans sounding like "Luba, I… Luba, you…" However, those phrases did not express any meaningful information to speak of.

Doc Stoim attempted to pour oil on troubled waters, administering sedatives to the patient as a result of which David got the hiccups. The drunkards, desperately loyal to the miniscule manager, could hear his moans of grief. They made a collective decision to use sandpaper and scrape off the obscene statements; however, no one had the guts to climb to the second floor: Anno stood at the door, a rifle in hand, big as mountain peak. He informed his customers he was not a good shot; he would take aim at human heads only, therefore be warned, everyone. The drinking talents could go to the devil for all he cared. Then Anno added politely that if they didn't beat it, he, in the name of God, would coerce every single alcoholic into paying for the drinks he had consumed, villains, black hats, etc., all of them.

The minute the revelers realized that the pub owner was speaking about immediate payments from their own pockets, even the most loyal among them dispersed like patchy fog. It was only the dust swirling through the street and the rousing chorus of the song "The Bulgarian Soldier Is a Hero" that showed where the guys were: near the railway station, and feeling immortal after fifty-gallons of stony booze. At a certain point, Doc Stoim said *Let's shove off*, and shoved off, a dignified gentleman of average height, his hair pepper, salt, dust and drops of brandy, a dancing spring in his altogether hesitant step, and a flower vase in hand, from which he drank, his face abstracted and luminous. The doc was so deeply absorbed in thought that he walked past his car, failing to notice it. Soon, his powerful baritone joined the bloodthirsty chorus of "The Bulgarian Soldier Is a Hero".

Anno entered the room, bent down and took off David's shoes. Then, a wet towel in hand, he set about cleaning his manager's swollen and badly bruised face, feeling sick at heart, unable to keep his grief under control. His manager's cheeks were an eyesore, his lips cut, scratched and bloody; the idiot who had poured turnip poison into David's throat was a criminal. The honest manager slept and snored, occasionally moaning "Luba… Luba!"

Anno relieved his friend of his enormous jacket, in which David was lost like a worm in an ocean, wiped his neck and noticed — it was impossible to miss it — a sentence printed in lilac ink, glittering on David's puny chest "I love Luba". Luba was tattooed on his left arm and above his ankles, seven times altogether.

David's telephone was bursting with photographs of Luba: Luba, a bundle of books in hand, looking like a hound thrown off the scent; Luba in a shabby room, her pocket-size posterior perched on Kenneth Clark's *Civilization;* Luba, staring at the Struma River, a sharp knee, rather a pair of compasses covered with human skin that jutted out above the water. Anno's throat constricted, a bitter taste dusted his mouth. He stopped staring at the lilac statement. He had failed, he had not rescued the wonderful lad from Luba, and the winter winds would find him again all alone in the backwater village deep in snow. David lay, his face gray ashes, half-dead.

"I don't want to lose you," Anno whispered.

He had to put David's tangled hair right, without delay. First, he ran the big comb through the manager's locks. He used this one every time he took care of Drum, the stray dog. The Cat had recently adopted the beast and now his coat glowed with health. Then Anno arranged his first mate's hair with the small comb intended for small mammals; the truth was that kittens did throng The Cat, mewing softly at the bartender, and especially a ginger tomcat, a regal specimen, heavy as a sky full of storm clouds, Anno's favorite.

The comb was too weak for David's hair, flattened, starched and plastered to his skull after the long soak in turnip brandy. David smacked his lips, burped loudly as Anno patted him on the back. The pub owner covered his manager with a yellow hand-woven quilt, an heirloom his dear grandmother Yana had left him, may she rest in peace!

"Life is solitude, David," Anno said.

§

Vasil had stopped reading old newspapers. At nightfall, he headed for the fork in the road to the railway station. Years ago, there used to be a small beer factory, and the path to it was strewn with broken beer bottles like a field sewn with barley. The maternity ward was on the second floor, just above the offices of the factory managers and supervisors. His daughter Sara was born there, a beautiful bundle of swaddling clothes, the prettiest baby he had seen in his life. A ten-month old tot, she learned to walk and talked like a radio host after she turned three. Sara grew into a beautiful girl. A knot of youngsters shuffled their feet loudly behind her on her way back from school. At times, she dropped her pen, and the boys fought who'd pick it up for her, the winner in the squabble reaping a reward. What was it, what? No one would say. Every afternoon, Sara's mom made an educated guess as to what had happened.

"You kissed somebody," the woman said accusingly.

"I didn't," Sara vehemently denied the charges made against her, but her mother, swimming amidst smells of baked peppers and garlic, hurried out of the kitchen and sniffed at their daughter.

"You did!" she insisted.

Sara didn't say another word.

Although the girl had bought all her dresses from the Second, or more precisely, the twenty second-hand Boutique and made no efforts to spruce up, the boys tailed her like a bomb squad. The truth was Sara didn't feel like washing or ironing her clothes too often, and stank of disinfectants popular with the second-hand shop as she walked in the street. Vasil had seen it with his own eyes: Sara said she wanted to eat a couple of plums straight off the tree, looked at the lads' hands, grabbed the cleanest one among them, then took its owner to the clump of plum trees. His daughter chose the deepest shadow of a tree, sat down on the shirt the lad had pulled off, his sweaty back shining anxiously as Sara showed him, "This branch."

Stripped to the waist, the sixth grader climbed up and up to the clouds, the plum thorns scratching his chest, pricking holes in his neck, yet he shinned up the tree, dropped the plums into the plastic bag that Sara had tied around his neck, or threw the fruit, like firing a projectile, directly on the grass. Sara, however, didn't stir a finger, let alone go collect plums; she sat on the poor boy's shirt queening it over the whole world, at times even opening her Bulgarian grammar textbook. It seemed highly improbable she read anything having to do with Bulgarian grammar, for Miss Petrova pleaded with her mother to help Sara, "Please do something for this girl. She won't be able to spell her own family name, I'm telling you."

After about an hour or perhaps a century, the boy came down from the tree, squatted down beside Sara and waited, not venturing to touch her, not even look into her face. Sara was made of thorns, and you never knew if she'd drive a barb into your eye or kiss you. At times, she frowned for no reason at all and said, "Give me the plums and wait."

Looking guilty, the lad handed her the plastic bag and, not looking up, she spilled out the plums in front of him then trampled them underfoot. This happened quite often and Romeo, his eyes as empty as the empty plastic thing, walked off with his tail between his legs. Sara came back to the street where the flock of lads patiently waited for her, praying this time she'd make the right choice. Everyone was itching to shin up a tree for her, take off his shirt, hoping she'd sit on it and leave her aroma in the fabric, the most beautiful girl in the village of Staro, in Dupni and Sofia, oh, come off it, in the whole universe. They knew what "universe" meant, Petrova had repeated this word a thousand times.

But Sara never chose another boy on the same day.

When she was pleased for no reason at all, she held hands with the boy. No one told his friends what happened under the branches of that cold-hardy plum tree; the lucky dog's face glowed like the fire exit sign in the Town Hall, even more fiercely did his cheeks shine, much like the red mailbox, in which the old townsfolk possessing no computer skills dropped their Christmas cards. Sara walked home alone, and the young guy, his happy head raised like a flag in the air, trailed along behind her.

A boy never stops hoping for the best. Very rarely, after she passed by the Community Center, Sara turned around. She said nothing to her classmate, just looked — not into his eyes or face — just stared into the space above his shoulders, her feet sinking into the shadow of the Community Center.

The Community Center was an old solid building with a library and a small dancing floor, on which no one danced. No one used the library except for a couple of geezers like old Vasil and Luba, his scrawny daughter who talked to nobody. The citizens believed she was born deaf and dumb.

It was the first time that Vasil had seen Miss Petrova, or was she Mrs., his daughters' Bulgarian teacher, in the warm library room where the bookshelves were lost under layers of dust. The folks were not sure how to address the educator and anxious to avoid any possible misunderstanding or insult, called to her, "Hey, Petrova" or "Ahoy, Petrova."

She and Vasil talked about the weather, the kids, about Vasil's wife and how she cooked homemade compote for the winter. This short conversation didn't leave thoughts. He saw her face among the words printed in the old newspapers, he watched as Miss Petrova strode across the square towards the library; that was how he'd came to know that Sara, his eldest daughter, vanished behind the Community Center. Dog roses, sloes, nettles, haw-thorn and elderberry bushes grew behind the building, a twisted mass of thorns, spines and prickles, the worst of all, old man's beard, a brazen-faced climbing plant, coiled and wound around the tops of pear trees, drinking their sap until they withered and died. Nasty old man's beard did something else. It built a green, impenetrable wall, and Sara disappeared behind it.

"You've kissed somebody behind the Community Center," Vasil's wife hissed.

"No, I haven't," Sara said.

"Mitko, your classmate, has just passed by our backyard. He told me you did."

"He lied to you."

All the year around, their mother found sheets of paper in the fami-ly's mailbox; drawn in red pencil, hearts looked like ravens, punched by an arrow that glittered on these sheets. Somebody had printed *I love you sara* on the board fence. No comma after "you" and "Sara" beginning with a small letter! Old Vasil was outraged. The youth of today are ignorant and illiterate. Sara was impressed neither by the mistakes nor by the guy's decla-ration. On the following morning, the flock of oiled forelocks waited for her in front of their garage, some of the boys fighting again who was to carry her bag. Majestically, although her dress cost 20 cents in the Second-hand Boutique, and her shoes were clumpy, too big and impossible to kick off, Sara handed her bag — definitely a fifth-hand one — to the tallest boy then bent her steps toward school.

The throng of kids bubbled with excitement, Sara in the lead, the boys following her, the lucky tall dog carrying her bag, not daring take her hand. Five yards behind this parade, Luba dragged along, quietly, like a stray dog. No one volunteered to carry her bag filled to overflowing with books.

"Soon, they will draw my face in a church," Sara said one day. They all were eating dinner, her mom, her sisters and Vasil. "Did you hear me?"

"Shut up," Vasil's wife gave her the brush-off.

Vasil's heart sank. Having emerged from the small bakery, like a tide touching the shore, Miss Petrova walked along the street. Dark face, dark eyes, a sky heavy with a hailstorm were her eyes.

"Your bag is heavy," the teacher told Luba and took the backpack from Vasil's reading daughter's hands. Luba was as scrawny as their cat Gabriela after she'd had a litter of six kittens.

"I don't want a cat shelter in my house," Vasil's wife snapped. "We don't have anything to put in our mouths. I am not fattening any tabbies or tom-cats here, so, sir," she collected the six furry balls in her apron and threw them in the trashcan.

Vasil's most compassionate child, Pirina, who came into the world in the maternity room above the office floor of the beer factory, let out such a mournful howl that Vasil's eyes brimmed with tears. She and he ran to the trashcan, and Vasil lifted the little one high in the air. The kid crept into the bin, rummaged through the garbage and gave him the newborn kittens one by one, all of them blind, bedraggled, more dust than fur on their backs. Vasil took the six scared critters to the cellar, and when they started to thinly mew, his wife cornered him. "Did you bring the yowling vermin along?" she asked.

"I did," he admitted.

"He didn't. I did," Pirina stood in front, protecting him.

His wife Slava collected the tiny wriggling backs of fur in a bag and chucked them in the trashcan again.

"You have beautiful daughters, Vasil," Miss Petrova had said. "Luba is a smart kid. I haven't taught Bulgarian literature to such a clever student before."

"How long have you been a teacher?" Vasil asked.

"For fifteen years."

"And why do you live alone? You look good…" Vasil blurted out. "I mean…" He was at a loss. Was it his stupidity or his courage that had made him prattle on?

"I haven't met the one yet," Miss Petrova said, her face burning like those automobile tires the youngsters put on fire on the first Sunday before Lent, then jumping over the flames, hoping to be happy in love.

"You'll meet him," Vasil muttered under his breath, against his will.

"I won't."

He attended the parent-teacher conferences and felt shame for what Sara had done: day in day out, boys came to blows over her attention, brawled outside the schoolyard, locked horns, the likely outcome being bleeding noses or bruised chins. Vasil blushed at Pirina's flagrant disregard for school rules. Somebody called her a "cow," an eighth grader, a lad forty pounds heavier and a head taller than her. Pirina had cracked his head open with a stone.

Vasil knew the history of this stone. He, her father, was to blame. It was his fault.

"Don't become anybody's slave, girl. Ever. The minute they notice you bend your head, you'll be crushed under foot."

"How could I keep my head up, Dad? Petar is much stronger than me."

"No one is stronger than a stone, my girl. Nobody is as loyal as one. Take this stone. Keep it." Vasil picked a piece of granite from the ground, the first one he clapped eyes on, and thrust it into his strongest daughter's hand. "This stone is stronger than anybody's head, and much harder than Petar's."

Now, Pirina's stone was spotted by reddish-brown stains.

"This is from Petar's head," Pirina said as she pointed to one of the stains. "He wanted to make me his slave. 'Kiss the soles of my shoes,' he ordered me." His daughter shut up, a thin girl, fleet of foot, all sinew and jumps, her eyes as dark as the instant when death comes. "Can you see this blotch, Dad? It is Petar's dried blood. He'll never order me to kiss the soles of his shoes again."

Vasil counted the stains on the piece of granite he had given his girl.

"What about this spot?" he asked.

Pirina didn't say anything. She stared at her boots, then at his sneakers.

"I won't tell you. You'll punish me if I do," she said at last.

"We are friends, aren't we?" he began. "I am your father and I am your friend. Friends don't lie to each other."

"You'll punish me."

"I won't."

"Promise me."

"I promise you."

"Swear on Mom's, Sara's, Luba's and on my life you won't beat me."

"I swear on your mother's, Sara's, Luba's and on your life," Vasil took a solemn oath. "Let all of us die if I beat you."

"You've never beaten me anyway," Pirina objected.

"Come on, tell me," Vasil insisted, his weak smile a wound on his face.

The river, a small mole amidst the willow trees, burrowed into the clay in the heat. The sun watched from above, so furious all clouds had fled, letting the blue blanket of the sky, not a bead of moisture in it, hang over the village of Staro like a puppet on a chain.

"Miss Petrova's blood," Pirina snapped.

"What!" Vasil said, bristling at her words.

His daughter thrust her chest out, a tough kid, her eyes dark in this black afternoon, a girl quieter than the mice in the cellar, strong like the brandy ripening in the old mulberry barrel. His daughter didn't budge an inch.

"You like her a lot," Pirina said evenly, slowly as if she was walking past the second-hand shop. "You like her, and Mom knows it."

"But…" Vasil started. It felt as if an earthquake shook the grass beneath his feet.

"I let Miss Petrtova know this is a warning," his youngest daughter said. "The next time, the stain will be much bigger. You told me this stone is harder than any man's head, Dad."

Pirina fell silent, her words worse than the bloodstains. At a certain point, she made up her mind. "This stone is harder than your head, Dad. Stop fooling around with Miss Petrova. If Mom gets ill… Then… you know what… your blood will stain the stone."

He raised his hand against her. Pirina didn't flinch away, her eyes refusing to flee as she tightened her grip on the piece of granite. He had thrust it into her hand. The girl stared her father in the face. In the afternoon, Vasil had run to school. He knew it was unnecessary to ask anybody any questions. The teacher's head was bandaged, her neck was bluish and ugly, almost purple.

"I am sorry. Forgive my daughter Pirina. Please, Petrova!" Vasil said. "She didn't mean any harm. Petrova, don't expel her from school. We don't have money. She can't travel to the school in Radomir. We can't pay for her to stay in town. Forget what's happened, Petrova. I'll clean your cellar for free… I can plaster the wall of your kitchen. I'll fix the tile roof leak. They say you've complained the roof of your hut was no good."

Miss Petrova, her neck purple, a tight bandage on her head, didn't say anything, didn't even look at him, and he thought — didn't even think, he saw it in his mind the way lightning flashed and cut the backyard, letting thunderclap loose and crashing. His youngest daughter would be expelled from school. They would kick her out. Where could she go? Pernik was at the back of beyond, and Sofia looked like another universe. Uneducated — that was what his child would be. And what could an ignorant woman do? Become a slave. He hated the thought somebody would make Pirina tuck tail. He wouldn't allow his own flesh and blood to fawn at a boss and kiss his dirty shoes. Vasil read newspapers because he wanted to see what they'd tell him about freedom. *Freedom is a fat bundle of cash,* mass media said. No. To Vasil, freedom was something else. Don't let anyone treat you like dirt. If a badass tries to, pick up a stone from the ground. This stone is your freedom. This stone is your way out. But the newspapers didn't say so maybe because they were old.

Vasil was scared to look at the teacher, no, he felt ashamed for her.

Suddenly, her lips pressed to his. She was not kissing him, she bit him the way the rain lashed against the land that was sick with the heat, the way a peal of thunder kicked the house before it set on fire. He'd stared at the old newspapers that didn't say anything about freedom, and he saw her. He thought about the family's daily bread and saw her. *Your blood will stain the stone*, his daughter Pirina had said. That was what freedom was: blood.

Mom knows. He thought… no, he had no time to think. He was kissing the teacher. He had been dreaming of her for so long. She didn't believe in old newspapers. She taught the children Bulgarian literature, she struggled. She taught even the ones like Sara who went to school because of the boys. *Mom knows…* Petrova taught his smart daughter Luba. Don't become slaves, she taught her classes, and his daughter Pirina listened to her. She taught Sara not to give in. Don't put up with lies, kids. Vasil kissed the teacher. This was the happiest secret of his life, of his blood.

Back home, Slava weeded the pepper, cooked potatoes for supper, washed the dishes, picked strawberries. Slava cut the meat into twelve tiny pieces, calculating how to make it last until Monday the 20th, the payday. The woman had dumped that miner from the town of Bobov Dol, his legs strong as steel scaffolding, and two heads taller than Vasil. At home, Vasil's wife carried buckets of water from the river to water the peppers… Miss Petrova had kissed Vasil so darkly, so beautifully he wanted to die.

"No," he breathed.

He couldn't say how he pushed the dark face away. His lips killed the kiss that had made him the happiest man. The sky above him was as old and blue as Pirina's canvas shoes. "No!"

And yet, Vasil lived for the minutes when Miss Petrova passed along the street on her way to school. He sat on the bench in front of his house, a stack of forgotten newspapers in his lap, a shabby, quiet man, waiting. Miss Petrova walked quickly, her swarthy face a beautiful scar in his memory, still throbbing, soft and distant at the end of Vasil's world. Happiness didn't stop at his bench, but he knew. He knew this was his girl.

Miss Petrova left the village of Staro. Without her, the school went deaf. Its windows seemed to run dry, without her, its front door did go blind. Reading newspapers made no sense anymore. Now he knew what freedom was: a dark face, the sunset a memory of a kiss still warm on his lips. To be free was to see her walking past his hut. So many years in the coalmine, his busted leg, the children who were born above the office of the beer factory… Even when he saw their tiny faces for the first time, he was not that happy. His daughters were freedom too. And Miss Petrova would not come to Staro again.

After Yakob took Pirina to his citadel, Vasil drank only tap water in the evening. He was itching for a drink, no, he was dying to sip at the yellow brandy he himself distilled. Instead, he sold his four bottles to coal miners and bought bread. He also paid money for drugs to make his wife less scared and anxious. A bottle of tap water in hand, his old coat a flag of a defeated army on his back, Vasil went to the cemetery. He himself carved his daughter's name into her headstone — **Pirina Vasileva, 2001-2018.** He sat at her grave, opened, by force of habit, an old newspaper he didn't read, and slowly drank water. At times, he fished a stone out of his pocket — a grayish one like all others in these parts. But there were dark stains on it. Pirina's stone… Don't be anybody's slave, Vasil said as he put his hand on her grave. He didn't say anything else just sat there, staring at letters of his daughter's name. He saw her — a wiry kid, a willow stick. No, she was a tough dogwood branch with dark eyes, like his wife's black kerchief. Pirina. Pirina.

On Thursday, or was it Saturday, he sat in front of his hut, pressing the tap water bottle against his heart, the sun a pale penny above him, and he saw her: her face distant in the shadow of the months he hadn't seen her, so pretty… She had made him the happiest and the saddest man at the same time.

"Miss Petrova," Vasil whispered. "Miss Petrova!" He was scared to look into her eyes.

She hugged him close, her body against his chest and it felt the Struma River was on fire.

"I saw Pirina yesterday," Miss Petrova whispered through his kisses. She was as light as a shadow of a peony, warm as rain in July, beautiful as the early autumn frosts set in Vasil's hair. "I saw her in Sofia. Pirina is alive. She talked to me."

Vasil cupped her dark face in his hands. He knew his wife was in the backyard, cutting corn stalks, chopping cabbage or peeling potatoes under the mulberry tree. No matter where his wife was, she could see him hold the dark woman, kiss her arms, caress the tiny wrinkles on her neck that smelled of spring. He kissed happiness. He knew happiness had many faces. Pirina was alive. His Pirina who'd never be a slave… his Pirina who knew what freedom meant.

"Miss Petrova," Vasil breathed. He pressed her to his shirt, to his blood he pressed her, to his skin and misery, to the afternoons he'd lived through watching Pirina's headstone he himself had carved, to his despair the tomato plants had died early this year. His wife, a black shadow under the black mulberry tree, looked, and looked, and looked, unable to stir, unable to breathe.

"Pirina told me," Miss Petrova spoke sharply between his dark kisses. "Pirina said, 'Don't forget my stone, teacher. I feel bad for you. I'll be sorry for your blood on the stone. That's what freedom is about.'"

"You are pretty," Vasil whispered. He couldn't stop holding her close to his blood. He didn't want to stop. But there was something much more important than him. "Pirina is alive!" he roared.

§

He had melted away like a wax candle, his face thin and white — a white rag hung on a branch to dry in the autumn wind. Koyna, his mother, sat by his side, a tall gray-haired woman, her coarse work-roughened hands dead in her lap. She ran her drug-store, dug and tidied up her garden, roamed the hills and woods collecting herbs, brewed teas and infusions for the local folks that didn't have money to pay her; they could only dig up potatoes or prune trees for her. Now the Roma families, dark, quiet caravans of children, women and men, stopped by her place.

"How's your boy, Aunt Koyna?" they asked. Some brought a handful of wild raspberries, others a bunch of dill, still others quail lard. They entered the room. Kalcho sat at the table behind a bowl with a biscuit mashed up in it, his eyes' wells gone dry. He smiled at the tots, no, it was his sallow skin that smiled while Kalcho crept at the bottom of those deep wells. He didn't say anything, just sat there, and if he'd eaten some yogurt, he'd throw up. His face, like a stream in August, had run dry.

Koyna sold her cornfield and took him to different doctors. The man she lived with sold the only valuable thing he possessed, a gold ring that weighed as much as a sigh, almost nothing. He had hoped one day he'd give it to his daughter. Maybe his daughter had already married some good-for-nothing, maybe she was knocking around Europe or had flown to Spain to live off the fat of land with a passionate Spaniard, under banana trees.

His daughter was a pretty girl he knew, and hoped Kalcho would fall for her. The drunk's heart, a mole trapped in its underground burrow, leapt with joy. He had hoped against hope, putting aside any dime and nickel he could, saving up his cents and bucks, buckling down to every job he was lucky to get -— a factory night guard, construction worker, Jack-of-all-trades at the Best Tire and Auto Service, gravedigger and whatnot. He tried hard not to squander everything he'd earned on booze. He wrote a letter to his daughter and sent it to her mother's old postal address, but received no answer; he called her on her mobile phone, and it turned out the number was dead. He'd told the drunks at The Cat he wanted to find his daughter and give her his gold ring, and one day she did come to see him. Slim as a sorrel leaf she was, her face plastered with layers of makeup, her green eyes looking black.

"You said you wanted to give me your ring," the girl said. She didn't ask, "How are things with you, Dad?" Didn't even call him "Dad." "Come on, give me the ring. I don't have time to waste."

"I'd rather you saw Kalcho," her father said. "The boy got really sick, cannot keep food in his stomach. Go talk to him. Maybe you'll like him."

"Give me the ring," the girl said. Her voice was cold beer that cut your guts. You'd been dreaming of a pint, and that kid David in his huge white jacket served you a good glass in The Cat. After you swilled it down, your throat turned to mud. You coughed and coughed, and failed to get to the bottom of your chest. It hurt badly.

And it broke you down.

"Girl, go talk to Kalcho first," the father muttered. "The ring won't run away."

The day she was born, he was as happy as a clam — eyes that smiled at him all the time, a sweet happy tot. Now his daughter didn't even look at him.

"Where is that wretch Kalcho?"

The sick man's room stank of stale air, of crow's herb and other smelly concoctions, nasty all of them.

"You'll be pushing up the daisies long before I eat dinner tonight," the girl said to the sick man.

"Yes," answered the wax candle from its bed. "I probably will."

"Not a big deal," said the girl. Then an idea seemed to cross her mind. "They say your name is Kalcho. You've got cash, haven't you? Give it to me. At any rate, you're dying."

"I have some money, yes," Kalcho said.

She had left the bedroom door ajar and her father could hear her talking to the boy. Although he was a drinking numbskull, a lowly thief that had robbed Koyna of all she had to live on, and slept for two weeks in front of her hut on a threadbare rug she'd thrown away, Kamen was ashamed of his daughter. How come his girl had turned into a handful of expensive makeup bottles? Where had she lost her green eyes?

"Give me twenty levs," she said.

"Okay," Kalcho agreed. Then he felt queasy and vomited up the dry bread he ate five minutes ago. "Go take two ten lev bills. I keep my money in that drawer over there."

His daughter rummaged through Kalcho's drawer. She routed out mittens, socks, her fingers rapid like thunder, light as a thief's who'd take your sweatshirt from your back and you wouldn't notice. You'd wonder why Koyna held the gypsies, these cheats and liars, in high regard, why she treated them with herbs and teas when they pretended they didn't have a penny to bless themselves with. They kissed her hand, double-tongued all of them. Kamen the drunk also wondered why she let them enter her sick son's room; especially an old Gypsy woman, Mariza by name who weighed two hundred pounds. She had long curved scars from her shoulders to her wrists, and a gaping wound on her right arm that smelled as if the whole village had dumped gallons and gallons of sewage into her blood. This old Gypsy never brought Kalcho anything, just sat by his bed and sang.

She didn't have any voice to speak of. It creaked between her teeth like an old door, and her Gypsy song didn't have any words in it. You could ask why Kalcho grinned, not only his lips, his eyes grinned as he held out his arm as thin as the Gypsy woman's walking stick, to shake her hand. The drunkard felt sorry for Kalcho, very sorry indeed. When Kamen slept on that threadbare rug in front of Koyna's hut, he was starving and tried to eat the bark off the apple trees. He went and begged for a cigarette end or a chunk of stale bread from the Gypsies, and Kalcho, flushed and disheveled, his head in the clouds, came to Kamen, sat by the threadbare rug and the two of them talked. The kid gave Kamen things crammed into a plastic bag: a piece of apple pie with a dusting of sugar on it; two roasted bones, probably chicken for Koyna bred chickens; a couple of prunes and a handful of cherries with little worms in most of them. The drunk bolted down the food, munching on prunes and apples together, smacking his lips so noisily that the bats — kerchiefs that had seized the night — squeaked like old chairs. A wonderful holiday began every time Kalcho brought the alkie a cigarette.

"You're a good man," the drunk told him. "I wish I had a son like you."

Kalcho said nothing, a shallow smile on his face.

"I was scared when you started to throw up the night I moved in with your mom," the drunk admitted. "To be honest with you, Kalcho, I wanted you to die, so I could live with your mom; if you were dead and cold you wouldn't poke your nose into our business. Let's make sure everything between you and me is clear and aboveboard. Your mom Koyna is as green as a gooseberry, I tell you, Kalcho, very easily led. Anybody can turn her head. I did, and it says a lot. A babe in arms can trick her out of her money. How can I put it," Kamen the drunk went on. "She's a naive woman, your mom is. So naive that a man has to protect her. Drive away the thieves and conmen. Everybody around here is a criminal, put that down in your notebook and read it twice a day. On the days they work in factories, folks aren't criminals, but after they get back home, the only thing they're itching to do is steal something or beat somebody to a pulp. Honestly, Kalcho, at a certain point, I thought to strangle you while you lay asleep on your bed," Kamen sighed. "I'm glad I didn't. You are my only friend, man. Your mom is my only friend, too. I can't explain this to you, but it is true."

Silent, Kalcho smiled at the bats or perhaps at the clouds invisible in the night. Now the kid was going to breathe his last like the hound that died at their front door. Had some jerk poisoned the beast, or did the dog cash in his chips like old men do, because of old age? The drunkard didn't know, but he was ready to cut his own wrists and pour his blood into the boy's blood. Kalcho and his mom, Koyna, were his best and only friends.

Now Kamen's daughter dug and delved and scavenged for cash everywhere in the room. She took not only the twenty lev bill, she pocketed everything she found; the drunk knew exactly how much money Kalcho had tucked in that drawer. He himself had stashed away most of the bills, hoping to save up enough levs to buy the most powerful medicine the druggists had in Germany. They showed it on TV: the thing was so strong that it was enough to just look at it, and on the following day you became as sturdy as the hill opposite the Town Hall.

His daughter stole everything, seventy-nine levs altogether; she lifted the penknife and the flashlight Kalcho had given the drunk, hoping that his drinking friend would be less scared in the night when frogs jumped at his side. And if a hedgehog rolled up into a ball — the dusty road was teeming with those sly fellows — or a snake hissed like a grenade about to explode, then Kamen's flashlight could illuminate the fauna invasion and frighten it away, and everything would be ok. Although the moon often lingered above Koyna's hut, its light turning the night into a silver brandy bottle, the drunk had accepted the flashlight with gratitude. He didn't use it to light his way to the pub, not at all. The electric thing hammered home the basic point that Kamen had a pal under that moon. At times, it looked like Koyna and the next minute like a glass of beer.

"Leave the boy alone. Give him his money and his flashlight back," the drunk told his daughter.

"Give me the ring," she snapped.

"I'll sell it and I'll buy medicine for him," the drunkard said — so slowly as if he already saw what that medicine from Germany would do: cure his friend, and they'd go fishing in the Struma. What a pity that the river had become small and shallow, a stretched piece of gum, and they'd catch nothing. They'd sit together in silence; however, if you kept silent with a friend, it felt like you'd caught the best trout, even if you didn't see a minnow. You knew at home a bowl of bean soup waited for you on the kitchen table. Koyna had cooked it for you and for Kalcho, adding a lot of mint and hot chili peppers to it.

"Give me the ring," his daughter snarled. "You fat boozer."

The drunk shook his head, sighed. He rarely did this because his chest ached every time he took a deep breath, and in the mornings Koyna made elderberry tea for him.

"I'll buy medicine for the boy," he said, his eyes fixed on the door of the room in which Kalcho had just thrown up the chunk of bread he'd had for lunch.

His daughter grabbed the money, all seventy-nine levs that the drunkard had saved up to buy meds for his friend, shoved the flashlight and the
penknife into her bag, opened the drawer again, pulled out two handker-
chiefs and stuffed them into her pocket. Then she sneaked a look at the sick
man's room.

"I hope you die today, faggot!" she said.

In the heat of August, the street looked like liquid chocolate as the girl
strutted across, her nose in the air.

"Don't listen to her, son," the drunk said to Kalcho. "You'll get well soon.
I'll buy you that medicine from Germany. I watched it on the TV with my
own eyes. They said the thing could bring dead folks back to life. You're
alive, Kalcho. Don't be afraid, son."

"I'll get better," Kalcho muttered, dropping his words onto the floor.
Kamen wasn't sure if the kid believed what he'd just said. Kalcho was still
there, at the bottom of these dried-up wells in his eyes.

Koyna had invented a little trick to cheer him up. She invited the girls
from the Roma houses, thin and dark like black sparks all of them, to her
place. They brought laughter to Kalcho's room; some danced for him, a lass,
very pretty, her face swarthy like an oven in which a loaf of bread had just
been baked, her legs dusk falling late in the afternoon, kissed Kalcho, but he
didn't take a turn for the better. The sick boy asked his mother and Kamen
the drunk to bring old Grandma Mariza. Her hands reminded him of the
moss-covered branches of that huge, endless willow by the river. The tree
had dried out in a night; in the evening its leaves and sprigs were all green,
in the morning the branches drooped, withered and shrunken, and the
trunk had split into two tinder-dry colossal chunks. Had lightning struck
it? It might have happened the way the old gypsy Mariza said it had: the
roots had touched a treasure buried in an earthen jar, and the tree warned
the town folks it was high time young men went and dug it up. Kamen the
drunkard feared the dead willow was a bad omen.

When Kalcho lay awake, Kamen kept him company in his room,

imagining the two of them were fishing in the Struma River that was as thin as a pant leg in front of them. It had to be different, the drunkard thought, it should feel totally different when you were about to close the world behind you with an old friend at your side. Your buddy would give you rosehip tea to drink or some bread to eat, although Kalcho couldn't keep his food in his stomach. When in the evening Koyna closed the door to the boy's room, the drunkard took the threadbare rug — the same one on which he slept on in the summer the druggist had thrown him out — and snoozed through much of the night under his friend's window. Koyna's hair turned white overnight. The woman, like the willow, chose the night to lose the color on her face. In the morning, Kalcho was running a fever again. But I have a gold ring, the drunkard said to himself, and his eyes found hope in the strong crags on the hill opposite their hut. He'd sell the gold thing and he'd buy that German medication for his friend.

He was still thinking of that German medicine when a gigantic car, not an automobile, a Godzilla of some sort, made its tires screech in Koyna's backyard. The monster didn't pause in front of the drugstore, it thrust its way through the dry yellow grass instead. The drunkard rubbed his eyes and pinched his own cheek because he saw the thing was Yakov's ugly Jeep Grand Cherokee, the recurring nightmare of young and old in these parts. This idiot will set the drugstore on fire, the drunk thought. He'll kick Koyna out of her hut the way he's kicked out dozens of guys, then he'll sell her place to weak-chested money man from the capital. They said the air in Staro was very good. It was a cure-all for everything from cancer to cuts and bruises. Cure-all my foot! But I'll break his neck. I'll...

It was Yakob that got out of the car first, a broad chest, strong trouser legs, a donkey in a designer suit. That's the end of it, the drunkard thought. That smart suit means he'll burn the hut down. Kamen had to save Koyna. He tiptoed to the board fence and clutched at an iron rod; he had thought to hammer it into the ground next to a young apple tree bent to the grass, in need of support. Had woodworm eaten the tree or a stray dog knocked against it? The drunk tightened his grip on the rod as he took a step to Yakob. I should've given the ring to the boy, a thought raced through his mind. You're a bonehead, Kamen, yes, you are.

They wouldn't find a single bleached bone of the man who'd raised a rod against Yakob. They said the bigwig had hounds which he fed on men's bones, and he melted men's nails in a special-purpose oven. *But the rod, my iron rod, is stronger than a special-purpose oven. We'll see who's gonna be dead meat, Yakob, me or you. Don't you dare touch my Koyna.* The iron rod jutted out like death in the scraggy man's hands, a drunk; and a very neat and unnaturally clean one. The rod could smash any man's head as long as the guy who was clutching it didn't give a damn about a thing in the world. But the drunk cared about a gold ring he still hadn't given to his friend.

A young woman jumped out of Jeep Grand Cherokee, a slim and svelte thing, her hair as black as a field that had just been plowed, her hands white-blooming cherry trees, all clean and glowing. Give me a break! Kamen the drunk knew that lass. She was Vasil's daughter, wasn't she? One of his three girls. Give me a break, man. Hadn't the gypsies dug her grave on the hill, overlooking the drugstore, the most prominent spot had they chosen for the kid, in the shadow of the only juniper bush that had survived the fierce heat of July? The two of them, Kalcho and the drunk, had visited her grave. Kalcho knew he was going to throw up, but every time they went to the graveyard together, the boy took a sip of brandy small as a grain of wheat as he sat on his haunches by the wooden cross, then gave the rest of the *eau de vie* in the bottle to the drunkard, and prayed that God would send the girl to his troubled dreams. The two of them sat by the juniper bush, saying no word to each other. But when you kept silent with a friend, loneliness didn't taste bitter in your mouth. You wanted to be a juniper bush and give Kalcho your shadow, but most of all, you wanted — although you were the foulest drunk in these parts — you wanted just for a split second to become God Almighty and bring Vasil's daughter back to life, and you wanted to see Kalcho's eyes grow wide and happy.

Now we're in for it, Kamen gasped. Lo and behold! Pirina, flesh and blood and good looks, all rolled into one, strode toward the sick man's room.

Perhaps the drunkard had actually turned into God Almighty for a second: it was evident the girl had no intention of lying in any grave, let alone the one the gypsies had dug for her in the shadow of the juniper bush.

"Pirina! Is that you?" the drunkard wheezed. He rubbed his eyes and spat on the ground, scratching his thin neck. Yea, a man could be God Almighty for a while, but after that, the poor bugger had no way of knowing when he'd turn back into an ordinary fella, his chest giving him trouble, and he had to slowly sip at his hot elderberry tea. It was good that Koyna brewed it for him.

"Yes, it's me, Uncle Kamen. Where is Kalcho?"

The drunk didn't show her the way, Vasil's daughter seemed to know where the sick man's place was. She passed by Kamen as noiselessly as if she were a cat or a mouse, and entered his friend's room.

"Hi," said barrel-chested Yakob dressed in an expensive black suit.

The drunk choked on his own tongue, coughed and tried to spit one more time on the ground, and failed.

"How long have you been waiting for this boy to die?" Yakob asked. His voice was one of those huge dump trucks full of dead pine wood logs. A month ago, thick forest stretched as far as the eye could see, then it was a caravan of dump trucks loaded with logs. Yakob had no voice to speak of. His throat produced woodworm.

"We aren't waiting for the kid to die," the drunk said. "We're waiting for him to get better."

"Your neighbors tell me a different story," said the dead pine logs from the dump truck.

"You haven't listened carefully to them," the drunk snapped. This time, he didn't spit on the ground. He spat on the cobblestones an inch away from the trouser legs of the black designer suit.

Koyna showed up in front of her drugstore.

"What can I do for you, Mr. Yakob?" she asked, her gray hair a cotton roll ready to dress a wound in case the man in the black suit clobbered somebody in her backyard.

"Pirina went to see your son. I'm waiting for her," the black suit said. "Make me some coffee."

"I don't sell coffee here," Koyna said, turned her back on him, a broad back that had a lot of muscle because it had bent over to brew herbal medicines and infusions, to dig the tomato beds and weed the peppers. The woman had bowed before every single strawberry in her garden.

The druggist's hands, like the old gypsy woman's, looked like rakes. Her fingers were roots that no hoe under the sun could cut no matter how hard the tempered steel bit them. It was only the drunk who knew how many times the gypsies had kissed these hands: when the six-month old baby survived the flu; when an old grandpa could feel the pain go; when a woman who had had a miscarriage stopped bleeding and had wanted that baby so much. Babies were like trees: they loved the sun and hated the axes.

Pirina showed up, a beautiful thing that even now, burning at the stake of the August heat, smelled like spring.

"Yakob, I won't come back to you," the spring girl said. "I don't care about you."

The big man in the black suit, a shirt as white as death and a dark-blue necktie, sat on the grass like gypsies did. He, too, had plucked a blade of grass and was chewing on its end.

"Think about it," he said. "You'll lose the mansion. I'll buy you a yacht. A new laptop and a new telephone. I'll take you to Paris."

"I don't care about you, Yakob," the girl said. "Buy another woman a yacht and go to Paris with her."

"Martusha will die without you," the man said.

"Don't be so sure," the girl said, her back as light as a dandelion seed, and she hid again in Kalcho's room.

After a while, the drunkard heard a horrible noise and rapidly rushed to the other end of the corridor, but that didn't help, so he plugged his fingers deep into his ears. Hissing snakes and screaming lizards crawled and writhed on the upper deck of the yacht: that was what happened in Pirina's roar. If you were a tiny kid like Kamen's daughter, on her first birthday, her eyes the color of fresh sorrel, Pirina's energetic wailing would positively drive you crazy.

"Pirina, shut up!" the drunk shouted. The girl had no intention of obeying his reasonable orders. This was the ugliest song the drunk had heard. It scratched and clawed at the air, thundered and rumbled until the wild tune finally slashed the hill with Pirina's grave near the only juniper bush that had survived the heat. The sky hung helplessly from its clouds above the drunk's head, unable to muffle the screeching sounds.

Yakob — something bad must have happened to this man — pressed his big hands against his belly, opened his mouth and vomited, but the wild wailing sounds didn't give a tinker's damn about the man's plight. On the contrary, the weird piece of music, all edges, false teeth and nails dug into Kamen's ears, plowed the ground, stunning even the worms that had hidden deep under the grass.

Yakob puked all over the cobblestones behind the Grand Cherokee's left front tire as big as a hill, or even bigger.

The drunk couldn't say when exactly Pirina shut up in sick Kalcho's room. However, after the nasty sounds died away, he felt much better, removed his pinkies from his ears and thought, *it's no good.* He wished he had a bottle of brandy in his hand, well, let's be realistic, a vase, not even a vase, a snifter or at least a small glass of brandy, but now he had no drop at all to drink. The man who had filled the designer suit with his muscles sat by his vehicle dangerously green around the gills as if somebody had stomped on his face. His pale and twisted features didn't even resemble a face; in his mind, the drunk compared them to an counterfeit banknote, one of those five-thousand lev bills in circulation twenty or thirty years ago in Bulgaria that folks didn't bother to remember anymore. However, the drunk took pride in the fact that he was able to pay 30,000 levs for a glass of plum brandy, the happiest purchase he'd made in his life.

"Pirina, I feel bad without you," Yakob said.

In these parts, you didn't believe what Yakob said.

§

"You're hiding her, Vasil!" Kiro did not roar. His voice wobbled like a steamroller in the quiet backyard with the pepper beds, crashed into the house, its walls whitewashed and glowing. The building reminded you of a porcelain marmalade saucer although Slava and Uncle Vasil didn't make marmalade. "Are you sick or what, man!" the steamroller wanted to know without delay.

By force of habit, Kiro's powerful hand rubbed the limping miner's forehead. "You're not running a temperature. Ok. Where're you hiding her, Vasil?" Then the thick voce pushed off, lock stock and barrel, for a more hospitable location. Kiro wasn't good at shooting the breeze, so his paws squeezed the miner's neck, letting the miner kick his legs in the air. Uncle Vasil hung like a catfish that had swallowed a big hook; although the man tried hard not to wriggle and squirm, his lame leg trembled, a string pulled tight ready to snap. Now Kiro clutched the miner's denim coat and shook the man like a bag of coal. Vasil was heavy, the denim cloth ripped and the old man plummeted towards the dust. He'd have thudded to the ground if Kiro hadn't grabbed the old wrinkled neck. "Where're you hiding her? Where's Luba?"

Vasil had either bitten his lips or had choked on his tongue. His face, usually ash-colored, was now a water bottle full of gray mud.

"Let him go!" Even before Slava shouted she charged like a bull. Clenched fists was all she had, then she changed her mind, her nails digging deep into Kiro's neck. The giant didn't budge. It seemed a butterfly had just perched on his shoulder. Vasil's face filled the mineral water bottle with blood. The old man wheezed, his lame leg trembling no more, his arms, a second ago raised to the sky, drooped as if someone had wrenched them from his shoulders.

Without warning, Kiro dropped the clubfooted man on the ground, letting him tumble backwards in an untidy groaning heap of old clothes in front of the house. Slava lunged forward, a hissing torpedo that struck Kiro's huge chest. He didn't even register the blow, just waved his hand. His thick fingers happened to graze Slava's arm, sending her sprawling across the yard next to her husband. A smaller bristling heap she was, a mess of hair and teeth, a crazy woman who struggled to her feet, shook her fists at Kiro's face and thundered, "I'll kill you!"

Not a wife, no, Slava was an explosion that ripped through the giant's chest one more time. He didn't even stir the way he did to get rid of a mosquito. His left hand grabbed her hair and lifted her in the air, his right hand gave her a box on the ear. It was a little slap in the face, something like, "Hi, how're you doing," but the woman reeled, flailed wildly, bled from the nose, yet rapidly staggered to her feet and lunged at him again, a wasp, a devil, lava, flowing magma, an avalanche of thin muscles and poisonous eyes hungry for Kiro's blood. He didn't bother to tighten his grip on her shoulder. Perhaps he hit her in the chest with his thumb, or probably in the stomach for Slava was bent double and collapsed like an old cottage ceiling next to her husband. Kiro lifted up his heel against her and his huge training shoe landed on her chest.

"Where's Luba? Tell me!" he repeated.

"If she were here, she'd come running out to spit in your face, idiot," Slava snapped through the blood coming out of her nose. "She'd have none of your insults, dimwit."

"I… well I… I mean well…" Kiro started. "It is my intention to… my intention to marry her," he spat on the ground, spat one more time, scratched his head, leg and then his neck. "I have a house. I have a car. I have twenty acres of land and a vineyard. Yakob promised he'd buy me a flat in Pernik if I get married. I want Luba. I don't want anybody else. You are hiding her from me."

"Luba is not here."

"Come off it."

Vasil, too, spat blood and slowly, like a donkey loaded with too many bags, tried to stagger to his feet. He failed, crashed down to the ground, but went on struggling to stand up, holding his head high all the time. Kiro grabbed his hand and left him standing on his feet as if the clubfooted man weighed less than a shoebox.

"Kiro, when you were a little boy, you and I found three newborn puppies," Vasil started.

"They were puny, all the three were," the big man's head nodded in agreement. "White, black spots, cute little doggies."

"They were small. Somebody had thrown them not far from the Struma River."

Kiro nodded again.

"The winter was bitter and ice cold. Slava didn't give me any food for them," Vasil went on slowly as if a bulldozer was digging the words out of his mouth. "I collected bones, chunks of stale bread and brought them to the puppies. Didn't tell Slava a word about this. Well, they got used to me and started yelping even before I crossed the bridge over the Struma. Summer came and there was a lot of food. The restaurant cooks must have given them something to eat."

"I gave them food," Kiro corrected him. "Spoke to the cook too. Told him what would happen if he didn't give the beasts something good to gobble down..."

"Then winter came again, much worse than the previous one, Kiro. The puppies grew up and now a pack of stray mongrels roamed the street to the railway station."

"Where's Luba? Tell me!" Kiro cut him short.

"One evening, I was on my way back home from the station," Vasil went on. "I could hardly trudge down the muddy road, had no penny to bless myself with. The pack of dogs attacked me. Three huge beasts led the way, howling and growling, all white with black spots. Hungry, angry. This is the end, I thought. They'll be crunching on my neck and skull. But the three mutts came up to me and licked my hands. How come? Then it dawned on me that maybe those were the three puppies I'd given bread to. All grown up, their fangs as big as claw-hammers. But they didn't bite off my nose."

"Where's Luba?" Kiro hissed and spat.

"You, what did you do," Vasil muttered. "It was you, Kiro, that bit off my nose." The old one held still as he looked up at the whitewashed house that resembled a white porcelain cup, then spoke slowly on as if he was thinking out loud: "A simple man that I am, I ask myself: who was the kid I gave apples to and picked bunches of sorrel for? Wasn't that you, Kiro?"

Kiro kicked him in the shin, not very hard. If he'd let his foot do the kicking properly, the whole Urgent Medical Care Hospital in Sofia wouldn't be able to stitch Vasil up and make a proper man out of him. The clubfooted miner reeled back, and even before Slava, her clenched fists big as chicken eggs, pounced on the giant, a blue coat showed up in front of the house that now looked more beautiful than a whole set of porcelain teacups. The piece of clothing was old and faded. It almost covered the ankles, and its sleeves were so long that they concealed the hands as far as the fingernails. Luba. A dimpled chin, dark hair, a face that tried hard to hide its beauty in the shadow of the small house, and failed; a very beautiful face that at the same time looked like Slava and Vasil; however, first and foremost, it resembled a tiny cloud because it had everything in it: a storm and heat, thirst and moisture, rains and children, playing in the warm dust. You had to be a kid who Luba had taught the letters of the Bulgarian alphabet in order to notice all this. None of those kids were here now.

"Come with me." Kiro neither spoke nor growled. The iron steam-roller in his voice hit the girl, but Luba wasn't scared of iron. Slava jerked her head as she pushed her daughter to the house.

"She is not for you, idiot!"

Kiro ignored her. He made a dash for Luba, his dirty T-shirt, his elbows, his knees hungry for the girl's blue coat. He grabbed her, not by the hair, pushed her, but didn't knock her down. He lifted her up under her armpits the way a father would to carry his toddler to the bathtub. He made sure he hadn't broken her neck.

"Luba, listen to me! I mean well," the giant said. "I am going to marry you," then he carefully — as if he was washing Yakob's jeep by hand — left Luba on the ground. His right hand slid down the faded cloth of her coat, paused, hesitating whether or not to pluck the two apples there. The man made up his mind to measure their size first. His fingers slid further down to the buttons, and froze nailed to the spot they most wanted to research. "I'll marry you here and now, Luba," he said. A dribble of saliva came out of the corner of his mouth, but he didn't know that. His hand dug for something just under the third button of the faded coat, failed to find it, so the other hand swooped down and tore at the blue cloth. Buttons, like small change, clinked against the cobblestone walkway. "Luba, I... you...and I," the giant muttered. "Luba, you know that... that I..."

He couldn't say "Luba" for a third time because Slava smashed the milking bucket against his head. However, Kiro didn't budge. For a second, his fingers strayed from the faded fabric, gripped the bucket and flung it into the pepper beds.

"Kiro, I will not marry you," the girl said.

Kiro didn't hear her say this, or maybe he had, but what use were a crazy girl's words? She chewed and swallowed one book after another, packs and bundles of lies all of them. If she went on passing smartass remarks, he'd set fire to her tomes, every single one of them. Yes, he would. Kiro squeezed Luba's hand and pulled it so hard that her ribs rammed into him. She groaned, lost her balance and, if he hadn't caught her as if she were a newborn lamb, she'd have collapsed at his feet.

"Are you okay?" Kiro asked, his huge hand landing on her forehead. Her skin was cold, so she had nothing to complain about. "You're okay." He grabbed her arms and dragged her towards a big vehicle, Yakob's old jeep.

"Leave her alone!" Vasil shouted. The giant gave him the cold shoulder, then, on second thought, he stared at the miner.

"I'll break your good leg. Your head too, if you don't shut up."

Then, as slowly as the moon that didn't know her way among the clouds, like the sun beaten by a storm, like the last ten levs in the pocket of a guy who had lost his job, in front of the house, a girl showed up. So pretty she was that the road straightened out its curves, and the yellow field opened up to build a grass path for her.

"Let go of Luba," the girl said.

Her eyes were beautiful, although a dangerous glint had dug a dark pit in them. Everything this girl wore was expensive: her shoes cost probably more than the whitewashed house that resembled a Chinese teacup. Her dress, her gold necklace, her gold ring… You asked yourself how come this beauty queen landed in your backwater wasteland. Not even mosquitoes hung around here long; it was only natural they'd rather drink something nutritious, calorie-dense from noble veins in Sofia, the capital, than barely survive on limping Vasil's blood.

Kiro swallowed a couple of times, swallowed a couple of times more as he kept Luba so tight against him that the bones under the faded blue fabric nearly cracked.

"I told you something," the girl in gold said. "Let her go."

A miracle happened. Kiro, as big as a heap of paving stones, his head brushing against the eaves of the teacup house, slackened his grip. It was only his nails that held Luba. The strong fingers that twisted horseshoes with ease now didn't know what to do. Kiro's nails had sunk so deep into the faded blue coat that Luba couldn't squirm free. Slava plucked up courage, took the washtub, rushed to the huge man and crushed down tub and dirty laundry against his back.

Kiro was about to knock some sense into her by swatting her across the face, when the girl with the gold necklace took a step toward him.

"Don't make it hard on yourself, Kiro," she said. "Leave the girl alone."

The big man stared at her, his gaze slowly falling apart, collapsing, scared to stray away from the ground under his feet.

"Luba, come here."

The blue coat obeyed. It came up to the young beauty with the gold necklace. She was more beautiful than the necklace, the shoes, the bracelet, the gold ring, the village and the sky. She was the most magnificent girl in these parts who had her own room in the Venice Motel. Come off it, the owner of the Venice Motel built a brand new establishment for her, the New Venice Inn it was called, dazzling pink marble, aluminum and glass all over the place. Guys who could move seas from Bulgaria to the other end of the world and took baths in kangaroo milk spent many a night at this delightful hotel. The owner of the New Venice Inn himself was crazy about this girl, although his third wife was pregnant with his first and only child.

"Look here, Sara," he said a week ago. "I'll kick out my wife. I don't love her. I love you."

But the man stank of garlic and unwashed underwear. He showered once a week. At the New Venice Inn, Sara met gentlemen who brushed their teeth after every meal. It was mere coincidence that one of these well-dressed gents suffered from a debilitating man's disease of unclear origin, which Sara addressed and cured within six months. The bigwig who took baths in mare and nanny goat milk several times a day could not believe his own body. He himself put his sexual prowess to the test, happily amazed, then underwent a thorough and comprehensive medical examination. The man had the cleanest bill of health. He was as fit as a fiddle. As healthy and tough as an iron rod, that was what the doc said. What the doctor didn't know was this happened only when Sara breathed softly by his side.

At the end of their first week together, the VIP bought her a new car, at the end of their first month, the grateful guy purchased the New Venice Inn and gave it to Sara. Young and old, from the village of Staro up to the hill where Bulgaria ended and Greece began, were gossiping about Sara who transformed a filthy rich squirt into a normal man like you and me. She'd given him so much strength that… but when she was not near him, the wretch couldn't breathe and choked on his own teeth. Both townsfolk and villagers discussed the long story about this foreign dimwit. Thanks to Sara, he got into good manly shape and paid masons and bricklayers to build a church for her. And so they did! Could you beat this one? They built the thing in the village of Staro exactly on the spot where Sara fell in love for the first time. Venerable dames declared it was extremely difficult for Sara to remember when and where this event happened. Sara was rumored to think deeply ten days and ten nights in a row, and at long last she led the builders to the top of the greenest hill.

Clergymen conducted cheap, most wonderful funerals in this area. Just above the graveyard, in a pit — as to the origin of which the old geezers strongly disagreed, was it a bomb shelter or a goat shelter — exactly there, in this deep ditch, Sara's key love event unfolded.

Now, instead of a bomb shelter, the builders did some trenching and excavation work, laid secure foundations, and the church grew up within 240 days, from its marble floor to its marble ceiling. An artist, his hair as gray as mist, took to painting its walls and used Sara as his model for the Virgin Mary. The said boneheaded artist told his wife, "I don't want you. I want Sara. I'll give you the whole house, my studio, my boat, my chest of drawers and my car. Please leave me in peace. I'll go away this afternoon."

The artist's wife was by no means bigoted or small-minded. She knew the ropes of financial operations and wanted to enjoy her husband's company and resources at home. The foreign bonehead who took baths in mare milk, the one who recovered from the incurable masculine compliant and became a normal guy thanks to Sara's efforts, fired, in a fit of jealousy, the wayward artist and hired another one to paint the church to the end. In this instance, however, the big wheel gave the master painter only Sara's picture, seven feet long by five feet wide.

"Look at her face and paint it," he ordered the artist.

Within nine months, the church was spick and span, completely plastered, painted, white and strong, so neat and clean that now God knew where He could take shelter in these parts. He would be safe here because Sara watched out for Him from the wall. Sara from the village of Staro had eyes that put your mind at ease, Sara on the icon could heal the sick and bring people together. For months, Sara had been driving a black car, a better and sturdier one than Yakob's Jeep Grand Cherokee.

The church had no name, so what? Many folks walked around the area, and no one cared about them, names or no names. Did they drop dead on account of being obscure? Not by a long shot. Gypsies and Bulgarians from the village of Staro called the building "our little church," If you named your baby boy Atanas, his grandma called him Tanas, his mommy called him Nas, but everyone knew the suckling in question wailed no matter how you chose to address him.

This village is a failure, no more, no less, Slavka thought. What are you up to, God? Hussies protect us from Kiro, namely my daughter Sara. Sara, the nimblest fingers, the prettiest of all, turned out to be some kind of Jezebel, a bag of chaff! Let me not choose a nastier name for her. See how she's looking at me in the church! Guys come, bow down before Sara's icon and stare at it. They pray, the idiots. That bad egg, the foreigner, must have gone off his rocker, the poor soul… had money to burn and built a church… had even more money to burn and paid a goat of an artist… I'm sure there's soup in his foreign skull instead of brains, that's why he went and named the icon after my daughter, Saint Sara. Oh, give me a break.

Tell me how I can pray to you in this church, God. How could I? I know Sara, my firstborn, very well. She barely earned a D in Bulgarian literature and how she earned her C in math is an issue Mr. Ivan, the math teacher, should be thoroughly ashamed of. Sara must have cured his disease too.

"Let her go, Kiro," Sara said. So deeply and powerfully did her daughter speak as if all her life she'd earned As in Bulgarian literature. It was as if Slava hadn't bludgeoned Miss Petrova, the Bulgarian teacher, with a fence picket on account of her lazy firstborn daughter.

Now Kiro's face writhed, blushed scarlet, a water bottle full of blood. Slava thought she hadn't seen so deep red color on a human face, although she'd seen pools of blood all her life. In the good times, when they bred pigs, it was she that slaughtered the porkers because Vasil was no good at killing anything, couldn't hurt a flea.

"I'm gonna marry her," Kiro rumbled as his eyes went to his dirty gym shoes. "I mean well. I've chosen her. Don't need anybody else. That's all there's to it."

Sara stared at him as intently as if she had not only a gold ring and necklace, but her chewing gum was pure gold, too. Her eyes came down on the giant like a ton of bricks. Slava's eldest girl was made of marble, strong blood and pigheadedness: from her trendy heeled sandals to the last square inch of her white hat. It looked so beautiful on her head that, yes, the artists nutty as fruit cakes though they were, had the right to dub the icon *Saint Sara* in "our little church."

"I am the first man she's had," Kiro shouted. "Ask Luba and she'll tell you."

Sara kept mum so long that the big man was sweating bullets as he barked, "I'll bump off any idiot that touches her. I'll bump you off, Sara."

"Kiro, go hang the clothes up to dry," Slava, the beautiful girl's mother, hissed, pointing to the washtub.

It was a miracle that Sara's beauty had cured a wretch of a severe malady. After the guy got well, he went and built a roof above God's head in Staro. Years ago, there was an old church in the village, but crooks stole the brass bell, the incense-burners, the candle wax and the priest's robes. They took everything they could lift from inside of the church; then, one by one, the roof tiles vanished and the stones from the walls melted into thin air. At last, some drifters who probably were in on the job wrenched the big marble slabs from the floor. Only the wooden cross remained, lying sprawled on the ground in the yard, eaten by woodworms and slugs. The old wives were superstitious, and although the winter was evil like dogwood brandy that had just been brewed, none of them dared chop and burn the cross. Now, a board was nailed to the church fence which said in black and white that the site was guarded by a security camera system. It didn't make clear who did the guarding, so the Roma lads, old hands at implementing appropriating measures, experts all, were not convinced that cameras had been installed on every remaining brick, stone or roof tile.

"Start hanging out the laundry!" Slava hissed.

Kiro slowly picked up Vasil's wet undershirt and chucked it on the clothesline.

"Wring it out first." Slava, small like a kennel, gave him the rough side of her tongue.

Kiro picked up the undershirt, wrung the water from it, and a tattered piece of cloth, rolled out like sticky dough, remained in his hand. Slavka, unperturbed, icy blood through and through, took a couple of steps towards the big man. She stood on one leg, checking if she could keep her balance, then tried to kick the big man to the ground. Her foot couldn't reach his ass, her clumpy shoe grazed his thigh, and her ankle hurt. The woman didn't stop kicking and pummeling the giant's chest with her fists. She hissed, clawed at his eyes, banged on his ribs, hit and bashed the side of his body while Kiro, his forehead reaching the roof tiles, went on hanging out Vasil's underpants, Vasil's faded blue shirt, Vasil's old black socks. They would dry on the clothesline.

§

"She used to work at the Venice Motel just like us!"

The young Roma girls often focused on this topic, and one of them, tall and slim like a moonbeam, said, "I worked with clients in her room."

Now, at the Venice Motel, a magnificent walnut door opened to Sara's room, with its walnut panel walls. A sun carved into the white wood on the ceiling by a famous woodcutter shone on an imposing four-poster bed that the owner of the motel had bought for Sara from Vienna. A crystal top table, a work of art, glowed in the middle of the room, a silver vase glittered on it, and even a book, the only one Sara could remember from her school days, *Under the Yoke*, a novel by Vazov, the Bulgarian classic author, gathered dust on the walnut bookshelf.

Truckers and other insignificant squirts that paid according to the pricelist nailed conspicuously on the wall in the lobby of the Venice Motel were not allowed to set foot in Sara's sanctuary. Only the moneyed gents, well-heeled bigwigs all, enjoyed free access to the room with the stunning woodcarvings, which reminded one of Sara's beautiful face. The common people in Staro ate kale and turnips; only the glamorous snakeskin wallets could inspire the brothel owner's respect, curtsies and bows. All customers, even those who didn't speak foreign languages, unanimously maintained that the room had a century of French style in it, i.e. you couldn't find a canopy bed like that in other bordellos; the connoisseurs believed that every inch of space here was loaded with radiant energies, which worked wonders with their *libido*. No one in these parts knew what this word meant, although some guys made believe they did. Even the Roma girl, the moonbeam, could feel the radiant energy and knew that therefore she did nothing bad. On the contrary, the guys all behaved like gentlemen in Sara's room: they didn't beat or bite her, didn't use dirty language, didn't stick knives in her throat or below. Delicate blossoms in the wind, that's how customers behaved. Nevertheless, the Roma girl admitted she didn't know exactly what "delicate" meant. Maybe the man didn't smell of garlic or had taken a shower recently. Yes, these too, but that was not the most delicate thing she imagined one did.

In her heart of hearts, she knew what truckers thought; the dark girl had the feeling she labored like a saint in this motel, and the customers talked about it. One of her clients had given her a small silver cross. It was true that only top bananas visited her in Sara's room with the walnut sun, which blazed down on her four-poster bed. Its red canopy, in the Roma girl's opinion, was just gathering dust, could gouge your eye out, and made you cough so hard that your tooth fillings could come out. The truth was she suffered from bronchitis while she honestly accommodated plasterers, stonemasons, farmers and plumbers in accordance with the pricelist nailed in the lobby, another proof the girl was on the verge of becoming a genuine saint. She dreamed of chancing on a quiet and profoundly religious client. Maybe one day it would dawn on him to build a church for her, not as big as Sara's. Ok, let it be a tiny chapel, the Roma girl wouldn't say no to it, and please let the religious guy pay for a new icon of Saint Mariza (the moon-beam girl was named Mariza after her grandma). O, the way young Mariza would look and smile at the townsfolk from her icon! The girl was sure she had a kind heart, and an artist should positively paint the picture of her face and soul truthfully.

Young Mariza bought her sisters sweet baggy T-shirts on the money she earned in Sara's room at the Venice Motel. She even bought an ABC book for Valia, the youngest, the baby of the family, a silly thing, who sat in the shade of *Our Little Church* spelling out words all day long: *F-A-T-H-E-R, M-O-T-H-E-R.* Every time the kid managed to read all the letters printed below a drawing, she'd burst into song and caroled on big and hard until she yelled herself hoarse. One couldn't make out a single word, but the girl said she was performing in English. The words in her song were embers, dust and rain, and this was the kind of music she made for Luba, her teacher. Mariza had taken an oath: on her next client's money she'd choose the brightest and most interesting book, with a picture on every page, even if she had to pay fifteen levs for it. Mariza knew what she had to do to extract fifteen levs from a client's pocket especially if the creep was a stingy son of a bitch.

In these parts, and, Mariza suspected, in all other places under the sun, men were as tight-fisted as graves, but a woman should accommodate a customer even if he was a grave. Mariza was not a big wheel to frown on guys, was she? She was old Mariza's granddaughter, and the old lady could sing. It was true her tunes hit you like a ton of bricks to say the least, but they kept poor Kalcho alive. The determined grandma went and thundered her songs as Kalcho, the druggist's son, lay on his deathbed, while young Mariza sat by the open window, listening and learning to sing. She too thundered a tune or two to her more delicate clients, and they gave her three times more than the fee on the pricelist.

Mariza often walked to the nameless church and prayed in front of the Saint Sara icon. She pleaded with Sara to give her good health, money and considerate clients. When the girl didn't feel like a shirt wrung out bone-dry by her customers, she prayed to chance on a sick man. *Let my love make him normal again, normal and kind!* she prayed. *Let him build a chapel for me. Not a big one, a tiny chapel would do.* Then God could come visit her. Perhaps God would help her meet a decent man. She'd have two kids, okay, three kids, and they all would look for ABC books like her sister Valia. Mariza knew half of the letters of the Bulgarian alphabet and could read, well, after a fashion. She knew the numbers as well so she could calculate how much money the clients gave her and how much she had saved up in the shoebox she'd hidden in the cellar amidst the old battered suitcases.

This secret shoebox made young Mariza feel so strong, so courageous that she for no reason at all, lacking any sympathetic clients whatsoever, struck up with "Happy Birthday to You", after which she went on roaring all her grandma's songs. They were beautiful and so gutsy they made her fly with joy like a sparrow, even though no client alive was in sight.

Oh, that magnificent chapel! There would be a smiling Saint Mariza icon on its wall. By all means, Saint Mariza would need a lev or two to give to the sick and the poor; the girl felt like sobbing after she saw a guy dig in his pockets and find no coins in them. She'd do her best to connect people with the good God. Her grandma did it with ease because she kept His icon on the chest of drawers next to the beanbag. God, although he was a deity and not an ordinary man, had an ordinary heart full of kindness and mercy. A heart like this would understand you had to accommodate clients because your mom had a bad cough and her asthma was blacker than the road to Pernik. He would know that some roof tiles were broken, and seven people lived in one room at home. However, even God didn't know how much Mariza enjoyed listening to her little sister Valia. Valia was the runt of the family, yet she read as smoothly as the redhead on the TV. Where had Valia found that precious fairytale about the snow rabbit?

It was so cold in the forest that even the most thoughtful clients' ears had frozen and turned into icicles. The little rabbit too nearly froze to death. He didn't have any bread to eat, let alone meatballs. He had no house, *consequently* he was in a worse situation than Mariza, and this was as clear as the sky above her head. The rabbit just sat on his ass, knowing a blizzard was brewing in his stomach and he'd sure meet his maker soon. Brooding hard about death, the rabbit collapsed from exhaustion and fell asleep. Mariza often got off to sleep like that especially when she had loads of work to do: eight or nine clients were a bitter pill to swallow even though she accommodated them in Saint Sara's best luxury motel room. The rabbit slept, drained of energy and courage, under a briar bush. In the morning, he woke up and lo and behold! A silver roof glittered above his head. It had been snowing all night, the snowflakes as brilliant and sweet as hand-made chocolates. A client from Greece had given Mariza a box of hand-made Greek chocolates all big like bells, so she knew. *Consequently,* the snowflakes had built a house for the rabbit while he slept through the night. Mariza had not heard a more beautiful tale in her entire life. The truth was she could read it all by herself, but with only half of the letters of the Bulgarian alphabet you understood only a half of the fairytale, not the whole thing.

"Study, Valia, study, little heart," Mariza instructed her sister, showing her a particularly good picture in the ABC book, and if her customers hadn't put too much pressure on her during the night, she tenderly added, "Read a fairytale to me, will you?"

The kid stuttered, hummed and hawed, soon sweating profusely, although her dress was good and loose-fitting. Mariza's younger sisters Arda, Struma and Bistra — all of them named after big Bulgarian rivers

— had worn this baggy item of clothing. Grandma Mariza said she loved rivers so she gave all her beautiful granddaughters names with lots of water in them.

"No one can trample water underfoot, my pretty girls," Grandma Mariza explained. "The water flows and sings all the time the way I do. It's true a river may run dry in the fierce heat. A river is like joy. Every day, joy runs dry a little bit, but don't you be afraid, sweetheart. The sky is always above your head. A cloud will show up, another cloud will soon join it, the two of them will let their rain pour down on the meadows, and there's the river, big and strong, galloping amidst the frogs and the mud. Remember, among mud and frogs, joy comes back. If a river flows nearby, pretty girls, we'll have plenty of bean soup, and there will be a good sky above our house. It will keep us warm better than any blanket. That's why I named all of you, my treasures, after large rivers," their grandma Mariza often told them. "I didn't know, my beauties, that Arda, Struma, Bistra and Mariza were rivers. Once I kissed a learned man. On the following day, I went on kissing him, and I kissed him, as many times as there are rivers in the world. That man told me the names of the most beautiful rivers in Bulgaria and I went and named you after them. And that's why you are so pretty, my magnificent girls."

Kalcho, the guy who was expected to cash in his chips — Ivo, Mariza's brother, was ready to dig the most wonderful grave for him — but the chap didn't need it anymore. Look at Kalcho now! He didn't seem to care about the grave that Ivo was keen on accommodating him with, had no intention of even looking at it.

Kalcho was holding hands with one of Vasil's daughters. What was her name? Mariza scratched her head. This girl's name just slipped out of her mind like a client sneaking off without paying. Pirina. Yes, her name was Pirina. Folks' names ran away from you like thieves. Well, even if a thug hit Mariza on the head with an iron rod, she wouldn't forget the way Slava, Pirina's mom, baked potato chips for all children. The woman put the round raw circles on the hotplate, paying utmost attention to their color as she turned the thin slices around with a knife. Thus, the round things didn't turn into cinders. How magnificent these baked potato chips smelled! Maybe God himself caught their aroma, which flew skywards from aunt Slava's hotplate! The woman, silent and very serious, baked and baked new delicious chips. Obviously, that year was rich. Even stones and sand must have yielded truckloads of potatoes. Slava chucked the round slices on the hotplate, and when they became brown and crisp, she gave them to her three daughters, their mouths open widely like bills of jackdaws.

Mariza and her sister Arda sat outside by the window and breathed in as hard as they could, their skins, bones and heels sucking up the magnificent fragrance. One day, Slava who was — let's be honest about it, a notoriously pesky and peppery battle-axe — threw lumps of earth at Arda, Mariza and Struma as the girls tried to sneak their way into her garden. The three of them were not thieves, for from it! They would by no means steal all straw-berries. No, sir. They'd leave some behind, but stingy Slava wouldn't have that. The woman baked those golden potato circles; it was true, although her soul was as black as mud after a rain shower. One day, the battle-axe let out a whoop as she beckoned them over.

"Come here, kids. I've got plenty of potatoes for you."

Arda and Mariza took seats across from Slava's three daughters, their mouths, too, gaping like jackdaw bills. Oh, the loads of marvelous potatoes they'd been guzzling all afternoon! Never in her honest life — even after her most caring clients asked her out to dinner at Venice restaurant and bought her fried chicken nuggets — had Mariza tasted anything so gor-geous as those superb potatoes. Slava's daughters didn't protest against the newcomers, not in the least. There were so many baked chips, tons of them, and everybody was happy as if God Himself had reached his hand down for his baked potato chip on the hotplate. Mariza was sure he swallowed hard together with the kids.

Now Pirina, the most courageous among Slava's daughters, as dashing as her sister Pretty Sara (Pirina too was slim, but no slimmer than Mariza!)

— Slava's most courageous daughter held sick Kalcho's hand, and the two of them ran like mad to the church with Saint Sara icon in it. These two ain't got the brains God gave a flea, grandma Mariza said. God Almighty, come and have a look at them! Kalcho wasn't on his deathbed, far from it! He was galloping like a horse to his bag of oats, like a client geeked to get Mariza even before she'd taken her slippers off, or like old grandmother Mariza, itching to slice the Easter bread in two. That was how Kalcho was loping across the field. He had obviously forgotten the fact that Ivo still counted on these 40 bucks for the future grave he was supposed to dig.

"Kalcho! Bully for you! I wish your mom Koyna saw you canter like a stallion. Ata boy!" This was the first time Mariza had been happy that her brother Ivo wouldn't earn forty levs for a new grave! She felt like jumping with joy. Koyna, the druggist's gray face would soon become pink like Saint Sara's on the icon in the church! Joy gave your skin light and strength as if you'd been eating baked potatoes ever since you were born.

"Kalcho!" Mariza was about to shout, and her voice was powerful enough to perform her grandma's songs. Well, she didn't shout and there was a reason behind this.

As timid as a calf, sick Kalcho bent down to Pirina, Slava's most unmanageable daughter. He didn't press any further the way a client would, didn't even dare kiss her square on the mouth. He kissed her hair instead, the poor soul, as birdbrained as a brush that he was. Ok, Slava's daughter did have good shoulder-length hair, but Mariza's wild locks were by far and wide the most magnificent and incomparable in these parts: as black as the Black Sea, that's how formidable Mariza's hair was, and no one had ever tried to deny this fact. Kalcho kissed Pirina's unremarkable hair and smiled so widely that his cheeks lit up. She'd commit — Mariza felt — an unforgivable sin if she shouted "Kalcho!" at that moment.

So, Mariza didn't shout at all, didn't even set out for their small nameless church with Saint Sara icon in it. The pair of fools had turned their steps towards it, and you could bet your life they didn't see a thing in front of them. Even if an elephant turned up under their noses, they wouldn't notice it.

§

I am Pirina, my eyes are strong and I notice everything.

Kalcho had lost weight and looked as thin as my forefinger. I stared at him, my heart thudded as if nails instead of blood were flowing to it.

"You are okay now, man. Why should you bend over double, huh? You'll be as strong as an ox soon." I tried to cheer him up and I held his hand as thin as a sheet of paper, yellowish, colorless even. It had never crossed my mind I could love a hand of yellow paper like that, or that I'd care about somebody, a man who wasn't strong enough to break a chicken's neck. I didn't believe my heart would shrink and turn into a hazelnut as I watched Kalcho. It did, though, it did. I touched his hair, thick, curly and tousled, smelling of sweat and sickness. His face that was lost in it. I wouldn't have that. No way! You don't know me, sickness.

"Take a seat, Kalcho, sugar," I said, but he didn't have the strength to take a seat. If he sank down on the grass, to which dewdrops stuck like leeches, he'd catch a cold for sure, so I took off my sweater — the truth was the thing cost five times as much as my mom's fridge. Yakob gave it me, he gave me everything under the stars, but I didn't care for Yakob's everything. I spread the sweater on the grass and said, "Sit down here, Kalcho, my dearest."

I'd never told anybody he was *my dearest*. It sounded downright ugly to me. My tongue wasn't a weathercock, and it didn't turn with the wind, buttering up the guy all over the place. My dearest jewel. O, come off it! The last jewel weighed more than an ox, and you had to keep your eyes open like the door of a village inn, otherwise the gemstone would corner you on the stairs or push you against the wall of your own living room. I could say *my dearest* to Kalcho. He was thinner than his own shirt, the same one I'd given him ages ago. I had bought it for 50 cents from the secondhand shop.

156

"I've asked my mom to put this shirt on me before I die," he said. "It keeps me warm in the night and it keeps my arms cool at noon."

"Kalcho, be careful," I snapped at him. "Say one more time something about pushing up the daisies, man, and I'll bust you one."

He smiled. Grandma Mariza's youngest grandchild beamed like that, a kid as large as your hand, his smile bigger than him. Every time he saw me, his face broke into a grin that began near his bootees and ended at the tiniest wisp of black velvet hair on his head. Kalcho was smiling at me exactly like that velvet baby. I tried hard to make my eyes sparkle happily and I failed. I kissed him — so quietly and gently as if he was the velvet baby. I feared I would hurt him and hated the thought of it.

"Kalcho, Kalcho," I whispered. "I will sing for you one hundred songs in a row. I'll sing for you day and night. I won't stop, I promise you. You will become as strong as the crags on Bare Hill, you can take my word for it."

He couldn't stop smiling, Kalcho the dear featherhead, and I suddenly was in a lighthearted mood, thinking, why should I sing to this guy, why not just kiss his smile as broad as a meadow? He may get better, who knows? Grandma Mariza, who was a very smart woman, told me once "When a man smiles, God is in his eyes, my girl. Look in his eyes and it's not necessary to go to church." And right she was. Kalcho caught my two hands and stooped down, his head curly like a fleecy rug. A rubbish-heap overgrown with nettles, that was all there was to Kalcho's hair. Yes, one more thing, it smelled bad. So what? Would an ugly smell scare me away? No way!

"A man is bigger than all wrong things in the world and smaller than the good ones. That's why man grows up, to grow toward goodness and justice," Grandma Mariza said.

Kalcho lifted my hands to his eyes and looked at them so intently, as if he'd lost a jewel and wanted to make sure if the thing had rolled down and stopped somewhere between my fingers.

He kissed the pinkie on my left hand first, then the ring finger, the middle finger, the index finger. He didn't say anything. He stroked my arm from elbow to wrist and flowers burst into bloom on my skin. O, come off it! Flowers my foot. Minor cuts and bruises all over the place, and I wasn't sure he noticed them. I must have gotten them while climbing the trees, clambering over slippery rocks and slithering like a grass snake down the wall that had tightened its noose on the mountain. No one had looked at my battered fingers with such tenderness. Very rarely, when I was a little kid, my father smiled at me like that before he put me up on his shoulders. However, I was heavier than Luba, so Dad always put her up on her shoulders.

"Look here," I said to Kalcho. "We'll have to take care of the crazy locks that keep falling over your eyes. I can't see you under this wild hair of yours. Wait for me, will you? I'll go fetch a pair of scissors. Our house is at a stone's throw from here."

"Don't go fetch a pair of scissors, golden-eyes Pirina" he said quietly.

No one had ever spoken to me that quietly. No one ever called me "golden-eyes Pirina."

Carefully, as if his unkempt hair was made of glass and was about to burst into a thousand pieces, I brushed it off his forehead, a high forehead, so yellow it frightened me. I began gently massaging it, kneading and pressing his skin as if I was rubbing Luba's heels, Luba, my puny sister, when she was ill and coughed, and Mom thought the kid would soon go. But I rubbed and kneaded her heels like a lion and I didn't let her go anywhere. Absolutely not! I learned to massage foreheads right away. Bit by bit, a pink hue squeezed its way under Kalcho's skin the way the day slowly grew above the river before the sun was up and strong.

I remembered: when I was a little girl, smaller than Gasho, our dog, and suffered badly from whooping coughs, Dad bent over me. At that time, he still hadn't got his leg broken and used to be the toughest guy in the world. He kissed my forehead and said, "I'll frighten your illness away, little Pirina."

He did, and I was in fine fettle again.

"I'll frighten your illness away, Kalcho dearest," I said to Kalcho and kissed the spot of color where the sun tried to rise on his pink forehead.

"Yes," he whispered. "I feel better now."

I started humming to him the tune about my dragons.

"If it's hard for you to stand the way I howl, I'll give you a fiver for making you go through a rough patch. Just tell me."

"I don't feel sick," he said. "I'll stop throwing up for good."

"Let's not bite off more than we can chew," I said. "For now, puke and take it easy. Little by little you'll stop feeling like throwing up altogether."

Kalcho told me he often went to the grave on the hill opposite the Town Hall. It was only there he didn't feel like puking.

Wait a minute. Which grave are you talking about?

Yours, golden eyes Pirina.

In the village of Staro, they thought that Yakob had bumped me off, so Ivo dug a grave for me under the juniper tree.

"And who did you lay to rest in the coffin?" I asked. "Do I look like a girl buried in a grave to you? Look at me."

Your mom said they buried Coalminer, your teddy bear.

How come they buried Coalminer! I'd grown up with him, at a certain time he was as tall as me, then gradually he became smaller, and I grew stronger and bigger. Coalminer melted away like an icicle and I loved him even more. I carried him everywhere, talked with him about everything on my mind. How could Mom come up with such a whacky plan? How could she go bury Coalminer? What a silly woman!

"I'll buy you another Coalminer," Kalcho said.

"Don't. Don't spend money for nothing. Be my Coalminer instead. I'll go everywhere with you, Kalcho, out in the cold and when it's scorching hot, too… when I have toothache and when I don't. I'll talk to you. You'll know everything that's on my mind. How good it is if somebody knows your good and bad thoughts. They're your best friend, and they'll be your best friend as long as they live."

"I've never been anybody's best friend…" Kalcho sighed.

"How come you haven't? What about me?" I cut him short. "You've always been my first and best friend and you'll go on being the one, whether you like it or not, at least as long as I live."

He kissed my left pinkie finger first, then the right one.

"Now I know," he said, and his disheveled hair again swooped down like a mudslide on his yellowish face. O, come off it! Stop babbling about yellowish faces, girl. Don't you know how to rub a baby's heels gently as silk, namely your sister Luba's? She was a clever little thing, and not a screaming infant like our neighbors' baby. You pressed gently, careful not to irritate the skin, you rubbed it with your finger pads, and your finger pads warmed up the baby's feet. The yellow skin slowly turned white and the finger pads felt so good that you thought, "Your hands are ballerinas, Pirina."

"Golden Eyes Pirina," Kalcho said, and exactly at that moment, his yellow cheeks decided they'd look much better if they became pink.

"I'm not Golden Eyes Pirina," I objected, although it felt awesome when a guy called you like that.

Kalcho went on repeating "Golden Eyes Pirina," said it too many times, and I, anxious to make him stop, kissed his lips. I drank his breath; I ate up all his "Golden Eyes Pirinas" and gave him all of my tough and powerful breath in return. Kalcho was leaner than my pinky finger that he'd just kissed, thinner than the shirt I'd given him. I felt like pressing his body against mine — I was strong, the strongest of Slava's and Vasil's three daughters. I was as headstrong as Mom, and her mulishness was fiercer that all February whirlwinds rolled into one. I was tough like Dad, and I was the tallest of us three. I wanted to press this disheveled man against my heart, clasp him tightly until his skin turned pink, but I was afraid I might break his chest. So carefully, as if he were a puny child like my younger sister Luba, I cuddled him close. I'd give him all my defiance, all my big strength I was going to give him.

"You know what, Golden Eyes Pirina," Kalcho said as he hid his smile in his beard. "They built a church without a name with Saint Sara icon in it."

I knew about it. They had built the best God's church in the village of

Staro. People in love went there, and Sara, my elder sister, the most beautiful girl who had ever walked under the sun and the moon, looked at them all the time. One wondered how come she was so beautiful. My father's face was wrinkled and gray; my Mom's was gray too, short and small. Sara…

Sara was different.

All day long, people flocked into the nameless church, old and young, middle-aged couples, twelve or thirteen-year old kids, a lad furtively giving a girl's hand a gentle squeeze. How funny they were! Sara watched from her icon, and I believed she said to them, "Okay, take it easy." I could read Sara's eyes and I was sure she was trying to encourage them, but the young pumpkins were still empty-heads and thought that kissing somebody was as challenging as higher mathematics. Gray-haired grandpas trudged up the hill; what would they want from my sister Sara? An old man kept plodding on, his walking stick dragging behind his feet, an old woman holding him by the hand. These two looked and looked, not for an instant taking their eyes off Sara as if they didn't know what a bad egg she was. My pretty sister hardly managed to scrape up a passing grade in Bulgarian language, and the thought of her getting a passing grade in biology gave me severe headaches.

A young man dressed to kill, sporting a mop-like beard, came to the nameless church and you'd be right to conclude his jacket cost as much as the building itself. Even I, who had lived at Yakob's place, was at a loss as to how much his true love had forked out for her lace-up shoes. The old couple lit a candle in front of Sara, the woman kissed the tail of my sister's dress painted on the icon and the man kissed it, too. That artist must have been as whacked as a brush. Sara would never put on such a blaring outfit, not if her life depended on it. The idiot painter deserved to have his ears cut off, baked and served to him at lunch. That artist snake positively had a dozen screws loose. Sara's eyes… I had to be honest here. He had painted her eyes exactly the way they looked at you. Sara's eyes found the words I kept only for Kalcho. They reached my fingertip pads, her good eyes, and I knew: I'd make his yellow skin turn pink. That was the reason why I said, "Thank you," to this addle-headed painting guy.

Mom allowed as how five painters worked their fingers to the bones and sweated bullets as they painted Sara's icon. The artistic leeches might have been two thousand for all I cared. Only one among them who was worth his salt was the artist who did Sara's eyes. There was plenty room for everyone there. I believed that every woman, no matter where she lived, had a secret hiding-place for somebody. Now I knew different. Sara's icon taught me Kalcho was not worth a hiding-place. He was worth all my life.

One day, I saw Mom and Dad. As always, she walked in front of him, for she was courageous as an explosion, mulish, flatly refusing to read old newspapers no matter what. Mom didn't even look at a book, only followed the news on our old TV, swearing like a trooper so heatedly I was embarrassed to listen to her. Behind her, Dad doddered along, moaning, throwing his injured leg back and forth, each step a laborious journey to agony, yet he finally caught up with her, a man as big as a barn, heavy, ungainly, his eyes gray with the dust of the old newspapers. They walked side by side for a while, and she often waited for him, otherwise no man under the poor clouds could ever catch up with Mom even if he rode a motorbike.

Dad took her hand. Then they stopped in front of the icon of Sara, their eldest daughter. What were they telling her? Who were they talking to? To Sara in the stinky hole at the Venice Motel, to pretty Sara the boys at school shed blood and fought for, or to Sara they both had known since the time she was a worm of a colicky baby, squirming and howling in pain?

Even I could not forget the day when Sara was about to die of pneumonia. Doc Stoim and gray-haired Koyna sprinted down the dirt track to our house. Surely, God himself must have descended the hill to give Sara these eyes. From the icon, they could see any room in which a little girl had been running a fever for days, and her mom was praying to God to save her. Maybe the Venice fleabag Motel had given Sara her eyes. Who knew?

Mom and Dad stood motionless in front of the icon. I noticed Dad trembling. He was not frail or shaky. He had dug wagons and wagons of coal that a whole town would not be able burn for a century to come. I saw him. His tears glowed like fireflies, like an open wound did these tears creep down my father's gray face.

"Forgive me, Slava," he said.

I could not understand if Mom forgave him or not, and why should she forgive him. She said neither "I forgive you" nor "I don't forgive you." She squeezed his hand and that was all.

What could I tell Kalcho about Sara and the church that had no name?

… One evening, I caught a glimpse of Petrova, my Bulgarian literature teacher, in front of Sara's icon. This woman had swept Luba off her feet, messed things up in her brain, turned her into a bag of books and a *Notre Dame* of Paris. Petrova was always harping on the same rusty string: everyone should read about some old man and the sea, and about a crazy white whale. Oh, give me a break. I hated the white whale's guts and didn't want to read anything about old men.

You'd better lead forth your dragons into battle than peruse a volume on an old geezer; better beat up a guy, break a nose or kiss a boyfriend than bury yourself in the dust of a lousy library, or become *Notre Dame* and die slowly the way Luba, my pretty loony sister, did. Luba, my dearest… I was like a mom to her for I had learned at an early age to rub a baby's feet and drive away whooping coughs. Only Sara's icon knew the exact number of times I had pulled Luba out of trouble. We, the three sisters, slept in the smallest room, and Sara was bitchy about the baby's bawling and wriggling in the middle of the night. I didn't mind.

Kalcho squeezed my hand, so weakly did he squeeze it, but I was grateful he had that much strength.

"Miss Petrova came to the church," I said to him. "No one accompanied her."

"In the spring I, too, went to Sara by myself," Kalcho said. "I fell twice while I was climbing the hill. Mom thought that I had died, but I was ok and I made it to Sara. On the way back, uncle Kamen and Mom carried me back home. The important thing was I made it to Sara."

"Why was it so important?" I asked him.

"Well…"

"What?"

"Because I asked her to bring you back to me," Kalcho blurted out and these were the sweetest words I'd heard in my life. How could this shabby boy think of them?

§

Why did this girl disappear?" David wondered as he watched the moon dissolve in Luba's faded blue coat. He ran to the cabin where a dozen books still lay on the floor, sat down in the dust and waited a couple of hours. Luba didn't show up, so he went to look for her in the kitchen of Venice Restaurant. Women in white caps were chopping onions there, the air clawed at his eyes, tears trickled down his cheeks as one of the white caps, the young cook, that stood near the kitchen door, asked, "Why are you whimpering, little David?"

Her eyes hit him in the ribs. "Oh, look at you! What a pretty boy you are! David, come here. Hurry up! How's you big friend Anno doing? I see he's bought you the sweetest little shirt! He's dolled you up all right. Oh, my, you are a real peach!"

"Where's Luba?" David asked. "Is she here?"

"What are you talking about, pretty?" the white cap sighed. "He grabbed her up in his strong arms and took her away. Now Luba walks on 100 dollar bills. I'm pretty sure she has her own huge Jaguar F-Pace car and she takes baths in kangaroo milk."

"Who took her away?" David muttered under his breath, his hands suddenly cold. His arms hurt and his knees were soft dandelion leaves. "Who? Tell me."

"Can't you guess, dolly?" the woman guffawed. The other two girls armed with knives, serious sentries in front of a huge heap of onions, gave faint smiles.

"You are very handsome," the cap said. "I'll poison Anno and I hope then you'll notice how pretty I am."

David took a step to the door. The smell of frying onions made him sick. His face was wet with onion tears. The cook in the white cap near him chucked the knife down on the table, unbuttoned her apron and wiped David's burning cheeks with the lower edge of her skirt. Like a deathly reef did her legs glare under his nose, muscled and sturdy legs full of heavy, threatening bones.

"You know what, Anno's right. You are very handsome indeed," the girl chuckled as she pinched him. Her fingers were evil and knew where it hurt a lot. She pinched him again. "I see. Anno's right to buy you nice clothes and things," concluded the young cook. "What do you want from Luba?" The cook's hand was as wet as a painter's brush. "Let me check what you hide down there," the wet hand went on. "There it is. Look at David's little worm."

"Don't pester the guy," the biggest of the three women said.

"Why not? He came here of his own free will," barked the girl whose thighs had thrown David into a blind panic. The white cap was an impregnable fortress, the Eiffel Tower in the kitchen. Her fingers went on investigating, squeezing here, pressing there or perhaps caressing, one never knew with cast iron ladies like her. Like a pickpocket, the cook's left hand was rummaging the space under his shirt.

"It hurts," David groaned unable to stir. The Eiffel Tower was taller than him, much heavier and stronger.

"The little doll smells like a donkey," the onion-cutting cook pointed out as she nibbled at his neck.

David tried hard to wrench himself free and failed. The pincers of her fingers that chased him, captured him and pinched his thigh again and again.

"The sexy flat stomach of yours…It's gorgeous."

He tripped and reeled back. Finally, her fingers let him be, the lingering onion smell, a cape on his shoulders, weighing him down, then her quick hands seized his belt, an expensive one Anno had bought him from Wien. Anno had paid a skilled leatherworker to engrave gold letters on the leather. **"The course of true love never did run smooth,"** said his trouser belt.

This sentence was wrong. Love was not a horse, therefore it could not run… Was Anno making fun of him? Love in the village of Staro, o, give me a break! The leather told David nothing but bald-faced lies.

"It's not a lie," Anno assured him. "I studied Shakespeare's plays trying to choose a good inscription for your belt."

"Who is that guy, Shakespeare, and why should he care about my belt?" David had flared up at his boss, but he liked his leather present very much.

Now, he was scared to ask the Eiffel Tower to give it back to him.

"Haven't you heard of Shakespeare?" Anno had asked him.

David gave him no answer. This Shakespeare was obviously a big fish, otherwise who'd allow him to make up lies for honest men's belts?

"He is a playwright and a poet," Anno had explained as his eyes went somewhere else far from the river, The Cat pub or the rails with their express train just now hurtling to Athens, Greece.

"I understand," David hissed angered by his boss's reaction. "A fat lot I care. Every Tom, Dick and Harry has an itch to grab a pen and write poems. None of this gang has done a stroke of work so far."

… He had thought long and hard about what he would buy Luba. He hadn't seen her for ages. Should he fork out a bundle on two pounds of fresh cherries? Ok, everybody likes fruit, but she could think to herself, *"Can David be so dumb? The only thing he can think about is spitting cherry pits. Why don't I get going and beat it for Spain on my own?"* At that point, it came down on David like a ton of bricks, *"The course of true love never did run smooth".*

Then he knew. He'd buy her a book. By Shakespeare. Wait a minute. True love? Give me a break! It was as clear and loud as a gunshot that Shakespeare was attracted to love and other smooth things, but what else would you expect from a crazy poet? David would follow a sensible course of action; he would run to a bookshop. He'd seen a small run-down one filled to the brim with books just next to the wholesale meat market he bought chicken wings and calf's liver from for The Cat.

He'd buy her a Shakespeare or two. If they let this guy scribble stuff and nonsense on five hundred dollar belts, then he wasn't some poor beggar or something. Anno praised the fella to the skies, too. Writers are like chicken wings, David reasoned. Some of them are juicy. Others smell. He was very knowledgeable about chicken wings, yet he wanted to forget everything related to chickens at least for an hour. He felt like buying her something big, a dress or some glad rag. It was high time this girl threw away her nasty apron. She looked downright crappy in it. That damned ankle-length apron was endless as a highway, but perhaps it was better that way. Her legs didn't frighten him, on the contrary, her snowdrop-white knees narrow as a fish's back calmed him down. David loved fish, they were docile and he compared her feet to minnows for, in his mind, minnows were gentle and kind.

When David was just a nipper, his fingers had a sea breeze in their bones, nimble and soft they were. He caught minnows like thunder, grabbing hold of slippery backs, then, lo and behold, the fish wriggled between his forefinger and thumb. He wanted to bring the catch to his grandma, so on the way back home he hid in the shadow of the bushes. Even as early as that, he steered clear of roads and paths because bigger and stronger boys not only walked off with his minnows, but also kicked him, slapped his face and punched him, trying to knock his teeth out. When finally David got home, he couldn't sit on his chair to eat dinner because his bones hurt. Fish and he got along very well, but no man alive understood him. David's boss was an exception to this nasty rule, the dear soul, excluding the fact that Anno went out of his way to civilize David and foster spiritual attraction between them. Attraction my foot! Anno trimmed and brushed David's hair, cut his fingernails and clipped his toenails, disinfected his wounds when David hurt himself, took him to the dentist and sprayed deodorant inside his shirt. He made David brush his teeth twice a day and tried hard to teach him English.

"Look here, David," Anno spoke quietly and his eyes ran away again to that distant place far beyond the railway line, two thousand miles from The Cat. "You and I will fly to London. We will sell The Cat. I am sick and tired of everything around me here. Ignorance, squalor… drunkards…"

David scratched behind his neck, feeling embarrassed. He and these drunkards had polished off a fifty-gallon bottle of turnip brandy, and he hated to calculate how much it cost. David often broke out in a cold sweat thinking he had cut the pub's profits to zero. He was the guilty party. He had drunk hard and ugly in The Cat. But oh, my foes, and oh, my friends! (as Anno was fond of saying) the bosom pals David made after the drinking binge! A man gave him a cigarette, another one bought him a pair of socks and a very nice fella, still partially sober, washed him, for Anno hated the guts of any T-shirts that smelled. He dedicated hours on end to sweaters, both to his own and David's. He washed them using softeners, catalysts, linen enhancing formulas, color fixing agents; in the course of nine consecutive days, he ironed David's shirts, putting various combination of scents on the fabric and using relevant chemicals to stabilize the flavor. "*The course of true love never did run smooth,*" Anno breathed, his nose buried in the collar of David's shirt then went on heaping loads of bunk about that Shakespeare guy as if the two of them had just got drunk together.

"Forget the old fart." One day David simply could no longer stand all this. "There's nothing smooth about love. Kick the big poetic cheese out of your head, and let's eat the chicken wings. They'll start rotting if we don't."

"We'll go to London together. We'll run a restaurant in London, you and I. With you by my side, I can undertake anything, David. My brother lives there," Anno spoke dreamily. Every time a dream sneaked into his skull, things took a turn for the worse, Anno either sobbed or threw a tantrum and threatened to arrange David's hair, using Drumm the dog's comb. Day in, day out, Anno cooked salt-free dishes, very good for your kidneys, he pointed out, but no, thank you, David's kidneys were as strong as granite slabs and didn't mind salty foods. Anno had an iron rule: he himself cooked all his own and David's meals. The minute the bowls of soup or the plates of salad were on the table, he produced golden spoons and forks, then they sat at table to have lunch. Anno kept close watch over David to make sure his manager had learned proper table manners. The little guy preferred to fall on the meat like everybody else and wanted to grab his steaks with his hands. He felt very happy in the company of his bosom friends, the drunks, although they gorged themselves on pork lard, onions, fat pies and stale bread, washing it down with turnip brandy.

On the days Anno visited his tailor, his beautician or his hair stylist in Sofia, David gathered his friends around him and their eyes were all fire and bliss. The bunch immediately came down to brass tacks as the honest men caught a dozen grass snakes. David didn't have the permission to catch animals, although some drunks argued a snake was not an animal since it couldn't walk. Actually, David was allowed to do whatever he pleased, but he hated to make Anno gaze off silently into space, his face, gray like an asphalt driveway after a heavy rain, tilted up to David's. Therefore, the turnip lovers learned to safely catch grass snakes and rapidly strip off their cool scaly skins. Then they sliced the meat into thin, long strips, which they sprinkled with crushed cloves of garlic they pilfered from the small vegetable gardens by the railroad track. Then the smelly brandy fans, all edgy, keyed up over the grass snake strips grilling over the open fire, stared intently at David. The manager of the drinking establishment produced a big bottle. At that instant, ferocious swilling and gobbling commenced, and happiness went on, culminating, very vocally indeed, in a song performed jointly in twenty-two big voices, all of them gruff and hoarse, "Brave Bulgarian Soldiers March Gloriously On!"

The drunks lifted David bodily into the air as they shouted at the tops of their drunken lungs "Atta bo-o-o-y!" The performance they put on was impressive and after it, the chaps, sloshed, drunk and blissful, rolled onto their stomachs on The Cat's terrace. Anno had found them several times like that: David sprawled out among three or four trusted friends, grinning at the cement floor. Anno was a strong healthy man. He didn't busy himself with kicking out the drunks, didn't break out into abuse, for he never swore at anybody. He grabbed David by the waist, tried to help his manager to his feet as carefully as a musician would lift his violin. Then he washed David's face and chest with mineral water, soaked up the glistening droplets with a soft towel and put him in the imposing four-poster bed. This piece of furniture purchased from Brussels, Belgium, could accommodate all the drunks, the cat, and Drum the dog who was the pub's talisman. On the following day, Anno refused to talk to David, didn't even glance at him, although he treated the short man to breakfast in bed, bringing gold forks, knives and spoons for him.

"Well…you see…I'm sorry, pal," David mumbled.

Anno refused to respond, dressed in black despite the fierce heat that boiled the water in the river — black shirt, black pants, black socks, black stone ring, black sunglasses, black necktie and a black watch on his right wrist. The world was midnight when Anno was angry with his manager. "I say I'm sorry, man," David insisted, intent on assuaging the pain in his boss's broken heart. Anno was an honorable man. He managed The Cat perfectly and helped its clientele grow, so finally David pronounced the words that healed the wound, "Ok, make some fondue for us."

Making fondue was a tricky task. First, Anno went to change his clothes. He took off his black shirt, black shoes, black pants, black socks, and put on a white dressing gown, white shoes and a matching white cap, on which a woman from the neighboring village had embroidered, "*The course of true love never did run smooth*". Oh, that saucebox Shakespeare again! It was evident his poor brain couldn't dwell on anything practical. Why should he ruin a guy's classy cap in the first place? Shakespeare-boy's head must have clogged up with love, and even Anno, a man after David's heart, went and embroidered his expensive outfits with smooth love ideas. Why didn't he tell his crazy friend from London to stop it?

Anno's fondness for chocolate was so exceptional that words in any human language could not describe it. He melted a mixture of cocoa and butter in small silver saucers, chopped walnuts and ground almonds and hazelnuts. Then he insisted David dab his lips with a cotton ball soaked in smelly liquid, which was supposed to be fragrant. Well, hunter's sausage with lots of garlic had a much better smell.

Would Luba like a fondue pot? David could make Anno prepare a kilo or two. No, although Luba was as thin as a screwdriver, she didn't care for chocolate. What should fondue want with her? David stopped at the meat market, bought good calf tripe, pork offal and chuck steaks, after that dropped in on the tiny bookstore he had picked out, and thundered, "Do you sell any Shakespeare here?"

"Yes, Sir, we offer the complete works of Shakespeare, 6th edition. Do you prefer a tragedy or a comedy?"

Tragedy? Comedy? Come off it, woman. A cat in a strange garret he was, nothing more, nothing less. It seemed wise to tell the old grandma who sold comedies and stuff here, "Give me the guy's thickest book!" He had learned from experience that the fattest thing meant the most precious one: the fattest pork chop, the fattest bundle in your pocket; however, he felt awkward about asking her this question. Wouldn't he make a fool of himself before this little old woman? Why not have a look at all the volumes and tragedies Anno's pal had sweated out?

"All these volumes are Shakespeare's works," the granny who had one foot in the grave said as she led him to huge shelves of books. "How come the poor soul is still breathing?" David wondered. Books and books, and volumes and nothing else. Not a trace of hunter's sausage and garlic, no smell of breath, no clean air. That must be the reason Luba was so scrawny. Pages and paper had really drained her; that was it. Gosh, so many books and all of them big like trucks. Not one looked normal to him. They surely cost a small fortune or a big one, the bastards.

"Give me the cheapest one," David ordered and the woman choked to death before his eyes. She must have thought he was a sleazy skinflint. Luba too would think David was a skinflint if she saw him, a slim cheap tragedy in hand. Might as well go the whole hog, he said to himself, patted the grandma on the shoulder to cheer her up, although it was evident the old sweetie already had both feet in the grave. He told her, "Ok, give the most expensive book you have. I'll buy it. Come on, old sweetheart, I am in a hurry."

The woman chose a volume for him, a dark-blue one, *William Shakespeare — Comedies* that cost eighty-two levs! O, come off it, man! For eighty-two levs, David himself would sit down in the shade and produce a comedy. It wouldn't be bad at all, so Shakespeare, stuffed shirt that he was, might take the hint and buy David a glass of plum brandy. Be that as it may, David wasn't going to split hairs. He was buying a present for Luba! He felt like kissing the smile on the girl's face and tried to imagine the moment when she'd glimpse the dark-blue slab of the book. Then perhaps she would show him her silver knees, gleaming like a school of minnows in the moonlight. He was not afraid of Luba, on the contrary, David was no fraidy cat. The boozers and he got along just fine, loyal, simple souls they were.

"Hey, sweetie, you read too much. Super smart, are you?" remarked the girl who had pinched him. She bent down and her dyed red hair pooled like the blood of a bad wound on his chest. The redhead grabbed the book and slowly, haltingly, spelled out the title *Sh-a-k-e-s-p-e-a-r-e. Co-me-dies*, eighty-two levs! You're nutty as a fruitcake! Forked out eighty-two bucks on a lump of paper as thick as two haystacks! Gosh! I'll tell you what I'll do if you gave me half the money you wasted on this Shake…whoever he is." Her hand again landed where it didn't belong. She wasn't being pushy this time, didn't pinch his thigh, just deposited the grease of her fingers close to the worm. The Eiffel tower dropped the book onto the floor, and it was fortunate for David she didn't hurl it because that would have ruined its splendid jacket. Rapid as lightning, David bent down and picked up the dark-blue tome.

"Luba doesn't work here anymore," the biggest and darkest cook said. Although she was a head taller than David her big hands didn't scare him. He somehow felt she was a decent woman.

"Where does Luba work now?" he asked the huge cook.

"She doesn't need to, honey, he took her away. How come you don't know who he is, sugar? Kiro pocketed Luba, Kiro the dude who broke a couple of your ribs. O, be a doll, Dave, I love you," blabbered on the granite wall of a girl who had gone and fingered his book. "Kiro has plenty of free time. I wonder which book they are reading now, Kiro and our chick Luba. Perhaps the couple is very interested in fat manuals like the one you paid so much money for, what do you think?"

At that moment, David was ashamed he was carrying Shakespeare the chatterbox with him, and the girls thought he had something to do with that scribbler. His arm gave in under the weight of the dark-blue tome, which was more of a gravestone than a book.

A total scumbag, that redhead was! David edged out of the kitchen. She had smeared grease all over his legs, and he had the feeling his pants were a trap he couldn't wiggle out of.

He had to see Luba. This suddenly seemed so important that spots swam before his eyes. She was the only girl who… Better not think about her now. He walked past the booze shop, silent and locked now, caught a glimpse of a shadow on its wall, but this wasn't Kiro; then David brushed by the fence of the Town Hall in front of which a couple of World War I guns jutted out. He enjoyed staring at their dark barrels. If he had had a gun, the lousy redhead wouldn't have taken the liberty to pinch or grope him. He hated her. Why hadn't he bought a gun! Then big Kiro the dinosaur wouldn't look that big.

David felt his footsteps melt behind his back as if they were wax. His feet were too weak to walk on. For a fleeting moment, he remembered the hourglass with golden sand Anno had given him on his birthday. Now David wanted to give it to Luba, but the sand, golden or not, wouldn't help. He was in the small street where Kiro the ogre's house stood a short distance from the wood. The short man stopped and hid Shakespeare behind his back, then he tucked in his shirt and hitched up his soiled pants, refusing to accept defeat. The mean redhead had stolen his genuine leather belt. David adored it despite the total fabrication the assertive English midget had printed on the genuine leather. David used to feel sturdy with an expensive thing curling around his waist. Maybe because of the missing belt, his determination went to the dogs. He turned around. Wouldn't it be better if he went back home? You shouldn't fight against a brick factory. David knew broken ribs hurt a lot. They did heal by themselves, it was true; however, Anno had wrapped him in a raw ram fleece for twenty consecutive days. His friend bought the priciest ram in the country, and the beast's fleece helped David to recuperate. The creamy thick soups that Anno cooked for David and the beefsteaks were delicious, and the 100 pipers of the Scotch whiskey constantly played their pipes as the two men ate and drank in the evenings.

David could imagine Luba's shoulders under her faded blue coat. Her knees would gleam before his eyes and he made up his mind. He *had to* give her the thick book no matter what. The thing cost eighty-two levs, but the price was of no consequence. No, Sir! Not by a long shot! He wanted to see this girl and hold her hand. Her fingers didn't scare him. He made for the front door, the house shining like a guillotine under the frowning sky. He followed the garden path for about a minute when suddenly a huge character towered over him, another brick factory — but the crackpot was not Kiro. An old codger he was, as big as a tractor with a seed-drill in tow, his fist the size of a loaf of bread. A giant woman trailed along behind him, her fat, strong buttocks enough to frighten a bear away.

"What do you want with me, idiot?" the old codger snapped at David. "I haven't asked you to bring your measly ass here."

"Hey, moron, who are you looking for?" the woman barked. Her voice was frozen rubble, but you tread on frozen rubble, couldn't you? It seemed big fat women weren't as rude as the small malicious ones, David thought and screwed his courage to the sticking place. Unlike the Eifel Tower, the huge cook in The Cat's kitchen had been quite kind to him.

"Speak up, moron," the woman thundered and David promptly found out she wasn't a good-natured grandma. A vicious vixen she was.

He plucked up enough courage to ask a simple question, feeling all his ribs sting, smart and hurt like hell. "Is Luba at home?"

"Luba's not under my roof." The big woman spat out the rubble she'd been chewing on.

David wouldn't go away with his tail between his legs the way the rats in The Cat did. Saucy vermin those rats were, he had seen them hundreds of times, scooting over cracks and corners the moment Anno's favorite tomcat slunk into the kitchen. David believed the tomcat was one of his best friends. The old codger clenched his fists and they were not loaves of bread. They were as big as hills.

"Luba!" David shouted, trying hard not to stare at the old geezer's fists. "Luba, it's me, David."

"My husband said she's not here," the huge woman's huge voice bit into his neck. "Wolf!"

A tousled mutt, or rather a thundercloud, a man-eating murderer, powerful, as silent as a grave, trotted out of the garden towards David, who stumbled and collapsed onto the grass as Shakespeare hit the ground with a thud, grazing his nose; perhaps this was what saved his life. Both the old codger and his gigantic wife burst out laughing. The old geezer shook and giggled, guffawed, spat and coughed as his crone waved her hands around the way a fat goose flapped her stubby wings.

"Wolf!" the old man screamed, and the mutt, his fangs hanging an inch from David's throat, froze in the air like a long nail driven halfway into a rafter.

"Beat it, idiot!" the old codger ordered and spat on the grass. "I don't want crazy Luba here."

"If Luba set foot in my house, with these two…" the big woman lifted her muscular arms in the air, and sounding quite businesslike, added, "I'll strangle her. My son the blockhead is out of his mind because of this lousy bitch."

David heaved a sigh of relief after he turned round, then dashed across the street as though he was being chased. Luba didn't live in the ogres' house. This was wonderful! He was so happy he jumped with joy. The two monsters hadn't captured his girl. He ran past the schoolyard where old linden trees and elms grew. Buses took the children to the school in the village of Opal, and behind the squat square building, waist-high nettles, clumps of thistles and brambles flourished on the clay soil.

David was already in the square yard when he saw her. Luba... A dozen of Gypsy kids, a flock of ravens that had perched on the dry grass around her, big and small children in faded T-shirts from the second-hand shop, all as pink as a watermelon, both girls and boys. Only one lad, a lamppost jutting out in the field, a head taller than the rest, was in a dark-blue T-shirt, neither faded nor dirty. He didn't wear torn flip-flops either. The kid had put on a pair of new shoes.

It looked as if the grandma who had cut the kids' hair had used a hand-saw: a wisp hanging like a tail here, a lock or a whole bunch sticking out an inch above the left ear and the rest of the skull shaved to the bone. The only exception was the tall boy's hairdo. It was very typical of these parts; the same barber arrived once every three months to cut everybody's hair. Young and old, Bulgarian and Gypsies used the service he offered, and the man did his job democratically indeed, going for the same haircut for everybody. He left a tuft of hair at the top of the head and nothing else. The hair stylist charged two levs per head.

Luba was in her long blue coat as ancient as a fairytale. Under the shabby fabric, her quiet ankles waited, making him think of pearl oysters. David had learned a lot about pearls. Anno had given him a gold tiepin with a pearl on it. The pearl, Anno maintained, cost more than Yakob's Jeep Grand Cherokee. Stop pulling my leg, man, David had said.

The tall boy with the new pair of shoes was staring at Luba as if someone had stuck a rod in him to stuff him like a stuffed owl. Luba was printing the letter Y with stick on the ground covered with sand. David hadn't seen her for ages. You're a bloody fool, David, he said to himself. Should've run to her a month ago. Why didn't he drag Shakespeare's slab of a book here before the end of summer?

"Luba!" he called out.

She had cut her hair short. It seemed to him she had become thinner and smaller and this was ok with him. Now David didn't feel uneasy or embarrassed. Perhaps he should have told her, "Look, I've brought you some Shakespeare." He blurted out instead, "Luba, I'm hungry."

The girl took her eyes off the letter Y she had printed on the sand, looked at David and did not smile. She slowly nodded, though.

"Come here, David, please."

David took a few uncertain steps over toward her. She didn't look pleased to see him; she seemed absentminded as if he hadn't thought of her all this time; as if she hadn't given him her own loaf of bread when his head spun with hunger and he had to live on 50 cents a day until April 20th.

"Hi, Uncle D," one of the kids chirped, perhaps a girl, for she had squeezed herself into a trouser leg transformed into a triangular dress. "I'm Valia. Don't you remember me?"

Some idiot had mercilessly chopped off the kid's hair, and her head looked as if a school of pikes had been gnawing on her skull for a week. Not a girl, a packet of ham was this kid, a small shabby packet after a drunk had cut off chunks of it, a bottle of turnip hogwash romping around in the man's stomach.

"Now I can read almost everything, Uncle D. I have to learn two more letters of the alphabet, U and V, that's all."

"Luba," David said. "I didn't come over after work to tell you I was hungry…"

She looked at him.

"I bought you this," he blurted out as he crammed dark-blue Shakespeare into her hands as if the tome were a hamburger bun.

"Comedies. I've read this," Luba said, but it didn't matter if she had read comedies or not. She was smiling.

"Luba, I didn't mean to give you comedies you had read," he explained.

Then she stopped smiling; Luba's quiet eyes, as peaceful as the banks of the Struma River, so gentle they could see only the letter Y on the sand, didn't mean to do him any harm.

"What?" she asked.

For a moment, her knee glowed like a sunset on her faded blue coat.

"Well… let's go pluck sorrel," David suggested, forgetting that in August sorrel leaves were as dry and hard as the genuine leather belt the redheaded shark from the kitchen had stolen from him. "I know a cool place where it grows… and I went to a bookstore in Sofia," he added his throat dry. "It's next to the butcher's shop I buy calf tripe from… a small bookstore with Shakespeare all over the place," David explained. "You could load a truck with the guy's stuff and comedies. I bought you the thickest volume," he declared firmly. "This was the most expensive book. Cost eighty-two levs."

Again a glimmer of a smile — perhaps it wasn't one, perhaps it was the shadow of an elderberry leaf or a white butterfly flitting about — played across her lips.

"Okay, Luba," he murmured reassuringly. "What do you say we get going? If we can't find sorrel then we'll pick something else. Look at the hill. We'll catch great grass snakes. I'll grill one over an open fire for you."

It wasn't a shadow of an elderberry leaf or a white butterfly flitting about in the trees. Luba was smiling and David wasn't surprised at all. He took her hand into his, and not for a split second did he think about the eighty-two levs he had paid for the most expensive book in the store packed to the gills with Shakespeare. Her hand was thin and scraggy like a five lev bill. It felt cold to the touch as if her thumb were a minnow.

"Your hand is a minnow," David said.

That boy, the tallest one in the gaggle of kids, his hair cropped for two levs so short his skull appeared blue, leapt up behind his back.

"If you touch her one more time," the kid hissed quietly, yet his words flitted to the upper end of the village of Staro. Perhaps the passengers who travelled on the express train to Athens had also heard what he said. The train trundled by, clattering down the rails the way a grumpy old man tapped his walking stick against the village square cobblestones. "If you touch her one more time… if you look at her again the way you're looking at her now, I'll crush you like a nut. Do I make myself clear?"

§

Kalcho would eat only when I sat by his side and told him tales. Kamen the drunk, Koyna's man, milked the goat and I gave Kalcho raw warm milk to drink. At times, I soaked dry bread in the goat milk and then my friend Kamen constantly nudged me in the ribs, "Come on, girl, put more bread in that saucer, I tell you."

"Uncle Kamen, he's not an elephant and can't eat so much."

Kalcho ate up all the food I gave him; if I cooked a horse trough full of soup, he'd wolf it down to the last drop. I hate cooking. After the Venice Motel's kitchen, everything that bore the slightest resemblance to a cooking stove was as disgusting to me as the mud on the road on a rainy day. However, for Kalcho's sake, I juggled with saucepans, baking tins and frying pans. In the beginning, he lay barely stirring, so I told him, "I won't have you sprawling out on the sofa, man. Get up. You have to eat, Kalcho, sugar."

He got up and I gave him the saucepan; he squeezed it between his knees and resolutely took to slurping down the broth. On the third day, the man stopped vomiting. I watched him as his face shyly, quietly turned rosy above his bushy beard.

"Let me shave your beard off," I suggested and slowly, cautiously I cut wisp after wisp of bristling, curly beard, setting his cheeks free, locks of thick hair perching on the floor. I was happy his skin under the beard wasn't pallid or ashen; it glowed palely golden. He was a frail, yellow-faced boy, his hair as thick and wry as the clumps of thistles in the field, his arms thinner than mine.

"I won't leave this house before you gain twenty-five pounds of muscle," I declared as I took his hand, trying to give him all my heart and all my strength.

"This is the right thing to do, Pirina. This is the way to give strength to a man. You help him get back on his feet. You hold his hands when he sleeps and when he stays awake, too," Grandma Mariza taught me.

To be honest, my love for that old woman wasn't that deep. She set the gypsy mutts on me every time I climbed her wild pear trees… not that I liked the flavor of the measly fruit, not by a long shot! I did it out of spite, to piss her off; she'd put the wrong idea in her head that I stole her pears. Grandma Mariza would sit under the tree, waiting for me to climb down. Then she would confiscate my bag filled to the brim with sour green fruit, grab my ear and pull it, saying, "Do you want me to give you a spanking, or shall I take you to your mom?" her slow and heavy voice like a ton of bricks. "I think you'd be better off if I whipped you with a bunch if nettles; then I believe you'll remember one thing until your very last breath. You make a grab at somebody else's pears when nobody is looking, foolish Pirina. Not when the lady who owns these pears is dozing off under the pear tree, especially if this lady is me."

However, Grandma Mariza was wrong in thinking that the nettles would be all I'd get. Mom would thrash me with iron tongs for a starter, then, to keep me going, she'd make me clean the whole house: my parents' room, the children's room in which Sara, Luba and I lived. Crazy Luba had dragged a truckload of paperbacks into it. You had to wade through knee-deep heaps of books, and if I put a tiny sheet of paper somewhere else, her eyes welled up with tears. She didn't say a word, but her eyes were like garden ponds overflowing from a heavy rain, and made me feel as if I had slit a toddler's throat. Luba's sad blue eyes were the reason I hated books.

Grandma Mariza squealed on me to Mom that I swore at townspeople. Her grandson Marincho taught me, mind you! The boy gave me one lev to swear at the postman, a guy as dark and silent as a November afternoon.

So I swore at the man, victoriously pocketed my lev and precisely at that moment, as ill luck would have it, Grandma Mariza heard what I was saying. She never beat children. She stared at you instead, and did it in such a way that you were willing to slap yourself across the face ten times if only she'd take her eyes off you.

"Hey, Pirina, you're swearing like a trooper," Grandma Mariza snapped at me. "So, thistles will grow on your tongue, frogs and lizards will spew from your ears."

I froze in my tracks.

"I'll let your mom know you swore at the postman who hadn't stolen anything from you."

Did I remember that day! Mom had gone off the deep end; half an hour earlier, she was angry with Dad, mad at the drought and most probably at the hailstorm, too, which had ruined twenty-seven of her tomato plants. Mom didn't say anything to Grandma Mariza. Losing no time, she grabbed me by the hair and the neck as if I were a ragdoll. I was heavier than her, stronger, too; however every time Mom got hopping mad, the woman seemed to grow two feet taller and towered over me, breathing so hard that the paving stones came loose in the street, the tiles fell off the roof of the house and the hens stopped laying eggs. Mom kept mum as she clutched a spoon, put it between my lips and pushed it through. I had to take a breath, so I opened my mouth. She rapidly stuck a long needle — we called it *bodkin* in these parts — into my tongue, and pressed it deeper. A bottomless sea of blood gushed from the wound Mom had dug in my tongue.

"If I catch you swearing at some honest guy, I'll plant an axe in your tongue. Do I make myself clear?"

It hurt so much that I couldn't even mumble, "Yes, Mom. You do."

Mom was so silent I thought she's go ballistic. She did. She stuck the needle into my tongue one more time.

"Do I make myself clear?"

It hurt and I couldn't tell the difference between a cow and Yakob's Jeep

Grand Cherokee if you asked me, but I put up with the throbbing pain as I shouted, my mouth full of blood, "Yes, Mom. You make yourself clear. Please no more needle!"

From that day onwards, I never swore at a guy or a girl. I didn't even swear in my mind — at Yakob or at snakes basking in the sun under my nose. However, I'd devised a way of showing Yakob what I was thinking about. I chose a shirt of his and slit its back open with a knife. The knife was very sharp, and to cut a 2000 lev shirt into ten crumpled rags was a pleasure. I collected the rags and destroyed them one by one, burning them in the flame of a candle.

"How's business, Yakob? How are you?" I asked before I stuck my belly like a tick to his skin. I'd been burning the rags of his shirt, watching the candle flames devour the cloth, the right sleeve first, then the front, which had covered his heart.

"Terrible," Yakob complained. "Stabbing pain under the left rib cage…"

I was too full of beans to sit still, I didn't feel like sleeping, and didn't suffer from pain under the left rib cage.

"You're magnificent," he mumbled.

Yes, I was. I was strong. I ate the best sirloin steaks for breakfast, lunched off Spanish tomatoes and Belgian strawberries and enjoyed the best Norwegian pies for dinner.

"I love you."

That was the reason why I had to give Kalcho sirloin steaks. He gobbled up a truckload of sirloin steaks a day, no, it would be more precise to say a trainload of steaks his mom Koyna hauled to his sickroom. I propped his head up and fed him on meat. Uncle Kamen the drunk, his mom's husband, pushed a sliver of sirloin steak into his mouth as well. Tears welled up in the poor guy's eyes, but I was patient like a paving stone, and kept on feeding and feeding him. Every bite he took appeared to make his skin harder and milkier. His hands looked for me, but didn't know what to do after they found me.

The nasty tall tales Mom made up! She said Grandma Mariza's grand-daughters paid Kalcho for the medicines in the field behind the fence. Behind the fence my foot! *Don't make it easy for a guy to find you, Pirina,* Mom had taught me; however, I made up my mind once and for all, *Pirina, make it easy for Kalcho without delay.*

He left me as happy as a lark. I was a 1st grader's notebook with an A the teacher gave the student on some difficult homework. It felt like Kalcho had no skin of his own and my skin was his. I was a river that flowed far and wide around him, I flowed through him and protected his heart. He had never wielded a hammer or an axe. His long-fingered hands had touched nothing but pills and cough syrup bottles in the drugstore. Once, I felt panicky he was about to die.

"You are very pretty," Kalcho said as he made room for me in the bed they prepared a month ago for his dying day.

"I'm pretty because I eat a lot of food," I said as I brought him a huge bowl of soup. "You must eat a lot too."

Make me weed strawberry patches, plant beans, shovel manure, dig a well, tell a tall tale, brew mulberry brandy, graft apple trees, but please don't make me cook! I had a terrible time washing burnt frying pans; I hated the stove's guts, but I made exception after exception for Kalcho: I cooked oatmeal gruel, made sorrel and nettle soups, roasted peppers with garlic and herbs, simmered beef stews. He was slowly recovering from the foul illness and he held my hand all the time. The silly sweetheart thought he was giving me courage. I won't die on you, his fingers told me. I didn't think even about it. A guy didn't get better if he was lying in bed all day long. Come on, Kalcho, get up, man! Let's go for a walk. We ambled down to the riverbank, bristling with willows, which to me, looked like Kalcho's three-day beard.

"Never tell a guy you are his girl or he'll dump you first thing in the morning," Mom coached us, her three daughters. Every Thursday night, she came back home after she worked a 12-hour shift at the bakery, and commanded, "Take a seat, all three of you."

If we had to "take a seat", then Mom would haul us over the coals big and hard. Sara, I, even Luba who was a brainy thing since the day she learned to walk, poor Luba, each of us three hoped against hope that we'd be tasked with shelling peas, so Mom wouldn't lecture us about the way we should proceed if we fell for a young man in a big way.

"Never admit you agree to be his girl. Tell him, 'I'll think about it.'"

Okay, I think faster and smarter than most folks, so what should I do?

"Little Pirina, do you want to be my girl?" Kalcho asked even before we started ambling through the fields.

"I'll think about it," I said. On the other hand, why think so long, you fool, I said to myself. Within a fraction of a second, I shouted, "Yes, I want to be your girl. What a load of rubbish! I've been your girl since the minute I saw you in your mom's drugstore, your hair as shaggy as Gasho our dog's coat. Then I immediately asked myself whose girl I was going to be. Yours, Kalcho!"

§

At noon, the leaves of grass felt warm and cozy. I still hadn't seen the Black Sea beach. Only Sara, one of us three sisters, had swum in the salty water with the bigwig who fell for her. I honestly thought she had become a saint because she restored the poor devil to health. In token of his gratitude, he built a church for her and hung Sara's portrait on its wall. Luba and I had seen the sea only on TV.

"Pirina, I wish you'd stop blabbering on about the sea," Grandma Mariza instructed me before she boxed my ears for pilfering pears from her fruit-trees. "If this is where your shoe pinches, go sprawl out in the meadow and you'll be ok. The dew on the grass is our sea, Pirina. Poor me, I was taken in by Grandpa Matey's claims he'd fallen head over heels in love with me. He taught me where the sea in the village of Staro rose and roared, he and I took a bath in the dew together and after nine months Ivan, my eldest son, was born," concluded Grandma Mariza.

Early in the morning, even before the hens woke up and started squawking, I edged my way into the meadow behind the sunflower field, took off all my clothes and sank into the grass. I hoped it felt the same in the sea, but I knew I wasn't there. The dew was icy to the touch, and I coughed as powerfully as Marko, the mayor's donkey. Mom used to rake me over the coals before she gave me snake's milk tea to sip. It was the nastiest concoction ever!

Kalcho was still weak and I feared he wouldn't make it to the grass sea of Staro. The dew was as cold as a horseshoe in January, but my Kalcho not only made it, he didn't fall ill after we swam in the grass, didn't even sneeze.

"Let's go to your sister Sara," he said as he held my hand, eager to give me part of his strength. Just imagine, Kalcho giving *me* part of his strength! Slowly and happily as if I was a crybaby, he led me to Saint Sara's church.

They never locked this church because folks arrived at night, workers who had toiled and moiled at the construction sites or in the fields, shop assistants and waiters, tailors and seamstresses who urgently needed advice. At dusk, they knelt down before the Saint Sara icon and prayed, asking Sara for help. Rumor had it that at midnight she most generously helped boys and girls in love.

Late into the night, after the midnight news on TV, loners came, mostly men. It was funny if you looked at the shabby flowers they'd picked in the field. The guys put their ragged bunches in front of the icon and my sister Sara watched, smiling. At night, her eyes gave me words you could say only to Kalcho. Young girls came to Sara, too, as young as the little gypsy lass with the funny haircut and her ABC book. Every time, the kid left a crumpled sheet of paper with a couple of words printed in big block letters on it. Once, Sara showed me the little girl's note. The letters appeared smudged; the kid must have used an eraser or maybe her own spit to remove the mistakes. She had scribbled, "santa SARA FINDE a good mann for LUBA she must not be lonnely like me."

Times and again, I swept the floor of the church — for free — because I loved watching the icon, and I knew everything there was to know about Sara.

The street urchins looked around scared that somebody might notice that they went to talk to the saint. They were too young to ask her for help. Old women, their heads as gray as the sky in the evening, trudged to the church through the grass, their walking sticks as heavy as death. They left flowers and buns. Gypsy boys sneaked up behind the grandmas and polished off any good eats they could lay their hands on. They ate as rapidly as fire engulfs a heap of paper scraps, leaving a smell of soot in its wake.

Kalcho and I didn't have flowers, so we left blades of grass in front of Sara. Mom would chop off my head if I picked one of her peonies. I was sure Sara liked grass. She had accompanied me to the meadow; we swam together in the dew and Sara, happy as a magpie, looked for a four-leaved clover.

"Try to imagine the field is not full of grass, little Pirina," she said. "It's full of fish."

My sister Sara was the most beautiful girl I knew — they built a church for her and this was the right thing to do. However, she was a little silly, to tell you the truth. How come the leaves of grass were fish? They were not! Had someone ever heard that a cow would eat fish?

In the evenings, I stayed with Kalcho on his deathbed that had nothing to do with death anymore. I didn't have to give him more of my strength, he gave me some of his instead. The guy regularly ate a big bowl of chicken soup I cooked specially for him, gorged himself on pork lard, guzzled honey and custard cakes, drank raw goat milk. His hands that a month ago hung down like the string of a broken kite, now seemed to have live coals under the nails, which is to say they could not stay peacefully in the same place, not that I wanted them to!

Was it a week or a fortnight later, I saw a shadow in the street just under the window of Kalcho's room? I thought to myself, this must be the man from the post office as sad as a dried-up stream. The poor bugger had complained he had no one to talk to. Has the cat got your tongue, man, eh? Go to the church and tell Sara, "You see, Sara, I collect and deliver letters all day long — to the blonde girl and her big guy at the filling station, to the old man in the grocery store and his wife, Grandma Mariza's sister. I am all alone like a rusty rail. Please, Sara, do something. I'd like to find a woman. Please."

Sara is a sensible saint; I'd grant her that, she'll help the mailman, I thought. But she's too pretty, and this means trouble. She doesn't know how to be wise, poor Sara… Well, if a girl was wise, she'd keep her head in the books the way Luba did and wouldn't think of anything but paper and letters. I was sure Luba hadn't asked our sister, Saint Sara for help. Nor was she looking for a man. She'd be afraid even of a weakling like Kalcho. Weakling my foot! Ask me about him.

The shadow came up to the window and I saw it wasn't that tall guy with the bad stoop, the mailman. It was Yakob. He said, "Pirina, I'll give you money."

I kept silent, and his shadow got longer as it leapt towards me.

"My house and… the mountain will be in your name."

"No," I said.

This was the first time I had felt sorry for Yakob. The man looked like Martusha.

"Will you stay with this worm?" Yakob balled his hands into fists and didn't look like an old crone anymore. I remembered that a month ago I was scared to death his fist would catch me in the mouth and send me sprawling.

"If you say one more time he's a worm," I started evenly, "I'll set the dog on you."

The uninvited guest produced a gun I knew very well; he had leveled it against my forehead once. Then Kalcho, a tall guy that looked like a rope hanging from the roof of an unfinished house, scrambled to his feet and shouted, "Leave her alone!"

The top of my messy man's head barely reached Yakob's nose. This looked bad, indeed, but, on the other hand, it was awesome that the skin below Kalcho's stubble was pink. It was awesome, too, that I had given Kalcho my stubborn strength while we held hands. On the other hand, I knew how much it hurt if Yakob threw a punch at your nose.

At this point, Kamen the drunk hurtled past the drugstore.

"Mr. Yakob, you are an important man," said Kamen who every night shared his pillow with Koyna. He spoke evenly, not wheezing or gasping as usual. "You are an important man, but you are in my house. I'll shoot you if you keep on pestering my son."

I could not believe my ears. I didn't know Kalcho had become a son to this man so strongly and inseparably attached to brandy.

"Pirina, come with me," Yakob's voice repeated, his face a dead gray fireplace.

"No," I said.

The sun strode like a rooster across the sky, and the drunk who I had perceived to be quite a good-natured though hardly brainy man, produced a gun. Its barrel was as thin as a cat's tongue.

"Yakob, I told you. If you don't beat it, I'll shoot you," Uncle Kamen the drunk said evenly as he leveled the gun at the important man's forehead.

At that point, I caught hold of Kalcho's hand. I wanted to give him all the strength I had in my blood and bones, but I was already shaking and he, my messy darling, gave me his courage. I knew Yakob always carried his gun on him. At times, he pressed it against a woman's head or thrust it under her skirt for a change. I didn't know why I thought then and there I was ready to give my life for Kalcho. Yes, I would shed my blood for him.

"Come off it, you fool," Mom would thunder. "Give him your life and shed your blood for him, eh! Stupid nanny-goat! If you dote on this Kalcho guy, ok. Make it easy on yourself. Give birth to his children and live with him for sixty years. But why die for Kalcho? Live with him!"

I was sure that my sister Sara was looking at me from her icon in the nameless church. They said God dropped in every day to get some rest there. Sara was looking at me from her icon, a sly smile on her pretty face.

§

His hand was as thick as an old pillow: scarred and bruised, a dozen wounds, some still open, others stuffed with black mud; it could scare even a strong man. Reddish and deep gashes, plastered with dust and calluses, jutting out like horns amidst the raw skin, dominated the frightening landscape of his palms. His fingers were long and fat, his bony powerful knuckles seemed able to splinter a wooden door or crush a wine barrel like an egg. Even sandstones as brown as shoe soles split under the fury of his hand.

First, his knuckles grazed Luba's chin, then the man unclenched his fist and the bundle of muscles relaxed. The hand with the scars, gashes and bruises landed on her forehead and lingered there like a bloodhound that had picked up a trail.

"You aren't running a temperature," a gruff voice, all scars and bruises, and granite, lashed a volley of deafening words. Then the hand, peaceful and calm, caressed Luba's scared forehead, and the voice, towering as a mountain, suddenly dropped and using one thousandth of its energy, said, "You don't have a fever, Luba. It means you aren't sick. Come on. Get up."

"I will not come with you," Luba said. "Let me go, Kiro."

"Shut up," he snapped. "Stand up!"

Luba remained seated on the ground by the path, a thin bundle of bones in a faded blue coat, the feet hidden in a pair of frazzled flat shoes, an ABC book with all thirty letters of the Bulgarian alphabet, the commas, the hyphens, a picture of Red Riding Hood and the Big Bad Wolf in it.

"I know this fairytale," the giant said. "*Grandmother, what big teeth you have*! It's a pity I wasn't there! I'd have cut the fucking wolf's head off. I'd have shoved it up his ass. Stand up."

"No."

Kiro touched her forehead one more time just in case. She wasn't running a fever, he was sure now.

"I don't want to beat you, girl. Don't make me. Come on."

"No."

He grabbed her around the waist, slung her over his shoulder and stomped off down the path.

"I'll take you to your sister's church," the man thundered. "You'll sit in a chair under her icon for a day. I'll lock and bolt the church door. No man or woman will set foot near Sara while you're there. I won't let anybody get a look. You'll be the only one in there. You'll wait near Sara's icon until love gets the better of you."

"No," the faded blue coat breathed. "No," said the frayed flat shoes.

"Love got the better of me," Kiro said, "because I always took the short-cut through the hill, fathead that I am! I thought I wouldn't have to trudge all the way up the valley road. How could I know it was your sister's place? This land is dangerous, mark my words! I passed by Sara's church, and look at me now. I'm not all there. Everywhere I look I see you. Honestly. I look at Arda, you know her, Grandma Mariza's eldest granddaughter, but I don't see Arda, I see you. I look at the pickup truck, its tires brand new, and a crate of red peppers on the backseat. I don't see a crate of red peppers. I see you. Idiot! Kiro, you're an idiot, I say to myself. The world is teeming with pretty women. They are all over the place. How come you were taken with this worm Luba? This worm has no curves and no ass. That's what I'm thinking about in my brain, but I have no brain anymore. You are in my head and you are everywhere," the colossus complained.

Kiro and Luba walked down the path, and as they approached the church, they passed by a bog.

"You know what, Luba? It's very dangerous to grab a handful of cattails if they are ripe. Their fluffy seeds get in your ears and make you deaf like a lamppost. I went deaf like a lamppost and they cut my ear. Here, have a look at the scar."

Luba didn't look up and didn't say anything.

"Luba, it feels so good talking to you. Hey, no one can listen to me the way you do. I want you to know this. Dudes say, 'Kiro, the stupid son of a bitch, is as dumb as a brick. Can't put two and two together.' But I can put two and two together, Luba, I can put ten thousand and ten thousand together and I'd be wanting some more of it. Honestly," he plucked a cattail and said, "Here, take this thing."

Luba obeyed, but the hulking man suddenly snatched the cattail from her hand. "No, stop! You'll get fluff stuck in your ear and they'll have to split your head open. You're thin like a frog, have to stand twice to make a shadow. Doc Stoim is a butcher. He splits your head open, you snuff it in the operating room and that's it. Mom says I was going to snuff it when I was a boy. I'm sure you'll snuff it too, look at you. You weigh as much as my elbow," the man declared as he hurled the cattail into the mud half a mile away from her.

In the middle of the bog, a tiny sliver of the moon shone — but it was not the daughter of that thick full moon, the old grandma of the stars, no! The old grandmas sat on the bench in front of the town hall in Staro, their ears hungry for the latest gossip: who was about to kick the bucket, and when would they bury the drinking wretch? No! A flake of the small moon gleamed thinly, a goat horn full of silver that made you speechless with joy. Perhaps it really was a wild goat, which had climbed to the sky and was jumping from cloud to cloud. Was this pretty moon glowing amidst the fat brown cigars of the cattails? No, it wasn't. It was a water lily.

"Can you see that thing over there?" Kiro asked as his forefinger, as big as a lamppost, pointed at the flower.

"Yes," Luba said.

Kiro reached to pluck the lily, but his hand could not touch its blossom. Two more flakes of the moon horn, their thin leaves drops of gold among the cattails, glittered on the soft wet ground. Wasting no time, Kiro threw himself over the mud, his chest puffing out, his heels pressing the hard shore, his fists grabbing at the few square inches of firm soil on the tiny island as his massive body became a bridge over the narrow marsh.

"Walk on me. Go pluck one of these," he told Luba.

She looked around, her blue coat shuddered, hesitating, breaking into a sweat below the collar. At last, Luba took off her faded canvas shoes and set out on her precarious journey. She stepped on one muscular calf first, then on the gigantic thigh; somewhere above the kidney area she steadied her posture against the wind, the silvery flowers a pool of soft anxiety in front of her. Luba bent down and looked at the three lilies. The biggest one looked like a baby's face: beaming and glowing, a small boat in the marsh, a light-house of bright gold for bugs and dragonflies. She didn't pick the big flower — one shouldn't plunder the best thing the narrow marsh had given birth to; her fingers touched the smallest lily as round as a beer cap. A gleaming handful of clouds, a speck of the sky, water that had sprouted leaves, that was what Luba saw. She didn't pick it. She slowly turned around, stepped on the left thigh of steel, then on the other, balanced her weight on the calves and made a little leap, landing on firm ground. It was hard to believe Kiro was able to tighten his muscles of iron, bend his chest and jump. He did it. What his shoulders and his shirt were up to would remain a mystery. His body soared above the marsh, flew off like enormous catfish as if he wanted to dive into the sun, then his muscles crackled again and flexed as he made a crash-landing. This man was a stone driven into the wet land next to Luba and the flower.

"Yeah, it's white.. and you didn't pick it." He ascertained the fact with a grunt, then carefully, his forefinger as slow as a metal detector, traced the curve of Luba's neck. It was a gentle curve like the trunk of his glass elephant. His dad bought him this toy a century ago. Kiro had squeezed the thing as he tried to see if the animal would squeal. It didn't; the glass broke to pieces, damn it! That was the reason why the big man touched the curve of her neck with the tip of his fingernail very carefully indeed. It was true that he enjoyed gnawing at his nails while he thought about something serious. His bitten and chewed fingertip urged the girl to make a decision.

"Come on, Luba," he said. "Tell me!"

"No," she said.

"You'll see, girl! If you stay with your sister's icon in the church, you'll start loving me. Honestly. I'm not lying to you. I don't care about lies and stuff. Love comes to you. Love doesn't care if you want it or not. This place is funny, if you know what I mean, and I mean this church. I took a shortcut, all the time I passed by your sister's church, and look at me now. I'm bumping around everywhere as if I'm blind. I'm blind without you. I'm telling you the truth. I don't know where I'm going, I don't know who I'll have to beat up next. I forget to drink water and I don't know if I've eaten my lunch. Time drags. Nothing ever goes right for me." For Kiro, babbling on felt like home. He'd kept his mouth shut all his life.

Every time he'd asked his mom a question, she smacked him in the face or boxed his ears. If he muttered a thing or complained, his dad snarled so viciously at him that Kiro wetted his pants a number of times. This was the reason his parents took him to Koyna the druggist. She always gave him a green pill. I spit on your pills, woman, Kiro told her. He went on wetting his pants every time he looked at his father even if old Dimitar didn't snarl at all. His dad, an old roving eye, fell for women, and this was all right, Kiro was sure of it, but his mom didn't think so. She hauled the old grouch hard over the coals after he chased a skirt or a petticoat. These two constantly fought. Kiro wondered who was bigger and heavier, his mom or his old man. Yea, Dosta was shorter than Dimitar by a head and a half, but if she hit the roof on account of the skirts and petticoats, the woman fumed and towered over his dad, often hitting him with a poker. Old Dimitar hated it when someone annoyed him, so he thrashed her with whatever came handy. If Kiro happened to blurt out a word, or, God forbid, fidgeted nervously between his mom's curses, both his parents fixed their eyes on him. One, usually his mom, boxed his ears, or his dad bludgeoned him with a broom.

The other kids kept a wide berth from Kiro. Whenever they noticed his hulking form, they spat on their chests to keep their courage up. He had taught them to bow down before him and they did it. But how could you be friends with a boy who kissed the shadow your ass cast, one who was scared to look you in the face? No way! The girls bowed down before Kiro too. He kissed them, or often didn't even bother to — why waste time and energy? He went straight ahead. He had broken the chicks in; if I look at you, I want no pants on you. Do I make myself clear? Well, how could you talk to a woman who first bowed before you, didn't even kiss you and went straight ahead? Could you tell her that all your life you'd been looking for a girl to listen to what you said? You wanted a field and a tractor, but not a field as big as a tablecloth, no sir. Kiro wanted land, rich, open and fat, a field that reached the hill, a plot as endless as Yakob's, but not one encircled by a moat and a stone wall. Yakob's wall looked like Emperor Trajan's fortress.

Miss Petrova had taken all her geography students, including Kiro, to Ihtiman to see it. Kiro liked the menacing building so much that five consecutive years, on Christmas Eve, he asked Santa for one and the same thing, "Santa, give me Trajan's Fortress!" Santa was a stingy guy and gave him nothing.

Now, Kiro wanted land as strong as Trajan's fortress, a tractor to plow it and wheat to sow on his share. Long ago, when he was a little kid, Miss Petrova took them to the Danube Plain. The Danube Plain was big, wheat and winds as far as the eye could see. The stalks towered over him, yellow ears of wheat were everywhere, behind him, in front of him, no end, and no shore in sight. Kiro wanted a plain like that, a vast prairie. He wanted to fire up the tractor and not beat common folks to death the way Yakob ordered him. Well, what could a guy do if he didn't get any other job, but beating other guys to death? Why talk about the Danube Plain at all if you lived in this rocky wasteland? Here, even mud was made of stones, and you found more moles than soil. You saw stones where guys' faces should be.

"I want the Danube Plain," Kiro blurted out. "And I want Trojan's Fortress."

Then he told Luba that he wanted a tractor, that he could take apart the engine piece by piece. He'd been restless at school, *Professional School for Cooks in Pernik, you know it, Luba, they call it The Soup.* He played hooky most afternoons and beat up the mechanics at Happy Repair Car Service for the sport of it. The Happy place was where they repaired tractors. Kiro punched the mechanics, week in, week out, knocked out a tooth or two, threw them out of "the premises" and took to removing the bolts from the newest tractor. Kiro liked one of the mechanics, a guy as old as the railroad track, hunched shoulders, no face, all furrows and wrinkles, stooping all over the place, a tobacco-pipe in his mouth. If you struck at a man like that, he'd give up the ghost before you hit him. He didn't bow before Kiro's shadow, he took a couple of steps back as he pointed to the tractor.

"This is the carburetor, kid. They call this thing a fuel pump. That box over there is the battery."

On the day the old mechanic died, Kiro ran a temperature, on the following day he ran a higher temperature, and it seemed his disease had no end. His old man and his mom were pissed off with him over his heart. It refused to beat. Koyna came over to treat the boy, all her medicines and pills in a bag as big as a bus. Her pills were no good. Now again, like ten years ago when he wetted his pants every time his dad glanced at him, especially if his mom suspected a woman was involved, things with Kiro went from bad to worse. Koyna, all her knowledge, herbs, treatment and medications couldn't cure him.

It was Grandma Mariza who helped him get on his feet when he was a boy. She chucked fifty cents on the ground and said, "Step on the coin, Kiro. Now, spit on it," then she wailed one of her nasty gypsy songs. You couldn't hear a word about men or beasts in her song, just mumbling, hemming and hawing — that was all. After the twenty-first hemming and hawing, Grandma Mariza spread red wine on Kiro's forehead and said, "Kid, you will not wet your pants anymore. You're not running a temperature and you won't be running one in years. Even if your old man hits you in the ribs with an iron bar, you will not wet your pants!"

Kiro wept and lo and behold! He stopped wetting his jeans and sheets on the following day.

…The old mechanic died and Kiro didn't attend his funeral. His mom didn't allow him to.

"You won't go bury this scoundrel in the churchyard," she said through her teeth. "Everybody will jeer at my family if you do. I hate the wretch's guts. His wife jilted him. His sons walked out on him, and they did right!"

Only Grandma Mariza and her granddaughters — the youngest a new-born infant, the eldest toiling and moiling at her ABC book — attended the funeral. Koyna's drunk, a chip on his shoulder, wouldn't stay out of anything, and trudged to the memorial service through the bone-dry grass.

"This idiot has made Koyna a laughingstock," Kiro's mother commented. "She goes and thinks she has a man under her roof. Man my foot! A wretch is all she has. Why? Look at her — she's a woman every inch of her, not scrawny, not paunchy, just a lady like me and my sister, that's what Koyna is! I can't find any fault with her drugstore either. We're still alive in this backwater village only because she's always stepped in. How can she put up with that drunken pig I wonder? A screw must've come loose in her head, or a part of her brain has turned sour, but you can't see it with your eyes." His mom spoke as she kept on milking the cow, glancing at Kiro. Of late, she had learned to stare at him the way his dad did, both frostily and fretfully, however, Grandma Mariza had already said her son wouldn't wet his pants. "If you dare go bury this crook in the churchyard, Kiro, I'll crush your skull like a nut. Do I make myself clear?"

Kiro didn't go anywhere. An hour later, he felt like biting his own head off. He rushed to the car service and found no one there. The mechanics he'd often beaten and pelted with rocks and bottles had vanished, or were probably drinking in The Cat. The big man retraced his steps back home and ran a temperature. Koyna still had her drunk under her roof and didn't make a secret of the fact he spent the night in her room. Even at Easter time she went to church with him, resting her head on his shoulder, not that there was much shoulder to speak of: all blotchy skin and bones. His sweater hung like an obituary note from his shoulder blade. The startling news, a show that was a real kick in the pants, featured Koyna and her drunk, walking hand in hand like kindergarten children, to the church with the Sara icon in it. The two of them planted themselves squarely in front of Saint Sara, keeping mum, now squinting at Sara, now exchanging glances. Kiro kept watch over them for ten minutes and could hardly believe his eyes.

Yes, there must be a screw loose somewhere in Koyna's head, one you couldn't see no matter how hard you looked. Perhaps only Saint Sara noticed it. She — one might rightly wonder if the poor girl had taken leave of her senses — gave a hand to any dull-witted boozer that couldn't get his bearings. There were many stupid folks in these parts, oodles of them, as thick as blackberries. They built Sara a church, hoping she'd help the weak, and the ones that had gone soft in the head. Guys and girls trickled into the church day and night, their faces hesitant yet glowing like glasses of expensive wine. Kiro had overheard a crowd talking about a young Italian couple; the kids had arrived here from Padua or somewhere. Greek couples went to Sara's church too, an old man and his missus, a Romanian young man and his Bulgarian girlfriend. At that point, Kiro got confused. He was sure Sara didn't speak Romanian or Greek. Perhaps she could get to the bottom of what the Italians told her; Italians talked pretty much with their hands like Bulgarians, but what about the Romanians? As luck would have it, a Greek couple, some dude and his woman, both young like green beans, got close to Kiro's jeep and shouted, "Bonjour, bonjour!"

Oh, come off it.

What was the Bulgarian for *Bonjour,* eh? Was it "I'll kick the shit out of you," or was it a worse word? However, the Greek dude and his girl were all smiles, both of them crazy as brushes, until finally the Greek chick said, "*Santa Sara! Santa Sara!*" At that point, it dawned on Kiro they were looking for the church the bigwig had built for Luba's sister.

"Follow your nose and keep walking for half an hour, then make a right turn and keep walking in a straight line. You'll be in front of the church soon enough." Kiro grasped what these loony Greeks wanted to know because he was smart. He was intelligent all right, although Miss Petrova's hair — Petrova, their Bulgarian teacher was an oddball, right? — turned gray within a month because Kiro couldn't say a word about some Spanish crackpot called Don Quixote. It was true Real Madrid won the 2016 FIFA Club Soccer World Cup. So what? They didn't have plum trees in Spain. It was also true that no plum trees grew in his grandma's backyard. Plenty of linden trees did, but you couldn't make brandy from linden blossoms.

Kiro's old man was a brainy brewer and a smart thinker, Kiro'd give him that. When his first and only son Kiro was born, his dad cut down the massive lindens and planted plum trees. Blue silver plums, El Dorados, Moyer plums, Greengages and Mirabelles, Black Amber plums, loads of them did father and son pick in the autumn. Their backyard was worth a fortune. In these parts, every living soul turned plums into plum brandy! Didn't his Bulgarian teacher know this? Even toddlers wouldn't care for linden tea. Okay, long story short: Miss Petrova's hair turned gray. Kiro had to repeat the 9th grade a couple of times; at long last he reached an agreement with Petrova, and read who Miguel de Cervantes, the crazy Spaniard, was. It turned out Don Quixote wasn't a soccer player as Kiro had believed. This Miguel guy, the son of a bitch, wrote a mean book, a huge pack of lies, about that Quixote dude. Kiro felt so sorry for the poor Don. If Kiro lived somewhere near Spain, the Don might've been his pal. Ok, at the end of the day, Kiro passed his literature exam and moved on to 10th grade.

However, he was speaking of something else: after the old mechanic breathed his last, Kiro had run a temperature for two weeks. The skinny old man was Kiro's only friend. Koyna hoisted the white flag, she was no good at healing Kiro, she said. Grandma Mariza was immediately sent for.

"What has happened to you, Kiro boy?" the old woman asked. "How come you fell ill, son? Tell me what you think about it."

He told her about the carburetor, the battery, the spark plug, he told her about the fuel and the way the old mechanic had explained to him: this is the engine. See how we'll take it apart. That's the accelerator pedal. It controls the throttle valve, ok?

He told Grandma Mariza everything; the old wrinkled darling had never boxed his ears, had never given him the evil eye. She hadn't scared him into rushing to the bathroom to take a leak. Kiro was speaking to Luba like that now, shared with her all the silly thoughts that crossed his mind, even the bad thoughts, which buffeted and poisoned him. He kept no secrets from her. His own mulishness and stupidity were to blame. Why should he take a shortcut home — like a bull? Kiro clumped up the hill in his boots and passed near the place where the rich fool from Sofia had built Sara a church. As a result of this, love nested in Kiro's head. Love drove him to panic and ruined him at the end of the day.

How could he be so dumb, damn it! It was as clear as a glass of brandy! Grandma Mariza lived not far from Sara's church; this explained why she was a good hand at brewing cures and making the sick folks as good as new, strong as stone fireplaces, too.

…He ran a temperature for twenty days after the old mechanic's funeral. Dry mouth and dry eyes, tired all the time… Kiro'd rather cash in his chips, honestly. At a certain point, Grandma Mariza cleared her throat as she stomped into his sickroom. The old darling produced fifty cents, gave him the coin and ordered, "Step on it, man. Now!"

Then she broke into that song of hers that had no tune in it, her voice thick with devils and saints, making your flesh crawl like a nest of ants. At some point she spoke to him, "You've lost an old friend, Kiro, and that's why your eyelids are drooping, and you're still pining away. Why don't you have any other friends, man? Listen to me. You must find a new friend." She produced another fifty cents. "Step on this coin, too, man. Now."

She hummed, wailed and howled for about an hour.

His dad paced up and down behind the sickroom window, swearing under his nose, fearful the sound of his voice could frighten the old gypsy crone. Kiro's mom bounded and jigged around her husband, and Kiro thought she was three heads taller than his old man. This could mean only one thing: his mom was scared stiff. The woman managed to keep her mouth shut even though she bit her lip so savagely it seemed she was planning to eat it. She paced up and down too, her big hand clutching the poker. Of late, the woman wouldn't leave their house unarmed, a spade, a poker or an air-pistol being her preferred weapons. The town's teeming with thieves, she said. Kiro was a little frightened by his disease. Oh, don't give me that! He was thoroughly frightened. Fear as powerful as a dust devil wrapped his heart as Grandma Mariza crooned her Mother Mary song, which didn't have anything, words or tune, in the red hot afternoon. The sun was a big red ball that angels and devils used for their world soccer championship in the sky.

Grandma Mariza didn't tremble or shudder. His mom's bitten lips, the poker in the woman's hand and his dad's curses failed to impress her. Kiro watched and slowly calmed down. An hour after midnight, he stopped sweating, his temperature went down and he said to Grandma Mariza, "Grandma Mariza, I'm hungry. Give me bread."

"Dosta, hey, hurry up, give the boy a loaf of bread," the old woman shouted, strong and beautiful, although the lines on her face were more numerous than the hairs on her head, and the stiff gray bristle that covered her skull was as thick as the grass in the field. Like a shoe brush was old Grandma Mariza's hair, and the wrinkles on her face were deeper than the gutters at the edge of the road.

His mom brought two loaves of bread and Kiro, who for three weeks had refused to put the tiniest bit of roasted lamb in his mouth, now tore off a chunk of bread and wolfed it down as if he'd never seen bread before. He scarfed the two loaves down within five minutes and shouted, "Mom, I'm still hungry!"

This time, his dad, mean old Dimitar, was quicker than his mom. The man, as impatient as a volcano, brought a massive platter of beefsteaks, smoked salmon and garlic they'd kept for the sick lad — the family saw luxury food like this at Christmas time. The people under the roof of this house were tough like the concrete columns of City Hall because of the lentil soups they constantly ate. His dad said it was more than mere chance that their place used to be army barracks where soldiers lived. Why should Kiro gorge himself on pork cracklings, have high blood pressure and give himself a heart attack? To make the neighbors happy? No, thanks! One would better pig out on lettuce. Kiro didn't think so. He gobbled up all the roasted lamb, bolted down the beefsteaks, guzzled four pints of linden tea and a pint of mineral water. The young man had refused point-blank to drink anything while he lay sick in bed, sweating and choking. It was the first time that Kiro had seen his father grin. No, Dimitar wasn't grinning; an endless smile had split his face in two. His dad came over, patted Kiro's shoulder and said, "I'm glad you are well. You scared the pants off of me, kid."

The big man squatted down, rearranged the boards under the cupboard, and produced a bundle of lev bills. In fact, it wasn't much of a bundle to speak of, just four fifty lev bills. He grabbed at a bill, trembling the way a fisherman's fingers shook when a huge trout had bitten the hook. After a while, his dad's hand stopped hesitating and extracted three bills from the wad.

"Take these," he said to Grandma Mariza. "Thanks a bunch. Thanks loads, old woman."

Kiro finally plucked up courage, so much of it, he feared he'd make the room burst.

"I… I… I want to ask Grandma Mariza a question in private."

Both his mom and his old man stared at Kiro as though roaring flames were burning on their heads.

"What do you want to know from her?" his mom said, pushing hard.

"Let the kid ask whatever he wants," his old man grumbled. "Get out of the room, woman."

When Kiro was left alone with old Mariza's wrinkles and lines, he was afraid to look her in the eyes. Finally he said, "Grandma Mariza, cast a spell. I want a girl to fall in love with me."

"Which girl?" the black lines asked, deep and heavy with nagging suspicion.

Kiro thought for an age before he spoke. He had to grasp his one chance, *it's now or in the netherworld* as his only friend, the mechanic used to say, may God rest his soul and may the mud above his coffin weigh lightly on his chest.

"Luba." Kiro breathed so thinly that Mariza made him repeat the name. After she heard it, her big mouth first curved into a smile, then the old crone burst out laughing, her teacup shaking in her hand and spilling tea on her crumpled skirt. All her wrinkles stretched like wires through which brandy flowed instead of electricity.

"You said Luba, didn't you?" she almost split her sides with laughter, her wrinkles clang-clanging like the wheels of the express train to Athens. "My goodness! God, come and take a look at this guy here. O, my God. Come running here!" Finally, she rummaged in her sleeve, produced a crumpled handkerchief, carefully unfolded it, glanced at the bills in her hand and gave him ten levs. "This is Luba, son. Give it to her and she'll be yours."

Kiro didn't believe her, by no means, yet he pocketed the money.

"Thanks a bunch," he said exactly the way his father had done, although he didn't feel like thanking the old woman.

"I found the right cure for your fever. It cost me fifty cents," the old goose declared firmly. "You know how much I gave you for that girl. Ten levs! She costs ten million. Do I make myself clear, Kiro?"

"O, much more than ten million," he muttered.

… Kiro watched Luba as she looked at the flower, the smallest of the three. He couldn't make heads or tails out of it; why should she choose the shabbiest one, eh? She must have gone around the bend, he thought, but she… she was a peach. A peach and a summer field Luba was. She listened to his twaddle so intently as if Kiro wasn't talking gibberish. She was as thin as the wild sunflower by the path, even thinner, and he had to be careful not to break her ribs. Ribs broke easily and took a long while to heal. Kiro carried *that* ten lev bill on him, day and night. He bought a leather wallet from Sofia especially for it.

"Grandma Mariza cured my fever as I lay dying," Kiro informed Luba and told her about the three fifty lev bills that his father gave Mariza, then went on telling her how the old woman grinned, and her wrinkles jingled like brass bracelets.

Luba listened to him. He noticed her smiling, but wasn't quite sure if it was a smile on her lips, or the shadow of the young oak tree that knitted its branches together just to pull the wool over his eyes. Kiro bent closer to her, and this time he was sure: Luba was smiling. She was beaming. She didn't have any wrinkles that could jingle like brass bracelets, but she did have eyebrows, and they lifted in surprise.

"Thanks," Kiro mumbled huskily. "Thanks a bunch, Luba."

Then he said quietly, if the big voice, bursting out of his mouth could speak quietly at all, "Let's go to your sister's church. You'll sit down under her icon, and I'll stand guard at the door. I won't let anybody from Greece, Germany or Bucharest enter the church. You will stay with your sister, okay? She'll teach you. She knows. Love is a handful of lentils, as simple as that. You're so smart, you'll soon get the hang of it. I learned it the hard way. You'll learn it ten times faster than me. I took a shortcut across the hill, you know. It never occurred to me this was your sister Sara's place..."

You couldn't tell for sure. You were off on the wrong track: she wasn't smiling. It was the shadow of the small oak tree, bending before the wind, unable to put its foot down, "You can't push me around, idiotic wind. Go blow your stack somewhere else. Let me cast my shadow for the pretty girl as long as I please." It seemed the small oak had done the right thing: it had sent the wind packing. Luba *was* smiling. There could be no doubt about it now.

"Let's go to your sister's church," Kiro said. He thought he spoke quietly, but both the half-deaf old wives in Staro and the passengers on the express train to Athens heard what he was speaking. "It's a funny place, this church," he went on. "No kidding, you came down on me like a ton of live coals. Maybe I am crazy, Luba. I fell hard for you. Can you beat it? It feels good to look at you. She's scrawny, I say to myself. I have to give her something to eat. I could bruise her ribs. A bruised rib hurts a lot. You know what? I'll watch out for you, Luba. Don't break her ribs, I say to myself. Your bones are thinner than toothpicks. Sorry, I didn't mean to insult you, you know."

Her smile was broader that the railway track to Athens, bigger than the wheat field which Kiro had dreamed about. He'd buy a tractor, a small and cheap one first. And I'll buy you a wagonload of books, what do you say, Luba? You'll become a clever woman like Miss Petrova. Just tell me you want a book and you'll have it. Honestly. You can count on me.

"Let's go to your sister's church."

Luba didn't say yes, but she stood up and ran away from the narrow marsh, taking her faded coat and frayed shoes with her.

"Luba, wait," Kiro yelled. "Wait for me."

He lifted her in his arms as if the girl weighed less than a handful of wheat. He was strong and he knew what he wanted, Luba and a sunny field. He carried her with utmost care, scared he might bruise her ribs. As thin as cobweb were her bones, so he hesitated.

"I'll carry you all the way, Luba. We'll get there quickly," Kiro said.

In front of him, the stones clattered; at that moment the express train from Sofia thundered along the rails.

In the Church of Saint Sara, a woman was kneeling in front of the icon. The intruder had managed to sneak in through the unlocked door. Kiro stared at her, fuming. Then he recognized her: Miss Petrova. Years ago, Miss Petrova's hair turned gray because he hadn't heard about a guy called Don. Was his family name Quitexe, Quixote? Yes, the woman was Miss Petrova.

She had died her hair dark brown.

§

Vasil coughed so violently that his wife Slava got frightened. *His heart will burst in his chest. What shall I do?* The truth was the woman wasn't asking what she was going to do. She knew. Slava, as small as a cherry stone, rushed to Koyna's drugstore.

"Koyna, Vasil has a fever. He's burning," she said. "He's been coughing badly for days. Give me something to help him, please."

Koyna cast her eyes over the shelves, fished out a box, then another, bigger one and gave it to the woman.

"No, no, come to my place," Slava said. "Let's rub him with your snake ointment."

"The snake mixture is not a cough remedy. We need coltsfoot," Koyna said as she searched through a drawer, pulled out a second, bigger box, took something from it, opened a small chest, produced yellow dry grass, then mixed the herbs in a wooden bowl. She crushed the grass with a pestle and poured some liquid, transparent like brandy onto it. The thing smelled like rotten meat.

"The mixture reeks," Koyna said reassuringly. "It helps to bring down the fever, though."

The two women pushed through the coarse thorns, the field in front of them bigger than the clods. The month of July had been a bit out to lunch lately; in the mornings, the heat seared your skin, in the afternoons, it rained pitchforks and, before you turned the corner, it was hailing outside. A rolling wave of slush crashed against the village of Staro. Koyna went from house to house, her ugly-smelling drugs in hand, and even the wind that came from the steep slope of Bare Hill stank of the cough remedy. The donkeys tethered to posts in the field were badly affected by the stench. Koyna's cough medicine smelled rotten to the cows, too. The beasts mooed chaotically and their eyes, usually meek and friendly, were now full of hurricanes. It was evident they we looking for a guy or two to jab their horns into.

Slava and Koyna passed by Saint Sara Church. The two neighbors didn't look inside, but they saw — it caught one's eye immediately — the thin, tall woman, her brown hair dye gone wrong, the hair roots on her head gray like asphalt driveway. Slava pursed her lips. Koyna looked away.

"I feel sorry for her," Slava blurted out. "She's all alone. She and Vasil, you know…"

"I know," Koyna said.

"Something happened to Vasil. I was ready to break up with him… put a stop to the family, you know. I'd snap out of it. 'Listen what, Vasil,' I told him. 'You lost your heart to someone. I understand. Go to her. One can't live without a heart,'" Slava shrugged her shoulders. "I packed his suitcase, Koyna. I ironed his shirts. He has two good shirts and a suit, an old good one. We kept these for our daughters' weddings, but… 'I washed your clothes and ironed them, Vasil,' I told him. 'The woman's waiting for you.' I watch her hang about in the field, Koyna. It hurts me. In the beginning, she loitered by the river, then loafed around in the cherry orchard not far from our house. She looked very thin to me. Finally, she passed along our street, must've just dyed her hair brown, sad brown… Vasil's hair is the color of burnt lime, not a single black hair on his head, not even a gray one. I told him, 'I hate you sinking fast like this. Go to her. You'll set me free, Vasil, you know.' I'm not that old, and I've lost only one tooth so far. If I put white clay and goat milk on my mug, I'll get rid of the deepest wrinkles. I'll look for some other guy. I can't lift the water pump and carry it to the well by myself. How will I water the pepper plants, if I don't have someone to give me a hand? You know how it is, Koyna."

"I know, Slava," the druggist said.

"I reckoned I'd go look for a job in Dupni or even in Spain. A cleaning woman in an office… I can work as a babysitter or I can look after an old woman. Folks in Dupni are wallowing in money, and every day, many babies are born there. I know a couple of well-to-do gypsy families, kind guys. Maybe they'll hire me to feed and wash their kids. I'll teach them to speak Bulgarian and I'll keep them clean the way I kept my own kids." Slava spat into the grass like a trooper and swore like a trooper as well. "Someday, a down-and-out loser like the drunk you sheltered, Koyna, will fall for me. I'll let him stay. What else can I do? I have to weed the peppers, dig the strawberries, and water the raspberries. I have to lug the water from the well…"

"A woman can't manage alone. It's hard to feed the kids," the druggist said.

"Oh, she'll be all right, but it is better for her if she has someone to have words with from time to time. If you don't fight, you can scratch his back for him. You pull the old newspaper out of his grip when he falls asleep. You ladle his soup into the deepest bowl, so you won't have to run twice to the pot on the stove."

"Maybe the guy you'll take in won't have a lame leg."

"I'd rather he had," Slava said. "I've gotten used to it, you know. He won't ramble around the hill when he gets drunk. He'll be scared of falling and breaking his head. If the guy doesn't limp, he'll go to the field after he gets tanked up. Any thief will rob him blind."

"Yes, that's right," Koyna agreed.

"I don't have a clue what went wrong," Slava went on. "The poor bugger from Sofia built Sara a church. I don't know what she's done to him. I asked her about it, Koyna, I did, honestly. She wouldn't tell me. She turned six, and the boys went crazy about her. She was no good at studying lessons. Heap of bad grades… the stick I beat her with broke, you know."

"I know," Koyna nodded. "You took her to me and I dressed her wounds."

"You are good at dressing wounds, Koyna. I was sure there was something special in the ointment you rubbed into her skin… which explains why they painted her face on the icon… all these crazy artists… I wonder how much the foreigner forked out on the church. A million? The poor bugger put a lightning rod on its roof."

"He must have spent more than a million," Koyna said, looking uncertainly at her feet.

"You are bad at figuring out how much things cost, Koyna, more than bad! You have no head for figures! When I paid you for the cough medicines, I gave you two or three levs less than they cost. I did it on purpose, you know, checking to see how you were coping with calculations. You couldn't cope at all."

"I could, but I thought you didn't have enough money."

"I said to myself, 'Slava, if you cheat Koyna out of her money, you are cheating God.' To be honest, I don't really know if God is in heaven, or there is no God at all. I haven't seen Him, but you're in front of my eyes, Koyna. 'When you steal money from our druggist, it's like you undress a newborn baby and throw her into a snow bank. That's what you did, Slava.' Then I said to myself again, 'Koyna is a silly woman, it's true. A snotty brat can fool her about anything.' For example, Kamen the drunk, has you turned around his finger, Koyna. I hate to say it, but it's true."

The druggist smiled. Grandma Mariza kept throwing this in her face, too, but one day the old woman whispered in her ear, "It's good when someone in your house loves you, woman."

Neighbors advised Koyna, "Kick him out, the sooner the better!"

Kamen was in the habit of producing a gun, an empty World War II Luger that used to belong to his grandfather, a corporal, 4th Sofia Infantry Regiment of the Bulgarian army. The drunk frightened the hell out of the village kids. What was the motive behind this load of nonsense? Well, Koyna would take a short nap after lunch, and the drunk didn't allow the cheeky teens to wake her up, harping on about blisters, draining pus and whooping cough. They could wait half an hour, couldn't they?

Koyna refused to kick the drunk out of her house. He called Kalcho "my son." His drunk eyes said it, his ancient gun said it and his blood said it, too, when a blood transfusion was given to the lad. On the other hand, Kamen got juiced up once a month.

"Today I'll be boozing it up, Koyna," he'd say to the woman. "My daughter has become a wolf. I feel bad for her."

He went to The Cat and drank all night. In the morning, Koyna found him lying prostrate on her rug. Kamen wouldn't let anybody touch that rug, neither would he swap it for anything in the world. Koyna was full of pity for the man. He was probably cold, so she left a comforter for him at the door. The brandy he had downed had toughened him up, but it was fortunate that when Kalcho woke up at night, he covered the drunk with his late father's shabby overcoat. Kalcho's dad was called Metodi. Poor

Metodi, God rest his soul. May he find peace and good brandy at God's honest table!

"That oddball — I don't care if he comes from Sofia or from a freaking rich city in the UK — after this blockhead went and built Sara a church," Slava went on, "all the time I had my doubts, gnawing a hole in my stomach. Is this a church in the first place? One day Vasil said, 'Slava, let's go meet up with God.' How come, man? You're not all there. It's all wrong. 'It's not,' he insisted. You know Vasil. How could I make this stubborn old man see sense? Why does he read all these newspapers if he can't explain himself to you? We went to the church and stood under the icon. The girl on the picture looked like Sara the way one saucer of the set resembles the next one. My firstborn daughter was looking at me out of the icon, Koyna. It felt good. I calmed down a bit. I would be years before I've paid off my water pump loan, I know, but Sara was looking at me. She was looking at me, and I forgot about the pump and the loan. You know her. She was a bonny bouncing baby. It was autumn, it was raining. She was running a fever in the dead of night. You, Koyna, rubbed snake's milk into her muscles… Perhaps you remember, eh? At the end of the school year, I went and collected my kids' school certificates. They were pretty girls, the three of them".

The druggist nodded.

"I tell you, Koyna, Sara's eyes helped me heave a sigh of relief," Slava went on. "At a certain point, I looked up and couldn't believe what I saw. Vasil was crying, I tell you the truth. What's wrong with him? I thought to myself. I was scared stiff! He must've taken wrong heart pills. Now, he was in for a heart attack. Or was it a brain stroke? Your teas aren't good for healing strokes, are they? Grandma Mariza has cured brain stokes only three times so far. I know many guys who kicked the bucket and were all dead like poisoned cats. I had the jitters and hated it. Vasil grabbed my hand. He kissed my hand, woman. He did it. I froze in my tracks. He's going to die, I thought. That's the end. He slowly said, 'Slava…. Forgive me.'"

When we returned home, Vasil opened the suitcase into which I'd crammed his two clean shirts, his black trousers and the jacket of his only suit. He hung his clothes back in the old closet where I had stored them for years. This was all. He didn't say a word about the brown-haired woman… about Petrova, you know. That day, she, too, prayed to our daughter's icon."

Koyna nodded again. The two women walked silently side by side, the druggist's thick gray hair heavier than she herself, Slava, a woman sharp and as agile as a squirrel.

"We'll find a cure for Vasil's whooping cough," Koyna said at last.

"Yes, we will," Slava said. She kept mum for a while, then suddenly blurted out, "I'm glad Pirina cured your Kalcho. I was afraid to talk to you about your boy, Koyna." Her thin smile grew up, her small teeth gleamed, good all of them. So far, she'd lost only one molar after giving birth to three daughters and years of toiling and moiling in the garden. She had dug peppers and lettuces, she had weeded tomatoes, string beans, raspberries, green peas and whatnot. Slava was smiling and at this moment — at least the druggist thought so — she looked like her daughter on the icon in the church. "Your Kalcho cured Pirina too," Slava said. "Pirina used to climb trees like a wild cat, and every time she saw a hilltop in the distance, she scooted off to it like the wind. Now she doesn't leave Kalcho's side, and I don't feel ill at ease. If she falls off her chair, she won't break her head. But if the she comes tumbling down a cliff, she'll be dead meat."

They walked effortlessly down the slope.

"Look!" It was Slava as accurate as a laser who noticed the couple first.

That idiot, Kiro the troll, who'd beaten black and blue more men he cared to remember, stood there, holding her youngest daughter, the thinnest, the most learned and stupidest kid in the family. He'd crushed her in his ugly arms, and he carried her, striding purposefully across the wasteland. Where was he taking her? Oh, come on, she knew. The ogre was taking the girl to the church. Sara's icon was the only thing of interest in this backwater village. Where else could you take anybody? For a second, Slava froze in her tracks then, as rapid as lightning, picked up a stone from the ground. Phew!

In these parts, nature was all mud. Mud as far as the eye could see. Slava's nature, however, was a horse of another color. She couldn't stand mud even under her rubber shoe soles.

She was going to kill him. Now. A thought raced through her mind: the idiot is too strong. He can bend a coin between his thumb and forefinger, they say. Come what may, no head is harder that the stone Slava clutched in her hand. She could sprint noiselessly as a raven's shadow. Slava caught grass snakes so expertly that the poor buggers didn't even wake up before she squeezed their fat scaly necks. She was on the verge of hitting him like a hailstorm, she was ready to hurl the stone at his thick head when Koyna reached out her hand. The druggist's veins were clearly visible. She had crushed loads of dried herbs and minerals, grasses and stones had deposited marks and stains on her fingers. Koyna put her finger to her lips.

Then Slava saw it.

Her daughter Luba, more knowledgeable about musty books than the TV, sat on Kiro's elbow and the ogre's arm was as robust as an iron rafter. She sat there, on the hairy rafter. Slava couldn't believe her eyes. Her silly daughter beamed like that when Miss Petrova gave her her first school certificate, and attached a band with the inscription *Excellent Student* on Luba's puny chest. Luba was the only one who got such a band among all children from the villages of Drugan, Staro, Opal and Vladimir.

Her foolish daughter was grinning from ear to ear. Why the dickens was she doing that! If only you listened, even if you didn't listen at all, it was crystal clear what this dodo was gabbling about at the top of his lungs. He was telling big lies about tractors, and he was spitting out loads of bullshit on engines, in short, drivel that could make you cut your own head off. Then Kiro blathered about the old mechanic, Hunchback Nikola, who bought the farm six years ago. How could Luba put up with it all? Her daughter sat like a baby in a cradle — the fool she was — in Numbskull Kiro's hairy paws, a smile on her face.

"God!" Slava whispered. "Help me!

Deep inside her heart she knew, although she'd never admit it — she loved Luba so much. Maybe the name was important too. Luba meant *best beloved*. Beloved or not, the girl was as thin as a clover leaf and wouldn't suckle like her other babies. Luba read books and things; she'd taken after her father and his dusty newspapers. Despite all the rotten newspapers, Slava held her husband in high esteem. Esteem? O, come off it, esteem my foot! She could hardly breathe until Vasil drove back home after a night shift at the coalmine. Luba was not only the spitting image of her father, her smile was a dead ringer for Vasil's. Slava would not forget the smile on Vasil's face when he bought her a bunch of violets. It was the only time her husband ever gave her flowers he'd spent a whopping fiver on. Magnificent they were, not shabby bluebottles you picked in the fields or stole from a neighbor's garden. So, Slava became resentfully attached to her youngest and weakest child, although she'd never admit this to anybody. She knew Luba was her silliest daughter.

§

David saw her smiling at the ogre. For a split second, he caught a glimpse of her knees, gleaming under her blue coat… Luba, the only girl he wasn't scared of. He should have bought her another book by that Shakespeare, he should have, then maybe… He sat down on the grass. He'd rather the month of July caught fire. Now it drizzled and the cold mist pushed its way to the bones under your shirt, now heat fried your lungs. In the afternoons, the sun blazed down hard. The grass shimmered, the new church on the hill glowed, clean and white like the party grill in the kitchen of The Cat restaurant.

His legs hurt.

His eyes fastened on the couple, the man as big as the brick factory and Luba, his Luba. The ogre carried her in his arms, striding across the field, careful not to drop her on the ground and break her head as he footed it over to the church. His voice, unbearable like the red-hot sky, hit David's ears. It wasn't this voice that hurt David. It was her laughter, so quiet he could hardly make out what it really was, laughter or a smile? He could see her face now. It wasn't sad. She had cried when she read *Notre Dame* to him, and he remembered her eyes. Her face didn't look lonely the way it did on that Thursday night when they lay on the *History of Bulgaria* and the dozen histories of Byzantium in her grandma's hut. Now her face was as quiet as the moon. Her knees waited hidden under her faded blue coat.

Her eyes were waiting, too. She had been waiting for him so long, and the afternoon above the railway station had turned yellow with fear. David got scared and didn't kiss her, his fingers didn't stroke the gentle path of the moon on her skin. He didn't tell her, "Come on! Let's get going. Now! We'll beat it for Spain. I've got one lev and 37 cents, but in Spain I'll make ten million euros. It's warm in Spain and you won't have to wear this old blue coat. I'll buy you a white house. I love your knees. I'm not afraid of them. I want to kiss you. Is this ok with you? Spain's not far from here. Let's go. Come on!"

He hadn't said anything. He could have rescued her from Kiro, could have grabbed a big stone. Could have broken his head! David hadn't grabbed a thing. The ogre kicked him and left him prostrate… three broken ribs. Every time David took a deep breath, it felt like he breathed in molten iron. And yet, he couldn't stop thinking about that white house in Spain. He thought and thought… He thought of Luba.

Luba was smiling as if she had just glimpsed the fantastic road to Spain. David fell on his back in the grass. He'd better punch himself and get a nose-bleed, so his misery wouldn't show on his face. Another fight, blood, just normal things, they'd say. There was a small vein or an artery in his nostrils. He clearly remembered what the teachers taught him: veins and arteries carried your blood. He got a B grade in biology, the highest one at school. No one envied him that he knew everything in the textbook! This meant he had read everything to the last page. David inserted his pinky deep into his nose, pushed the artery, and was gushing blood. His eyes had filled with tears much earlier, but folks around here didn't give a damn about your tears, they were after your blood.

"Here, wipe yourself off," someone said, pushing a handkerchief into his hand, a gray crumpled thing that looked dirtier than The Cat's backyard.

David looked up and saw him, a gypsy lad, as thin as Anno's sword in The Cat. At times, God dropped by there to admire the blade and its luster. The gypsy's face looked bad. It was evident the kid had tried to shave himself. His upper lip was an eyesore. Had a butcher tried to cut it with a handsaw? A few tiny hairs, resembling snail's tentacles, stuck out undamaged by the massacre. David knew this boy.

"Luba's gone," David said. He tried to swab the blood from his face with the gray handkerchief, but it was too small. He plucked a handful of grass and wiped his cheeks with it. The artery seemed to be hard at work in his nose. He had to use a load of hay in order to scrub the blood. David raised his head with an effort and glanced over the kid.

On the kid's cheek, a tear gleamed, a small one, like a lentil; they sold cheap lentils in the grocery store in Dupni, David knew. The boy banged his fist on the tear and smashed it.

"No whining!" said the boy, spat on the ground, kicked the grass and crushed it under his feet.

David caught sight of something in the shadow of the small oak tree. This shadow was narrower than the gray handkerchief, which had soaked up his blood. A small swarthy girl wormed her way behind the clump of prickly hawthorn bushes. Her head looked peculiar. At places, her hair had been whittled down and you could see the small bare skull glistening with sweat. Tufts of hair jutted out like ski poles under her ears. She had put on a skirt made from a pant leg, so tight the kid could hardly move in it. David remembered her, too.

"How are you doing, kiddie?" he asked the girl.

It was a pity David couldn't find any money in his pockets, not even a dime. The only truly magnificent thing he had now was the white shirt on his back, very expensive, its exuberant price stretching into the distance as far as the eye could see. The jewel in its crown were a dozen words, which Shakespeare had embroidered above the chest pocket for his friend Anno. The nipper could cut it into pieces, Shakespeare's instructions, too, and her mom could sew a blouse, a skirt, a dress and pants from it.

"Take it, kiddie," he told the girl. "It's for you."

The little one smiled, wiped her hands on the grass before she took the expensive gift then folded the shirt with utmost care. She took a hesitant step to the boy who had hacked away at his upper lip as he tried to shave. She pushed his leg and said in hushed tones, "Zachary, take this shirt. I give it to you."

The boy didn't look at her, didn't notice that the little one was trying in vain to thrust the shirt into his hands. The white silk glided over the grass like a magnificent parachute. The bent girl took the precious piece of clothing and folded it even more carefully than before. She got nearer the boy, half a step nearer, and timidly as if the ground would burst open under her feet, blurted out, "I've learned the alphabet." She took a short breath. "Now I can read like Luba, Zachary."

The big boy turned his back on the church that was as white as the clouds, and set out for a place no one knew. Where could that be? Probably the boy didn't know because after taking a step he ran slap bang into the young oak tree. The kid in the trouser leg skirt made from her dad's overalls didn't know the way either. The badly shaven kid pushed on as if he were a blind old man, and after a while tripped over something hidden in the thick grass. The girl took his hand nervously, expecting he'd shove her away, but no sound escaped his cut lips. Then the boy turned, a dried, dead thistle in the field. The girl stood on tiptoes, tossed the silver silk shirt onto his shoulders and led him forward. The two kids trudged through the heat to the grove of beech trees near the railway station.

David remembered that good edible mushrooms popped up there after a bout of rain.

David was wearing snow white cotton trousers imported from Marseilles, France. He had thrown out or lost his jacket. Did it really matter anyway? He collapsed on the grass near the oak tree, dead to the sun, which crawled along his back. He didn't want to breathe. For him, the end of the world had come. Where could he go? Luba was gone. Her knees were gone. The summer, the worst thief ever, walked off with the afternoon and sold it to a stranger. The oak leaves kept silent.

"Luba," David muttered.

His shoulders hurt. The sun blinded him. He didn't deserve to live. He would never get going for Spain, he'd never make ten million euros nor would he buy her a white house.

Somebody wrapped a towel around his shoulders. Even before David looked up, a small avalanche of hairy balls, kicking in a thin cotton bag, thudded into his lap. Claws sank into his flesh. Two kittens that still had not opened their eyes fidgeted amidst the white cloth.

"A woman has thrown them into the trash can," explained a voice he knew. The owner of The Cat spoke slowly, but David didn't glance at him. "I rescued the little fellows."

David tore out a tuft of grass. It was not an ordinary coarse bunch; the slope was overgrown with wild sorrel. David stuffed a handful of sour leaves into his mouth and chewed on them. He didn't notice that roots and crumbs of dirt clung to his lips.

"I should've given her a ring… I should have, but I didn't have one," David said.

The day waited. The field waited too. It didn't start to rain. The heat spoke in the language of frogs, and no roar of a passing train disturbed the grass snakes that were basking in the sun.

… Two shadows, the first one large, the second one thin, bent nearly double, slowly climbed the hill. At the top where no sorrel grew and the stone path ended, the white church towered over the slope.

"In idem flumen bis non descendimus," the large shadow whispered. "We do not go down in the same river twice, David."

The thin shadow didn't say anything.

It was very hot. The breeze crept up the hill, trying hard to hide behind the rocks. In these parts, the month of July hated the wind.

The two shadows entered the church. The icon gazed at them as if it knew everything about the dry sorrel, the faded blue coat and the book, which cost eighty-two levs. Maybe it liked the quiet afternoon and the express train for Athens. In front of the icon, a figure was kneeling, a very beautiful woman, her hair honey and chocolate. She wore a green dress, the same as the one the artist had painted Saint Sara in.

The large shadow gave a start.

The praying woman looked very much like Saint Sara, but her eyes were warmer and friendlier than the Saint's.

"Sara," the large shadow breathed.

The lady kneeling in front of the icon nodded, and the church brightened up.

"Sara!"

The woman who had the beauty of the whole world in her eyes winced. Perhaps she smiled, perhaps not. The wind had given her the warm July sunsets. The large shadow bent down and shyly, for a split second, its lips touched the hem of her dress.

"Sara! Pease! Please help my friend David!"

§

I saw them clearly, Yakob and his bodyguards, three or maybe four giants, standing in a row, like the teeth of a comb, like four heaps of manure. I stood far from them, yet I could hear them shout. The first tooth of the comb, the heaviest and the ugliest among them, ran headlong down the hill and gave clubs to each one of his team. I thought they were simple cudgels, but I was wrong. Within a minute, the clubs he'd given them burned fiercely. Torches. They had torches. The dark torsos made for the church, and the black bushes, which surrounded it, burst into flames.

Yakob charged towards me.

"Eh, Pirina?" he said, as he squeezed my chin between his thumb and forefinger.

The earth quaked. The grass leapt over my shoulders, uprooted trees squeaked, the sky collapsed. Stones were no more. The ground boiled. Birds shrieked. The air caved in. The wind fled. The church vanished, melted. Its walls were no more. Stones became dust.

"You love me, Pirina, don't you?" he said as he hit me in the face. His teeth dug into my chin.

Yakob spat. He spat out a part of my lip he'd bitten off.

"He'll be the first. I admit he's nasty, little Pirina."

Four teeth of the comb, four manure heaps surrounded me. The sky fell apart.

"You start," Yakob ordered the biggest manure heap. "The rest will take turns at her after he's done."

At the top of the hill, a huge pit gaped. The church stood there yesterday.

§

Down below Saint Sara's ugly pit, people were screaming. Many were running to me: Koyna the druggist, my mom, Grandma Mariza, her granddaughters, the gypsies, the Bulgarians, the children, Kamen the drunk, my sister Luba, Miss Petrova, my sister Sara, the men she had cured of their diseases. My mouth was hurting. So much blood was spurting from my mouth, that I wasn't sure if the clumsy shadow was my father's, or I had passed out.

Slowly, stone after stone, the walls grew. Every day, they rose up like a man recovering from a deadly disease. No foreigners showed up on the hill. Slava, the scraggy gnat, lugged stones up the slope, the druggist and Kamen, her drunk, pretty Sara, the small manager and waiter in The Cat, the owner of the restaurant in his silk suit, limping Vasil, everybody dragged rocks. The drunks, the gravediggers, the gypsies who worked here and had no time to steal anything, the teacher in Bulgarian literature Petrova, Luba thinner than a thorn, Grandma Mariza and her granddaughters, kids with their hair cut so badly their skulls shone, the postman, the highway maintenance workers, all, as much as they could, more than they could carry, everyone gave Kiro stones. He was the only one who could put up a stone wall.

They were building a church. It did not look like a church.

Rusted metal beams, yellow and gray sandstone slabs, edgy and dirty granite chunks, pieces of broken concrete columns: everything thrown out or stolen from somewhere. The walls grew bigger, crooked and formidable. They snapped at the sunset as strong as the sky.

The people had no church. They had no name for it. They had no icon for it.

They each knew one another. There were no strangers among them.

God had climbed the hill and was lugging stones up for the building like everybody else.

Even the children in the village of Staro knew him.

Up there where no path ran and the top of the hill was all dust and silence, the dim light cast two silhouettes. It was too early for the wolves to howl, and too late for the eagles to prey on wild goats. A young man with disheveled hair and a girl, her face pale like a crescent moon.

"I'll sing to you, Golden Eyes Pirina," the young man said. "Listen to me."

A song that tasted like the first raindrops after a long drought sounded in the air. It had no words and no tune, it had the end of summer in it, and it had the night.

"Please Kalcho, stop," the girl said. A shadow of a blackbird flitted over her face. It looked like a smile.

"I won't stop," the man with the tousled hair said. "I will sing to you until I make you happy."

The warm night dissolved in the song that had no tune and no words. The blackbird's shadow touched the girl's face again. It was not a shadow.

This time it was a smile.

About Fomite

A fomite is a medium capable of transmitting infectious organisms from one individual to another.

"The activity of art is based on the capacity of people to be infected by the feelings of others." Tolstoy, *What Is Art?*

Writing a review on Amazon, Good Reads, Shelfari, Library Thing or other social media sites for readers will help the progress of independent publishing. To submit a review, go to the book page on any of the sites and follow the links for reviews. Books from independent presses rely on reader-to-reader communications.

For more information or to order any of our books, visit:
http://www.fomitepress.com/our-books.html

More Titles from Fomite...

Novels
Joshua Amses — During This, Our Nadir
Joshua Amses — Ghatsr
Joshua Amses — Raven or Crow
Joshua Amses — The Moment Before an Injury
Jaysinh Birjepatel — Nothing Beside Remains
Jaysinh Birjepatel — The Good Muslim of Jackson Heights
David Brizer — Victor Rand
Paula Closson Buck — Summer on the Cold War Planet
Dan Chodorkoff — Loisaida
David Adams Cleveland — Time's Betrayal
Jaimee Wriston Colbert — Vanishing Acts
Roger Coleman — Skywreck Afternoons
Marc Estrin — Hyde
Marc Estrin — Kafka's Roach
Marc Estrin — Speckled Vanities
Zdravka Evtimova — In the Town of Joy and Peace
Zdravka Evtimova — Sinfonia Bulgarica
Daniel Forbes — Derail This Train Wreck
Greg Guma — Dons of Time
Richard Hawley — The Three Lives of Jonathan Force
Lamar Herrin — Father Figure
Michael Horner — Damage Control
Ron Jacobs — All the Sinners Saints
Ron Jacobs — Short Order Frame Up
Ron Jacobs — The Co-conspirator's Tale
Scott Archer Jones — And Throw Away the Skins
Scott Archer Jones — A Rising Tide of People Swept Away
Julie Justicz — Degrees of Difficulty
Maggie Kast — A Free Unsullied Land
Darrell Kastin — Shadowboxing with Bukowski
Coleen Kearon — #triggerwarning
Coleen Kearon — Feminist on Fire
Jan English Leary — Thicker Than Blood
Diane Lefer — Confessions of a Carnivore
Rob Lenihan — Born Speaking Lies
Douglas W. Milliken — Our Shadows' Voice
Colin Mitchell — Roadman
Ilan Mochari — Zinsky the Obscure

Peter Nash — Parsimony
Peter Nash — The Perfection of Things
George Ovitt — Stillpoint
George Ovitt — Tribunal
Gregory Papadoyiannis — The Baby Jazz
Pelham — The Walking Poor
Andy Potok — My Father's Keeper
Frederick Ramey — Comes A Time
Joseph Rathgeber — Mixedbloods
Kathryn Roberts — Companion Plants
Robert Rosenberg — Isles of the Blind
Fred Russell — Rafi's World
Ron Savage — Voyeur in Tangier
David Schein — The Adoption
Lynn Sloan — Principles of Navigation
L.E. Smith — The Consequence of Gesture
L.E. Smith — Travers' Inferno
L.E. Smith — Untimely RIPped
Bob Sommer — A Great Fullness
Tom Walker — A Day in the Life
Susan V. Weiss —My God, What Have We Done?
Peter M. Wheelwright — As It Is On Earth
Suzie Wizowaty — The Return of Jason Green

Poetry
Anna Blackmer — Hexagrams
Antonello Borra — Alfabestiario
Antonello Borra — AlphaBetaBestiaro
Antonello Borra — The Factory of Ideas
L. Brown — Loopholes
Sue D. Burton — Little Steel
David Cavanagh— Cycling in Plato's Cave
James Connolly — Picking Up the Bodies
Greg Delanty — Loosestrife
Mason Drukman — Drawing on Life
J. C. Ellefson — Foreign Tales of Exemplum and Woe
Tina Escaja/Mark Eisner — Caida Libre/Free Fall
Anna Faktorovich — Improvisational Arguments
Barry Goldensohn — Snake in the Spine, Wolf in the Heart
Barry Goldensohn — The Hundred Yard Dash Man
Barry Goldensohn — The Listener Aspires to the Condition of Music
R. L. Green — When You Remember Deir Yassin
Gail Holst-Warhaft — Lucky Country
Raymond Luczak — A Babble of Objects
Kate Magill — Roadworthy Creature, Roadworthy Craft
Tony Magistrale — Entanglements
Gary Mesick — General Discharge
Andreas Nolte — Mascha: The Poems of Mascha Kaléko
Sherry Olson — Four-Way Stop
Brett Ortler — Lessons of the Dead
Aristea Papalexandrou/Philip Ramp — Μας προσπερνά/It's Overtaking Us
Janice Miller Potter — Meanwell
Janice Miller Potter — Thoreau's Umbrella
Philip Ramp — The Melancholy of a Life as the Joy of Living It Slowly Chills
Joseph D. Reich — A Case Study of Werewolves
Joseph D. Reich — Connecting the Dots to Shangrila
Joseph D. Reich — The Derivation of Cowboys and Indians

Joseph D. Reich — The Hole That Runs Through Utopia
Joseph D. Reich — The Housing Market
Kenneth Rosen and Richard Wilson — Gomorrah
Fred Rosenblum — Vietnumb
David Schein — My Murder and Other Local News
Harold Schweizer — Miriam's Book
Scott T. Starbuck — Carbonfish Blues
Scott T. Starbuck — Hawk on Wire
Scott T. Starbuck — Industrial Oz
Seth Steinzor — Among the Lost
Seth Steinzor — To Join the Lost
Susan Thomas — In the Sadness Museum
Susan Thomas — The Empty Notebook Interrogates Itself
Paolo Valesio/Todd Portnowitz — La Mezzanotte di Spoleto/Midnight
                    in Spoleto
Sharon Webster — Everyone Lives Here
Tony Whedon — The Tres Riches Heures
Tony Whedon — The Falkland Quartet
Claire Zoghb — Dispatches from Everest

Stories
Jay Boyer — Flight
L. M Brown — Treading the Uneven Road
Michael Cocchiarale — Here Is Ware
Michael Cocchiarale — Still Time
Neil Connelly — In the Wake of Our Vows
Catherine Zobal Dent — Unfinished Stories of Girls
Zdravka Evtimova —Carts and Other Stories
John Michael Flynn — Off to the Next Wherever
Derek Furr — Semitones
Derek Furr — Suite for Three Voices
Elizabeth Genovise — Where There Are Two or More
Andrei Guriuanu — Body of Work
Zeke Jarvis — In A Family Way
Arya Jenkins — Blue Songs in an Open Key
Jan English Leary — Skating on the Vertical
Marjorie Maddox — What She Was Saying
William Marquess — Boom-shacka-lacka
Gary Miller — Museum of the Americas
Jennifer Anne Moses — Visiting Hours
Martin Ott — Interrogations
Christopher Peterson — Amoebic Simulacra
Jack Pulaski — Love's Labours
Charles Rafferty — Saturday Night at Magellan's
Ron Savage — What We Do For Love
Fred Skolnik— Americans and Other Stories
Lynn Sloan — This Far Is Not Far Enough
L.E. Smith — Views Cost Extra
Caitlin Hamilton Summie — To Lay To Rest Our Ghosts
Susan Thomas — Among Angelic Orders
Tom Walker — Signed Confessions
Silas Dent Zobal — The Inconvenience of the Wings

Odd Birds
William Benton — Eye Contact: Writing on Art
Micheal Breiner — the way none of this happened
J. C. Ellefson — Under the Influence: Shouting Out to Walt
David Ross Gunn — Cautionary Chronicles

Plays

Essays